THAT'S ALL, FOLKS....

The Looney Tunes ring tone on Meadow's phone went off, loudly. Meadow frowned. "That's the ring for Ramsay. Why would he be calling me? He knows I'm at a show."

"If you answer it," said Beatrice through gritted teeth as Looney Tunes merrily played on and on, "then maybe you'd find out."

Meadow put the phone up to her ear. "Ramsay? I'm sort of busy at this show here. Can I call you back . . . what? What!" She listened intently for a moment, her mouth rather comically agape. "Oh. Ohhh. Okay. Yes."

"Something wrong, Meadow? It wasn't bad news, was it?" asked Karen.

"Yes," said Meadow slowly. "Yes, actually, it was bad news. Jo is dead. Her car drove right off the side of the mountain."

The Southern Quilting Mystery Series
by Elizabeth Craig

Knot What It Seams

A SOUTHERN QUILTING MYSTERY

Elizabeth Craig *Spann*

AN OBSIDIAN MYSTERY

OBSIDIAN
Published by New American Library, a division of
Penguin Group (USA) Inc., 375 Hudson Street,
New York, New York 10014, USA
Penguin Group (Canada), 90 Eglinton Avenue East, Suite 700, Toronto,
Ontario M4P 2Y3, Canada (a division of Pearson Penguin Canada Inc.)
Penguin Books Ltd., 80 Strand, London WC2R 0RL, England
Penguin Ireland, 25 St. Stephen's Green, Dublin 2,
Ireland (a division of Penguin Books Ltd.)
Penguin Group (Australia), 250 Camberwell Road, Camberwell, Victoria 3124,
Australia (a division of Pearson Australia Group Pty. Ltd.)
Penguin Books India Pvt. Ltd., 11 Community Centre, Panchsheel Park,
New Delhi - 110 017, India
Penguin Group (NZ), 67 Apollo Drive, Rosedale, Auckland 0632,
New Zealand (a division of Pearson New Zealand Ltd.)
Penguin Books (South Africa) (Pty.) Ltd., 24 Sturdee Avenue,
Rosebank, Johannesburg 2196, South Africa

Penguin Books Ltd., Registered Offices:
80 Strand, London WC2R 0RL, England

First published by Obsidian, an imprint of New American Library,
a division of Penguin Group (USA) Inc.

First Printing, February 2013
10 9 8 7 6 5 4 3 2 1

PUBLISHER'S NOTE
This is a work of fiction. Names, characters, places, and incidents either are the
product of the author's imagination or are used fictitiously, and any resem-
blance to actual persons, living or dead, business establishments, events, or
locales is entirely coincidental.

The recipes contained in this book are to be followed exactly as written. The
publisher is not responsible for your specific health or allergy needs that may
require medical supervision. The publisher is not responsible for any adverse
reactions to the recipes contained in this book.

The publisher does not have any control over and does not assume any responsibility for author or third-party Web sites or their content.

ALWAYS LEARNING   PEARSON

For William and Caroline. Welcome to the world!

ACKNOWLEDGMENTS

Thanks, as always, to Coleman, Riley, and Elizabeth Ruth for their love and support. Thanks to my fantastic editor, Sandra Harding. To my agent, Ellen Pepus. Special thanks to my mother, Beth Spann, for being a wonderful beta reader (and mama.) And thanks to the quilting community and the writing community, for their support.

Chapter 1

"It's dying, Beatrice. A gasping, tragic death. And it's up to us to save it!"

Beatrice Coleman studied her neighbor Meadow Downey. To the casual eye, she didn't *look* fanatical. But when it came to the Village Quilters guild, Meadow was nothing less than obsessive. "I hardly think the guild is dying, Meadow. We're just hitting a little membership snag, that's all. More like a hiccup, really. It's the kind of thing that happens in all groups from time to time."

"A membership *crisis*, you mean! We must infuse new life into the Village Quilters!" Meadow's eyes gleamed maniacally behind the red frames of her glasses. "Beatrice, this guild has been around since the late 1800s. And it's our responsibility to keep it going. It won't die on my watch. We've lost two members recently—one to a retirement home and one to another town. And Piper's not even coming to guild meetings half the time," said Meadow with a meaningful look at Beatrice.

Piper was Beatrice's grown daughter. "She comes most of the time," protested Beatrice. "She's just really wrapped up right now in this staff development conference for her school. They've got to learn all the new state standards, and she's there all day and most of the night, listening to speakers."

Meadow didn't appear satisfied with this excuse. "Well, anyway, it's still not enough quilters. We've got to do something. Have you noticed what's been going on with the Cut-Ups guild, though?"

Beatrice thought this might be a rhetorical question but decided to answer, anyway. "I know they've got a couple of new members in their group."

"Not *just* a couple of new members, Beatrice. More like a couple of new, expert quilters in their guild. They'll be winning gobs of prizes at shows. Then we'll lose even *more* members because everyone will want to join the Cut-Ups," said Meadow, thumping Beatrice's coffee table emphatically.

"Clearly, you have someone in mind to invite. Considering your unexpected visit and your carefully practiced, impassioned speech," said Beatrice drily. "Who's your intended victim . . . er . . . your candidate?"

"Jo Paxton would be the perfect new member," said Meadow, sitting up straight and confident in one of Beatrice's armchairs. Her long gray braid swung off to the side. "She's smart, capable, reliable, and a fabulous quilter. She also judges quilting competitions throughout the Southeast. She's ideal."

"Jo Paxton? Isn't she our postal carrier?" asked Beatrice.

"The very one," said Meadow, beaming.

"Capable and reliable? Those are words you'd use to describe her? Really?"

"You wouldn't?" asked Meadow, her sunny face clouding up.

"Not if she's to be judged based on her mail delivery aptitude, I wouldn't. I've never been able to figure out when exactly the mail is supposed to be in my mailbox. And frequently, I end up with your mail and you've been getting mine. And I find Piper's mail in my mailbox almost every day." Not that her daughter usually got anything but catalogs.

Now Meadow's broad face creased with a frown. "I can't imagine where you got this impression of Jo. She seems like an incredibly efficient carrier to me. Prompt and accurate!"

"If the mail in your mailbox is correctly addressed, that's because I'm switching them out. They've already been corrected by the time you get your mail. And you apparently don't know when your mail is actually delivered. I promise it's frequently late," said Beatrice.

"Of course I know when the mail is delivered! And I'm very impressed that Jo brings it so early in the morning. She must be at my house by five a.m. to get it in the box by the time I go out to get the paper! And those Sunday deliveries . . . remarkable!"

Beatrice sat back and studied Meadow. She looked a little clueless, placidly sitting there with her mismatched clothes, red spectacles, and messy gray braid that fell to her waist. "Meadow, she doesn't deliver the mail at five in the morning. Or on Sundays. She delivers it sometime the day before. You're *checking* it that early in the morning, but you're getting the mail from the previous day."

Meadow waved her hands dismissively. "I don't even care. All I ever get in the mail is bills, anyway. Besides the delivery problems, do you have any other issues with Jo?"

Beatrice thought carefully. "Well—" She didn't even know the woman aside from receiving mail from her.

"Exactly! Me, either. That's why she's going to be such a great member of the group. I've gone ahead and asked her and she said she'd love to join up with us!"

Beatrice gritted her teeth, before taking a deep relaxing breath. That New Year's resolution to be patient was really getting put through its paces this year. "Then why did you ask me about it if you'd already invited Jo to join the Village Quilters?"

"I needed to be validated. We all need validation, Beatrice."

"But . . . isn't she in another quilting guild? I remember her being with another group at that last quilting bee."

"She *was* with the Cut-Ups, but she had a misunderstanding with them, so she ended up leaving the group. Or maybe they asked her to leave. Anyway, she's free to join our guild," said Meadow.

"That should be a red flag right there. Why was she asked to leave? Who did she upset? Why would we want someone like that in our group?"

"To make life interesting, of course!" Meadow slapped her hands on her thighs to loudly emphasize her point, and her huge beast, Boris, sprang up and started excitedly galloping around Beatrice's sofa.

Beatrice's head hurt. Her cottage living room was tiny enough without Meadow's larger-than-life presence. The fact that Meadow had brought Boris along for her breakfast time visit didn't help matters, either. Beatrice's corgi, Noo-noo, watched with concern. Meadow claimed that Boris was a mixture of Great Dane, Newfoundland . . . and corgi. If there *were* any corgi in Boris, it had gotten the short end of the genetic stick. And Noo-noo certainly didn't see evidence of it at all.

"Beatrice, I don't think it was any major disagreement. It was probably a matter of creative differences. As I mentioned, Jo is a quilt show judge, too, and is very highly regarded. She wanted the guild to be more competitive or something."

"Is that the direction that *we* want to go in, though? Is that what she wants for the Village Quilters? Most of our members are only quilting for the sheer love of it." Beatrice absently rubbed Boris' massive head as he laid it in her lap. For a moment she thought the beast might start purring.

Meadow shrugged. "We could probably handle more competition, Beatrice. I don't see it as a bad thing. Even you said that we could kick it up a notch. Remember? You have ideas for a few interesting designs that might help us in juried shows."

"I do have some design ideas. But I was figuring that we'd start out slowly with submitting our quilts for juried shows. Otherwise we could burn out—then the quilting isn't fun anymore," said Beatrice.

But Meadow had that stubborn expression now. There was no getting around her when she dug her heels in. For some reason she'd gotten a real bee in her bonnet with this membership drive. She must really not want the Cut-Ups to show up the Village Quilters. "I guess including Jo in the group is fine, Meadow," said Beatrice with a sigh. "After all, I don't really know the woman. Maybe she'll grow on me . . . it's not fair of me to judge her solely on her mail delivery capability." Or incapability.

Meadow said in a grateful voice, "Thanks for opening up your mind, Beatrice. That's what I always say, during my daily morning meditations. Open my mind! Help me live *mindfully*. I really do value your opinion, Beatrice. You have an incredibly discerning eye for people. And then there's the fact that you're the very smartest person I know."

Beatrice flushed and gave a dismissive wave of her hand. "Meadow . . . please. . . ."

"I'll admit that I've struggled over this decision. It's been tough for me. I did consider asking Karen Taylor to join our group. But honestly, I was a bit scared to," said Meadow, eyes wide. "She's *so good*."

Beatrice frowned. "I'm trying to remember exactly who Karen is." You'd think that, in a town as small as Dappled Hills, you'd know everyone immediately. It was amazing, though, how many people you didn't cross paths with.

"You'd probably know her if you saw her. She's

young, attractive. And—wow. She's just such an impressive quilter," said Meadow, looking as if she was struggling to find the words to describe Karen.

"She's not that young, is she?" asked Beatrice. "I don't remember any superyoung quilters here."

"Karen is in her early thirties. Age is a relative thing, of course, but at my age, that's young. She really has a gift, Beatrice. You need to see her work. Her quilts are simply stunning—she has the technique down perfectly, and her design is very innovative."

"And you didn't ask her to be part of the Village Quilters?"

Meadow looked around as if someone might hear. "She's sort of scary."

"Scary!"

Meadow nodded. "Just intimidating. Because she's so good and she wins all these quilt shows. You know. I didn't want to be rejected."

Now Beatrice was intrigued. There was someone who could make Meadow Downey as insecure as a teenager? This was a person she'd have to meet.

"Besides, she's in the Cut-Ups guild," said Meadow. "So it's not as if she was displaced or anything."

Meadow changed the subject. "But anyway, I think Jo will be perfect for our group. I do! And I can't wait to hear your recommendation. It will definitely give me some of that much-needed validation I mentioned. And I do feel it'll work out great to have Jo joining us— you'll see. I happen to know that Jo is going to drop by the Patchwork Cottage right before lunch today for some fat quarters," said Meadow, reaching out to rub

Boris. "It would give you a chance to spend some time with her before the first guild meeting. I do want it to go off without a hitch. Can you help me?"

"Okay. I'll see what I can do during the guild meeting." Beatrice rubbed her eyes. "What time will she be at the shop?"

"She said she'd be there at eleven, so let's meet then. You'll really love Jo, once you get to know her!"

She might be a little more loved if she delivered Beatrice's mail regularly. After Meadow left with Boris dragging her home, Beatrice walked out to her mailbox to see if the mail had come yet. It was empty except for a magazine that Beatrice's daughter, Piper, had stuck in the box. She'd starred one hot pink headline in the issue with a permanent marker: YOUR MIND-SET IS HAZARDOUS TO YOUR HEALTH. TAKE CONTROL OF YOUR LIFE, SURVIVE AND THRIVE.

These magazines always claimed to have the perfect prescription for every problem. The idea that they could take something as complex as a woman's life, her entire personal ecosystem, and transform it in two thousand words or fewer was laughable.

But intriguing. The article suggested that she look objectively at her life, think of one thing *she* could do to improve the quality of it (whatever thing was under her control) and then two things she could do to become a better person. Taking control. Yes, that would be a popular theme with women readers.

The article wasn't without its truths, though.

Retirement is for relaxing. She took a deep breath and released it slowly. She felt better, so she took another deep breath. She wondered for the hundredth time if it had just been too abrupt of a change—going from the fast-paced world of Atlanta to the long minutes in Dappled Hills. The quilting had definitely helped, she was sure of it. Because with quilting, she was not only sitting still to accomplish something, but creating art at the same time. And occasionally socializing while doing it. The multitasking aspect of it all was definitely pleasing.

The rest of her time tended to be more of a problem. Often she climbed into her hammock, prepared to read while listening to her corgi's snorting snores. But too frequently instead of settling into the story, she ended up thinking that she needed to refill the hummingbird feeder—so she'd leap up out of the hammock, startle the sleeping corgi, and dash inside to make nectar. Or else she'd realize that the knockout roses needed to be deadheaded and she'd pop inside for her pruners.

She was officially making a new goal—she was going to put more time into what was guaranteed to make her relax. The quilting. And she was going to make a conscious effort to keep hammock time as quiet time. That went for sofa time, as well, she decided abruptly. No jumping up to dust off the end table when she had her feet up. It was regretful that she had these compulsions, but she vowed to keep trying to work against them and have the peaceful retirement in the picturesque town that everyone wanted.

Of course, it might be difficult if Meadow Downey had anything to do with it. But at least she knew whom to go to in Dappled Hills if she ever started feeling bored.

Later that afternoon Beatrice walked into the welcoming environment of the quilt shop. Apparently, every single quilter in Dappled Hills had needed quilting supplies at once because the Patchwork Cottage was bustling with shoppers. But even full of quilters, the Patchwork Cottage was a peaceful oasis. Posy, the owner, always played soft music in the background, frequently featuring local musicians. Visually, it was a colorful feast for the eyes with bolts of fabric and beautiful quilts on display everywhere—draped over antique washstands and an old sewing machine, and hanging on the walls and ceiling to make the space as cozy and welcoming and homey as it could possibly be. Posy had also stocked the shop with every imaginable type of notion.

Jo was there, all right. She was the kind of person who stood out in a group because she was striking, not because she was attractive. She had black hair with white streaking through it, arched brows that gave her a condescending look, and a fondness for bright red lipstick. And she was already actively engaged in an argument with a younger woman.

"That's Karen Taylor," muttered Meadow. Her brow was furrowed with concern. Apparently, this wasn't the first impression she'd been hoping for.

Didn't Meadow say that Karen was in the Cut-Ups guild? No wonder Jo needed to find another guild. Karen, arms crossed and fire in her eyes, looked as if she might have single-handedly thrown Jo out herself. Aside from the ferocious expression on her face, Karen was a very attractive woman—tall and with the kind of carelessly tousled blond hair that had likely taken lots of time to achieve.

"All I'm saying," said Jo, wagging her finger at Karen, "is that you might want to reconsider that pattern combination. It's tacky."

Posy, the gentle and kindhearted shop owner, watched anxiously, her bright blue eyes clouded.

Karen's eyes narrowed. "Jo, you don't even know what I'm working on. It's an experimental quilt. I'm combining patterns and techniques to—"

"I don't need to know what you're working on to know it's going to be completely hideous," said Jo, hands on her hips. "Considering I'm probably going to end up judging it, I thought you'd want the heads-up."

Karen snorted. "I doubt you'll judge it. People talk, Jo, and you have a tendency to stir the pot wherever you judge. Making trouble won't win you friends and it sure won't get you invited to judge quilt shows."

"Then why do I already have three shows on my calendar?" asked Jo.

Karen's response was to turn her back to Jo and closely study Posy's new selection of fat quarters. Jo slapped down her purchases by the cash register and fumed as Posy fumbled through the checkout. Jo packed as much irritation as she could possibly fit into her small, rather stout frame. Posy, however, was even shorter than Jo—a fact that Jo seemed to be taking advantage of as she looked down her upturned nose at

Posy. Beatrice muttered to Meadow, "This isn't at all promising. I thought you said I'd *like* Jo once I got to know her."

Meadow shrugged. "Everyone's entitled to a bad day, Beatrice. We all wake up on the wrong side of the bed every now and then. Oh, and that reminds me that I need to introduce you to Karen. Maybe not right this second, though, since she's so unhappy. And busy. I forgot to tell you earlier that she mentioned that she was terribly interested in meeting you," she said in her noisy stage whisper. "She said she was very impressed with your background and stature in the art world. Imagine! Karen impressed!"

"Karen is the kind of person who isn't usually impressed, I take it?" murmured Beatrice drily.

"Never! The stuff that ordinarily impresses Karen Taylor is really *big*. Like national championship–winning quilters. Or maybe national-level judges. Or like astronauts. People like that. She did a search for you on her computer and said you were completely remarkable. Special!"

Beatrice shifted a little, uncomfortably. She didn't feel very special, especially struggling with her quilting.

Meadow squinted as the bell on the shop door rang, pushing her red glasses higher on her nose. "Uh-oh. This isn't going to make things better. It's Opal Woosley. Now, keep in mind, Beatrice, that these are a couple of people who don't coexist well. Everyone else loves Jo! Really!"

Opal was an elfish woman with a sharp chin and large ears that stuck out of her frizzy brown hair. Her genial expression transformed when she saw Jo. Jo's did, too, and became even grouchier.

"Why the long face, Jo?" The little woman was fairly bristling. "Aren't you happy to see me?"

Jo didn't deign to glance her way. Instead she grabbed her bag of supplies and shouldered her way through the gawking women customers and out the shop's door.

Opal burst into tears and several of the customers patted her as Posy hurried around the sales counter to give her a hug.

Beatrice muttered to Meadow, "Sorry, Meadow. I was wrong. Jo's obviously the perfect choice for our guild."

"So she's had a couple of misunderstandings," said Meadow with a shrug. "Haven't we all?"

Beatrice could see Jo stomping across the narrow main street. She raised her eyebrows when she saw a couple of different women scurry to the opposite side of the street after they caught sight of Jo. Clearly other members of the Jo Paxton fan club.

Beatrice turned back around to Opal, who was still quivering with indignation. "I don't know how she dares show her face around town after what she's done!"

Beatrice raised a questioning eyebrow at Meadow, who shook her head, making her long braid bob around. "Too long of a story," she hissed. "I'll tell you later."

Karen Taylor was commiserating with Opal. "Ignore Jo. I know you're mad, but if you try to argue with her, you'll get nowhere. Trust me, she'll only make your blood pressure go up. Want to help me decide between some patterns? I'm planning on doing the complete *opposite* of Jo's advice."

They moved their conversation to the other side of the shop, Opal's querulous voice still audible.

Posy walked over to Beatrice and Meadow. As usual, just seeing Posy put Beatrice in a better mood. She wore fluffy, cheerful pastel cardigans, no matter the weather, and always had a cute pin—today's pin was a hummingbird. But her sweet features were concerned. "I'm so glad Miss Sissy was asleep during that exchange," she whispered. "She thinks Jo is one of her best friends because Jo visits her house almost every day."

Beatrice turned to see the shop's sitting area. Miss Sissy, a cadaverous, fierce old woman, was snoring with gusto in one of the overstuffed floral love seats. "She really *visits* Miss Sissy that much? She must be a saint . . . or a relative."

Posy spread her hands out. "She's really just delivering the mail, I guess. But it seems like a visit to Miss Sissy. And sometimes she'll drive Miss Sissy with her to an out-of-town quilt show. Miss Sissy would have been yelling at Opal and Karen for sure." Posy, never one to dwell on trouble, then went on to change the subject. "Was there something in particular you were shopping for today, Beatrice? We've gotten some really fun patterns in."

Beatrice tried not to feel guilty. That Meadow. Always putting her in jams. She wasn't about to confess that she'd come to get the scoop on Jo and see what kind of mess the Village Quilters had gotten into. Although she *had* been thinking about getting some reference books on quilting techniques.

"She's not," said Meadow loudly. "She's here to give me some advice about the group quilt we're doing. Beatrice is so good with themes and design, you know. I asked her for a quilt design not long ago, and she came up with something absolutely amazing. The color palette she suggested was stunning—a crimson and deep raspberry that you'd never guess would go well together. And she put a fresh spin on a traditional design by taking a log cabin design and making it pop."

"You'll have to let me know if it ends up looking good whenever you make it, though." Beatrice was surprised to feel herself blushing a little.

Posy beamed at Beatrice. "That's your art background helping you out. You've got a wonderful eye for art."

Beatrice had been an art museum curator in Atlanta before moving to Dappled Hills to be closer to Piper. Although she gave herself a C-plus for learning how to quilt, she'd give herself an A for quilt design.

At that moment, Karen and Opal walked over to them. Opal's face was still blotchily flushed with distress. "I completely forgot one of the main reasons I'm here today," she said, her spindly fingers working nervously at the lace collar at her neck. "Seeing that horrid woman completely messed me up. I wanted to tell y'all that we need to make a special effort to go to the town meeting tonight. Mayor Grayson is bound and determined to collect taxes on our quilt show sales. And he even wants us to have a tax ID number to file taxes and fill out all kinds of permits! He might go as far as charging us for use of the town hall meeting room when we have quilt shows. I think he's flipped!"

Karen frowned. "Surely that's not necessary. Half the time the proceeds from our quilt shows go to charity, anyway. We're always supporting children's and women's organizations and other groups. Besides, it's not like we're making much money."

"He's completely determined to follow everything by the book. He's a very particular man! We need to put a little pressure on him at the meeting—remind him of all the good things the Village Quilters and the Cut-Ups do for Dappled Hills." Opal was visibly bristling now.

"I swear I simply don't know what this world is coming to," said Meadow. But her slightly faraway stare testified that her mind was still on the upcoming guild meeting and officially adding another name to the Village Quilters roster. Booth Grayson should count himself lucky. A focused Meadow would have been a dangerous thing for him.

Karen tilted her head and looked curiously at Beatrice. "Hi there. I don't believe we've met. Strange as that is, in a town this size."

"Oh, mercy! I completely forgot to introduce you. Karen, this is the Wonderful Beatrice Coleman. I know you were looking forward to—"

"I certainly *was*!" said Karen, interrupting Meadow. "It's such a pleasure to meet you, Mrs. Coleman. I've read so much about you. Atlanta has lost a real giant in the art world, I hear."

This kind of hyperbole always managed to fluster Beatrice. But she had to admit that it made her feel good. She hadn't actually felt proud of her abilities since she'd retired, and quilting's steep learning curve had been a real setback to her confidence. She said briskly, "No, I wouldn't say that. But you're very kind. Please call me Beatrice." She felt her smile falter a bit and cleared her throat as she thought of a diversion. "I'm excited about seeing some of your quilts at the upcoming show, Karen. Meadow has really praised your creativity and talent. I can't wait to check out your display."

Karen glowed with the praise. "And I'm eager to hear your opinion on them. I also want to introduce you around a little to some of the quilting world that's outside Dappled Hills. You're really going to be an asset to the community. Maybe you could consider becoming a judge. We could use an impartial judge with your eye and talent." Karen's face clouded—she was probably thinking of Jo's slanted views and aversion to Karen's quilts.

"Thanks, Karen," said Beatrice. "I'm still trying to get used to retirement and relaxing, though. I made a promise to my daughter, Piper, that I'd try to slow down—instead I keep charging around cleaning and doing yard work when I'm supposed to be taking life easy. Plus, I don't really think I'm qualified yet to judge a quilt show. I'll keep it in mind for later on, though."

"You're more qualified than most," muttered Karen.

* * *

That afternoon, Beatrice decided to retreat to the quiet of her backyard hammock with her book. One of Beatrice's favorite things about her cottage was its backyard. Private and well landscaped by the previous owner, it was proving to be a relaxing sanctuary. Posy had thoughtfully given her some bird feeders, and Beatrice loved hearing the chirping of the birds as part of the background. The yard had azaleas that blossomed most of the spring through the fall and was fenced in and bordered with luscious bushes. But the best part of the backyard was the hammock. Many times she'd come out with her book, curled up in the hammock, and promptly fallen asleep. She was prepared to do the same thing today. In fact, Noo-noo had already started snoozing.

Beatrice had just drifted off when her phone's chiming jerked her awake. Somehow, whenever she forgot to bring the cordless phone outside, it always seemed to ring.

Beatrice hurried inside and grabbed the phone, this time carrying it back outside with her to the hammock. It was Meadow. And Meadow sounded as if she was in a particularly scattered mood, which usually meant a longer phone conversation.

"I'm thinking about the guild meeting again." Of course. "I'm barely believing it's already time for it again! It really feels like we had the last meeting yesterday. Remember? Boris ate all the mini quiches I'd made?" Beatrice remembered very well. Those quiches smelled delicious. "Do you think time literally goes faster as we get older, or . . . ? No! Down, Boris! Bad! No cookie!"

Beatrice bit her tongue to keep what she wanted to say from slipping out, then asked in a voice that sounded tight to her ears, "You called me for something, Meadow?"

"Did I?" she asked in a blank voice. "But you called me, didn't you?"

Beatrice didn't bite her tongue this time. "Certainly not! I was dozing in the hammock."

"Do you walk in your sleep?" Meadow's voice was interested. "One of my cousins walks in her sleep. One night she woke up on her patio in the middle of the night. She was sitting outside in her nightgown with a raccoon staring at her. A raccoon!"

Beatrice waited. There was no point trying to get through to Meadow when she was like this. It was going to have to come from within her.

There was a sudden pause on Meadow's side of the line. "You know what? I *did* call you! What do you know? Okay, here's what I need," she said, quickly businesslike. "As I mentioned to you before, I really want Jo to like our group, so I thought a cake might make her feel welcome. But I can't pick it up today because I've got a dental cleaning in Lenoir, which I just remembered. So, could you pick it up for me? And this is the last thing I'll ask you to do, because I know you already said you'd help to make the meeting go smoothly today. Keeping feathers from getting ruffled, and that kind of thing."

And she'd also asked her to get acquainted with Jo

at the Patchwork Cottage. That certainly hadn't gone well. But she'd say anything to end the phone call and resume the nap.

"Do you think Piper can come? She always has a very peaceful aura about her. I hope that one day," said Meadow, sounding suspiciously sniffy on the phone, "that she'll be creating a peaceful oasis right in my own family."

Piper was dating Meadow's son, Ash. But it was a new relationship and a long-distance one . . . Ash lived on the West Coast. Beatrice liked Ash, but was glad that they were taking things slowly.

"Meadow, she told me she was going to try to make it for a little while. The teacher in-service is letting out early because the principal has a meeting. Piper would love to come. Quilting centers her, she says." Beatrice carefully steered away from the topic of Ash and Piper.

"I've really missed seeing Piper," said Meadow with a sigh. "Now, moving on to the cake—you're sure you don't mind?"

"No, it's fine. Who's the baker?"

"You know her, as a matter of fact," said Meadow, still sounding as if she was wrestling with Boris over something. "Opal. Well, I guess you don't actually know her, but you saw her today at the Patchwork Cottage. The small woman with the pointy chin. She makes amazing cakes from her home. Practically everyone in Dappled Hills uses her. Plus, she has the sight."

"The sight?"

"You know, she's psychic." Meadow's voice took on a respectful tone. "Opal can see the future."

Probably a future full of taking money from gullible Dappled Hills residents.

"Thanks for the warning. I'll go prepared to rebuff any offers to read my palms or anything."

Meadow clicked her tongue. "She's not like that, Beatrice. Opal isn't doing that hocus-pocus type of stuff with cards or palms or crystal balls or anything. She gets hit with these extraordinary visions sometimes, without warning and without encouraging them to come. It's not like she sits there in a turban and robes and tries to have spirits come talk to her. She doesn't take any money. Now, don't say anything negative about her gift! I wouldn't want to get on her bad side." Meadow sounded alarmed. "Who knows what other powers she might possess?"

"I wouldn't dream of disparaging her gift, Meadow. I simply don't plan on using it, that's all. I'm simply picking up a cake. Period."

Chapter 2

Opal's house resembled the gingerbread houses people made at Christmas: minus the gumdrops and other candies, but with the same white icing trim and brown color. Beatrice's hand was still raised from knocking at the front door when Opal yanked it open, beaming. "There you are!" She knit her brow. "Wait, *you* aren't Meadow! Who are you again? You seem familiar. You're not here to sell me something, are you? Because there's no soliciting, like the sign says." She pointed at a small white, curlicued sign with calligraphy that stated UNLESS YOU'RE A GIRL SCOUT, NO SOLICITING.

"No, actually," said Beatrice, clearing her throat. "I'm picking up the cake you made for Meadow—for our guild meeting. Meadow couldn't make it over here, so I told her I'd come by and pick it up. I'm in the Village Quilters."

"You don't mind if I call Meadow, to make sure? You

see, I really don't *know* you, so . . ." Opal's eyes were full of suspicion.

"That's fine, of course." Beatrice gave a small shrug.

Opal nodded, causing the frizzy halo of gray hair to bob around her head. Then she quickly backed into the gingerbread house and Beatrice heard the key turn in the lock. She walked back to her car and peered critically at herself in the rearview mirror. The same chin-length bob of shaggy, silvery ash-blond hair. The same high-cheekboned, solemn face that had stared back at her for the last sixty-odd years. Did she appear particularly dangerous today? Was it really necessary for Opal to lock the door?

Just as abruptly as the door had closed, it swung open again. This time Opal smiled at her, although the smile didn't quite make it to her eyes. "Kind of funny, isn't it? A cake for a quilting guild meeting? Y'all observing someone's birthday over there? I don't think we've ever had a cake at the Cut-Ups meetings."

Beatrice said, "Nothing like a birthday, no. I think the reasoning is that we're greeting a new member of the Village Quilters. We're welcoming her in with a cake, I guess, to make her like us more." She walked back up to Opal's door.

Opal beamed pleasantly at Beatrice, then while gazing steadily at her, opened her mouth to shriek, "June Bug!"

Beatrice was searching her clothing for a beetle when a small woman wearing an apron and a startled expression poked her head out of the gingerbread house.

"June Bug," said Opal in a milder voice. "Would you be so kind as to bring me Meadow Downey's cake? I've verified our visitor's identity," she said, as if reassuring the woman that the dessert wasn't being pilfered.

Still looking startled, the woman bounded off, returning in moments clutching a sheet cake that was ensconced in many layers of aluminum foil. "Thank you, June Bug," said Opal graciously. When the woman kept standing there and looking at her with wide, buggy eyes, Opal said sternly, "That will be all, June Bug."

After the little woman trotted off, Opal studied Beatrice with interest. "A new Village Quilter? And who might that be, if I could ask? Aren't any new quilters that have moved to town, are there? The guilds are pretty set in their ways with half the quilters in the Cut-Ups and half in the Village Quilters."

"Jo Paxton is the quilter. She's moving over from your guild." Shouldn't a psychic know this kind of thing without having to ask? And Opal, in particular, since that was her guild?

Opal frowned. "Why would you take on someone like her? Jo lives for making trouble. Why do you suppose she's not in the Cut-Ups anymore? If we were ever going to have a cake at a guild meeting, we'd have it to celebrate the fact that Jo is no longer with our group. In fact, I do believe I'll bring one to our next meeting for that very reason. I know Karen will be happy to eat a piece of cake to celebrate losing Jo."

"I noticed she and Jo didn't seem very happy with each other," said Beatrice.

"They aren't. That's because Jo is very competitive

and Karen is *super*competitive. Her mother kept telling her she was worthless at quilting, and now she's focused her whole life around proving her wrong."

Beatrice blinked. "That wasn't a very nice thing for her mother to tell her."

"Well, the woman's dead now. But she wasn't a great mother, that's for sure." Opal rolled her eyes, just thinking about Karen's mother. "But back to Jo. I think you'll end up with a whole host of problems if you let her join the Village Quilters."

The anti-Jo sentiment was getting to be a common refrain. "Oh, I'm not the mastermind of the recruiting effort. I'm only here picking up the cake. You know how Meadow is—she's a one-woman welcoming committee. I haven't been in Dappled Hills long enough to form an opinion of Jo one way or another. Although I'll admit I'm not a fan of her philosophy of mail delivery. Why don't you fill me in?"

Opal leaned forward. "I'm not usually the one to gossip." She pursed her mouth into a bow.

Sure she wasn't.

"But that woman makes me positively froth at the mouth." Opal did, in fact, appear right on the verge of frothing, eyes open wide and mouth in a snarl. "I have my own personal reasons for hating her, but other people have had issues with her, too. She knows all kinds of things about people in the town since she delivers their mail. What they do in their private lives, their interests, which doctors they see. I don't doubt she reads half the mail and makes educated guesses on the content of the other half."

Opal sounded as though she had personal knowledge of Jo's snooping. Jo couldn't be very popular in such a small town with this approach. "Does she?" asked Beatrice. "I suppose it's a good thing that my mail is as boring as it is."

The elfish woman suddenly appeared very tough and hard and not at all as fluffily innocuous as she had before. "Most of the time, it's just annoying things that you don't want the whole town to know about. All I'm saying is to watch yourself around Jo Paxton. She's not someone to be trusted." She paused. "*Especially* if you're a dog owner." She squinted at her omnisciently. "Which I believe you are."

"Meadow," said Jo, staring around Meadow's converted barn, "you sure do a lot of crazy quilts. Is that all you quilt now? It doesn't look like you've tried anything else in a long time." Jo squinted critically at the quilts, jabbing a finger to point at all the crazy quilts she saw.

Meadow and her police chief husband lived in a barn that had been converted into a house. Beatrice had been very doubtful when she'd first moved to Dappled Hills that the inside of their home could possibly be attractive. But ever since she'd first set foot in the barn, she'd fallen a little in love with it. The ceilings soared up to a skylight, and the kitchen and living room were all one room with beautiful hardwood floors. The feeling in the house was very loftlike and modern in some ways.

Meadow blinked at Jo. "I wouldn't say that crazy

quilts are *all* that I do. But I don't have room to put out all my quilts, of course. They're in cedar chests."

Meadow's wide-eyed expression told Beatrice that this guild meeting was not going exactly as planned. At least Opal's cake was delicious red velvet with a delightful buttercream frosting. That, in itself, was reason to enjoy being at the Village Quilters guild meeting. Beatrice was already contemplating asking Opal to bake her a cake just to enjoy at home. No special occasion was really needed for cakes, after all. And there were so many types of cakes. Considering possible different cake options was infinitely better than listening to Jo Paxton give unrequested critiques on everyone's quilts.

"And you're also stuck on particular colors. Most of your quilts use vibrant reds, blues, and yellows. Visually, it gets stale after a while. You spend so much time in Posy's store that you could easily find something totally different to inspire you." Jo continued peering at the quilts around the big living area. "Posy must be buying those colors by the truckload just for you."

Posy, quietly hand-piecing on the sofa, gazed anxiously at Jo. She clearly didn't want to be brought into this lecture.

"You've brought up food for thought, for sure," said Meadow eagerly. "Boy, it's good to have some fresh ideas for the group!" Meadow was clearly willing to squelch any irritation she felt to keep the meeting running smoothly.

Jo now eyed Savannah Potter's meticulously stitched quilt. Savannah and her sister Georgia's quilts were about as different as they could possibly be. Savannah's quilts were as tightly controlled as she was, and Georgia's quilts were free-spirit expressions of soft textures and comfort.

While Jo started explaining to Savannah that pinwheel, flying geese, and Polaris star patterns were too limiting, Beatrice's daughter, Piper, rolled her eyes at her. They were sitting next to each other on Meadow's long sofa that was draped with yet more crazy quilts. "Does Jo think she's judging a quilt show?" Piper whispered.

"Maybe she thinks she's here as a speaker," said Beatrice. "That's what she's acting like, anyway."

Savannah, usually a stern perfectionist who wouldn't take kindly to advice on the topic, was surprisingly docile, hanging on Jo's every word. It was almost as if this guild was starstruck at having a regional quilt show judge giving them feedback. It all made Beatrice feel fairly grouchy.

Miss Sissy, who had just polished off most of the hors d'oeuvres, grunted her agreement with Jo's assessment. "Crazy quilts! Geometric. Bah!"

Georgia and Posy got similar critiques and Piper took hers with good humor and a couple of winks at her mother when Jo wasn't paying attention. Piper grinned good-naturedly when Meadow teasingly proclaimed, "Go gently on Piper, Jo! You know she's my daughter-in-training. I won't have you insulting my future daughter-in-law's quilting abilities." Ash and Piper did have a nice little relationship going, although the fact that he lived on the other end of the country was a bit of an impediment.

Beatrice had listened to enough, though, and briskly interrupted Jo as she came over to study Beatrice's current project. "I have a ways to go, I know. There's no point in critiquing something that's flawed to this extent. Right now I'm trying to learn the basics and enjoy the process." Jo opened her mouth to interject some advice, and Beatrice stared her down firmly until Meadow intervened.

"We're pleased as punch to have you in the Village Quilters, Jo! It's such an honor for us."

Jo preened a little. "It's nice to be wanted. This is a much friendlier group than the Cut-Ups."

Or a more malleable one.

"They never really listened to my advice there. That Karen Taylor." Jo made a face as if she'd eaten something sour. "She always thought she knew best and is bent on making hideous quilts."

"Hideous!" echoed Miss Sissy, raising her arthritic fist in solidarity.

"I tell her she's never going to win shows with those things, but she keeps plugging away at them. And Opal." Jo shook her head as if Opal were completely beyond hope. Beatrice couldn't even imagine Opal and Jo being able to be in the same room together without having a blow-up.

Meadow clearly wanted to steer the subject into lighter, happier territory. Unfortunately, she chose the wrong tack to do it. "Opal. Yes, we saw Opal yesterday, didn't we, Beatrice."

At a memorable and conflict-ridden visit to the Patchwork Cottage. "We certainly did," said Beatrice.

"She was very concerned about something, wasn't she?" asked Posy, trying to remember. "What was it, again?"

Now Meadow's brow creased with worry. Because Opal had primarily been concerned about Jo.

"Oh, that's right," said Posy. "It was about the town hall meeting tonight. Dappled Hills is planning on levying some taxes and fees on the quilters and charging us for meeting space for the quilt shows. Or I suppose the mayor is. Something to do with a revenue issue for the town."

Meadow's cheery smile returned now they were out of Opal-versus-Jo territory.

Jo squawked, "What! Taxing and charging the quilters! But we're always giving proceeds to local charities!"

Meadow clasped her hands together anxiously. "Surely it won't be much of a hassle, though. It'll just be more of a pain to fill out the paperwork. It's not like he's going to be emptying out our coffers or anything." They were straying again from the happy, calming atmosphere that Meadow had been aiming for.

Jo was on a roll. "It's not the time or the money. It's the principle of the thing! There's a complete lack of respect behind his planning. It's not right." She sat back in her chair and crossed her arms across her chest, fuming. Then she wagged a finger. "I know what we'll do. I know the way to force Mayor Grayson to our point of view. But let's go to the town hall meeting tonight—all of us. Every quilter in each guild. I'll call them myself. A show of force!"

A cheer erupted from the normally placid ladies of the guild. Even Piper, who was as apolitical as possible, was planning to be there. Beatrice hoped that the police department had riot gear.

Beatrice had lived in the South her entire life and had seen a lot of Southern politicians. Many times they perfectly fit their jovial, good-old-boy-network stereotype. Booth Grayson didn't fit so neatly into a box, though. He was smart and acerbic with an accountant's sensibility and desire to stick to a budget. He solemnly regarded the group of quilters over his glasses as they took seats in the town hall meeting room before things started.

Beatrice raised her eyebrows as Jo entered the room several minutes later. Jo wore a pantsuit that implied she meant business and had pulled her hair into a ponytail so tight that Beatrice wondered if it was stretching her skin across her face. Opal froze at the sight. There was bound to be trouble. And Beatrice had thought that Dappled Hills seemed like such a quiet community to retire to.

After the minutes of the last meeting were read and the agenda followed, there came the moment in the meeting for public feedback, comments, and questions. Opal had a peach-colored piece of stationery in her hands, ready to deliver what she apparently considered a stern reproach to the mayor.

While Opal was still smoothing down her skirts, however, Jo had jumped up out of her seat and hurried over to stand belligerently in front of the council and address the mayor. "What's all this foolishness, Booth? Your proposal means you'll be drowning the quilt

guilds in paperwork, permits, and taxes. Are you trying to make it hard for us to meet? What have we ever
done to *you*?"

Booth studied her coolly. "There's nothing personal
about it—it's purely a revenue-based and legal-based
decision. Your groups are generating revenue. The
town of Dappled Hills could employ some of that revenue to help us meet our budget. Your groups should
have a tax ID number and pay taxes like other revenue-
generating entities. End of story."

The other council members fidgeted and their expressions were either nervous or wary. Maybe they'd
run across the wrath of Jo before. Or perhaps they
knew better than to have run-ins with quilters.

"It may be nothing personal on your end, but there's
something personal on mine. I have a problem with
people who do things that don't make sense. What
you're proposing enforcing won't bring in much revenue for the town, but could do a lot to harm the quilting guilds."

Booth set his jaw. "Thank you, Ms. Paxton. If that's the
end of your question, we'll hear from the next citizen."

"I don't think we will," said Jo in a cold voice. "I
have the advantage, you see, of knowing certain tidbits
of information about you. I know that you shouldn't be
as sanctimonious as you are. I happen to know things
about you that aren't so squeaky clean—"

"That's enough!" said Booth, an ugly red stain spat-
tering across his face.

"—and I'm thinking that maybe the people of Dappled Hills need a bit more information about the kind of person they've elected—"

Booth stood up, pushing back his rolling chair.

"—and the sorts of activities you're engaged in."

No longer the unruffled bureaucrat, Booth roared, "I said that's enough!"

Everyone in the room perched on the edge of their seats, breaths held, waiting for the next explosion. But there clearly weren't going to be any more explosions when Meadow's husband, Ramsay, Dappled Hills police chief, drawled, "I think that's enough, too. From both of y'all. Town meetings are supposed to be conducted in a particular way, and y'all are in complete violation of it. I need you both to take deep breaths."

Booth returned to his usual iciness and regarded Ramsay without speaking. Jo folded her arms tightly across her chest. Her mouth pulled unhappily down into a severe frown and she didn't appear to be making any efforts to relax.

Ramsay cleared his throat for effect.

"Isn't he so handsome when he's commanding like that?" said Meadow to Beatrice in her usual stage whisper. "It nearly makes me swoon. Even after all these years of marital bliss!"

Handsome wasn't exactly the word that came to mind when you met Ramsay Downey. He was a short, balding man with a stomach that had seen its share of hearty Southern meals. You wouldn't think he'd command attention in a room, but there was a quiet authority about him that seemed to work.

"Now, I don't know about Jo's allegations," said Ramsay, shifting from one foot to the other and looking as if he didn't really *want* to know about the allegations, "but I think the argument today boils down to a couple of different matters. The quilters think that Mayor Grayson doesn't fully understand the contributions they make to the community and that he's only seeing the group from a dollars-and-cents standpoint. Mayor Grayson states he is simply searching for ways to increase revenue for Dappled Hills. Maybe the mayor can go to the next quilt show. If my memory serves me," added Ramsay, "there's one this very weekend."

The mayor's mouth twisted as he stared coolly at the peacemaking police chief. Beatrice knew Ramsay would do anything to avoid trouble. All he wanted to do was lounge around in comfortable clothes reading Thoreau and making stabs at penning poetry. Frayed tempers and veiled threats only meant a necessary return to police work.

Booth had apparently come to the same conclusion as his gaze rested on Ramsay's anxious, supplicating face. "I suppose I could come to the quilt show before effecting the permit and tax change." He no longer glared at Jo, who'd smugly swept out of the meeting room. Now Opal was busily giving Booth the time and place for the quilt show, jotting it on a piece of paper and hurrying over to hand it to him as she babbled on.

Ramsay appeared vastly relieved at diffusing the tense situation, and the town council members appeared to share his relief, rushing on to the other items on the meeting's agenda.

Beatrice watched as Ramsay swabbed his face with a handkerchief. He was probably going directly home after the meeting, pouring himself a glass of Cabernet Sauvignon, and writing a celebratory poem. But if the tension in the town hall had been defused, the situation itself hadn't.

Chapter 3

Beatrice felt a little apprehensive when she walked from her car to enter the quilt show. She never looked forward to scenes, and she had a funny feeling that *someone* was going to cause a huge scene at this show. It actually started out being Beatrice that caused one—the car alarm for her new sedan started inexplicably going off when she was getting out of her car, causing several people to turn and stare, making her color a little.

But the scene inside the quilt show was either going to be Jo picking at Booth or Opal reproachfully telling the mayor the error of his ways. Or maybe it would even be a scene playing out between Opal and Jo or Karen and Jo. She'd dodge out if things got too heated.

Although she was tense when she got there, she felt herself relax as soon as she entered the quilt show. The event was being held at a historic school in nearby Blowing Rock. The school had been meticulously renovated with an eye to keeping the historic flavor of the building and was now used for traveling exhibits and art shows. The town kept the original tin ceiling and brick walls, and the hardwood floors gleamed. Quilts in every texture and with every color imaginable were carefully displayed with thoughtful lighting.

The first quilt she saw was one of Karen Taylor's. She gave a sigh of pleasure when she looked at it. It was absolutely stunning. Karen did indeed have a gift for quilting and a talent for design.

Fellow Village Quilter Georgia wasn't quite as sure about it. "So, you *like* this quilt?" asked Georgia dubiously. She pursed her mouth, staring at the quilt.

"Don't you?" asked Beatrice. "See the asymmetrical geometric pattern, the black-and-white scheme with the interesting copper shade Karen brought into the quilt? Art deco–inspired, obviously. It's straight out of the 1930s." She studied it, wistfully. If only she could get her quilting up to this level. She had great design ideas but couldn't implement them the way they needed to be.

"I wish it would go back to the 1930s," said Georgia with a little laugh. "What good is the quilt if you don't want to cuddle up in it?" Georgia's quilts exuded warmth and softness with their textures. "Of course, Savannah's are kind of prickly-looking, too, aren't they? All those precise stitches in the rigidly geometric patterns." She stared at one of her sister's quilts in a rather bemused way. "And Savannah is really so much quirkier than that."

The sisters both were, really. But what chance did

you have for *not* being quirky when your mother had named you and your twin Savannah and Georgia? Savannah, also, had an unfortunate problem with kleptomania. All the Dappled Hills store owners knew about it and kept a special, running, Savannah account that Georgia paid up each month. *Quirky* didn't quite go far enough.

Meadow bustled up in time to overhear Georgia mentioning her sister's quilts. "Your quilts are both beautiful, Georgia, just in different ways!"

"And you like Karen's quilt?" asked Georgia, nodding at the quilt.

Meadow beamed at the quilt. "I do! I do like it! It's modern and cool and sophisticated." She dropped her booming voice to what passed for a whisper for another. "But I'm glad I didn't invite Karen to be the new Village Quilters member if her quilts create division in the group! Much better to have someone like Jo."

Typical Meadow. She was either in happy denial of the friction Jo was creating in the group or else determined to ignore it.

"Speaking of our new member," continued Meadow, "where is Jo?"

"Probably kicking puppies or pinching babies," said Beatrice. Georgia gave a gasping laugh.

True to form, Meadow ignored this, too. "Judges of these events are incredibly busy, aren't they? So much to see, so many elements to judge each entry on. Mercy!"

This last was in response to a crashing boom of thunder outside the recreation center's window, followed by the sound of pouring rain.

Beatrice noticed the plate of brownies and fudge that Meadow was clutching. "Were you doing something with that?"

Meadow stared blankly down. "What? This? Yes . . . Oh, that's right. I was looking for the mayor. I figured, since we were trying to woo him, goodies might help. The quickest way to a man's heart and all that. Really, though, I probably should be pointing him toward Opal's cake. I think I saw her toting one in."

Beatrice glanced over Meadow shoulder. "You're in luck," Beatrice said drily. "Here he is."

A big smile stretched across Meadow's broad face as she caught sight of the mayor. "Hi, Mayor," said Meadow in the chirpy voice. "I thought while you are viewing this beautiful art here that you might enjoy some snacks."

Booth Grayson didn't appear to be enjoying himself. His clothes were sopping wet. He had a rather dour expression on his face. He was uncomfortable, he was bored, and Beatrice hoped that he would not take it out on the Village Quilters or quilting in general.

"No, thank you, Meadow. I had a large bowl of oatmeal before I came over. The quilts are . . . very nice. I've got to be leaving, though, because I've got some important business to take care of at the office." He took a precisely folded handkerchief out of his suit pocket and carefully dabbed at the raindrops on his clothes. "Maybe Posy can drive me back home in a few minutes. She was good enough to bring me here this morning since I wasn't sure of the location."

Meadow's face fell. "But that's no fun at all! I don't

think you've even seen all the quilts we have here. Besides, that's a lot of driving for Posy, considering that I'm sure Miss Sissy isn't ready to leave yet. And I know Posy must have brought Miss Sissy with her, too. She'd have to drop you off and come all the way back."

This thought didn't appear to bother the mayor in the slightest.

"Have you really *experienced* this show? There are tons of different styles. Karen has some really modern themes, Savannah has classic geometric patterns, and Georgia's quilts make you want to take the quilt off the wall, wrap yourself up in it, and watch some mind-numbing reality TV."

Booth's eyes narrowed. "I'm sure that's true, Meadow, but I've seen quite enough to make a decision about taxing the quilting group's proceeds and requiring permits. It was good of Ramsay to invite me here today. You'll have to thank him for me."

Georgia gave a small gasp. Her eyes clouded up, which, in Beatrice's experience, meant that the waterworks were about to turn on. Beatrice's head started to hurt. "But you haven't really given us a chance," said Georgia. "Did you notice that most of the proceeds from this event are going to fund local charities?"

Meadow's face was thunderous. She thrust her hands on her hips and glowered down at the shorter Booth. "You should eat something sweet," said Meadow pointedly, "to improve your sour disposition."

Meadow's stance and her booming voice were definitely drawing attention. Opal Woosley hurried over.

She clasped her hands and said anxiously, "Mayor Grayson! Would you like to have some caramel cake?"

Meadow said excitedly, "You've had Opal's cakes before, haven't you, Mayor?"

A spark of interest appeared in Booth's eyes. "Actually, I have. I will say that her cakes are positively amazing. I guess that it won't hurt to have caramel cake before I head out into the rain again. And I suppose I should give Posy a few more minutes at the quilt show. Maybe the rain will have let up a little by then."

Meadow, Opal, and Georgia all seemed to simultaneously exhale. Meadow grabbed Booth by the arm and pulled him toward the next room. Opal and Georgia scurried behind them.

Meadow got that mulishly determined cheerful expression again, and Beatrice knew Meadow was still stuck on Jo's absence. "She was probably held up at work. Jo said she'd come to the show right after she finished delivering the mail. Plus, you know, it's pouring down rain, so that's probably slowing her down, too. She said she was going to deliver it as fast as possible, though."

Beatrice could scarcely wait to see whose mail ended up in her mailbox today.

Karen joined them, sighing at the mention of Jo. "She's done an awful job delivering the mail even on the days when it's beautiful weather."

Meadow's pasted-on smile was strained. "Karen, Beatrice and I were admiring your quilt. We loved that art deco style, didn't we, Beatrice?"

Karen's shoulders relaxed from their stiff posture and she beamed at Beatrice with gratitude. "That's high praise coming from you, Beatrice. Thank you. You, too, Meadow," she added, in a bit of an afterthought. "Unlike Jo, y'all have some taste. It's absolutely astounding to me that she's a judge. It's sad because she's not even fit for judging a dog show. She's doing a real disservice to the quilting community."

Beatrice said, "Why exactly is Jo so critical of your quilts, Karen? I overheard her at the Patchwork Cottage, and it sounded like she was really going overboard with the feedback."

Karen lifted her chin up, then opened her mouth as if planning on really lambasting Jo . . . then apparently edited herself, with some difficulty, before she spoke. Instead she shrugged. "You know how it is. Some people like to pretend they know the best way to do everything. It's only natural, I guess. She's trying to change the way that I quilt and make it more traditional and less edgy. I think she has ulterior motives for doing it, though—when I'm experimental, I win shows. And Jo wants to win everything. Can't you tell? She's a very competitive woman. Her solution for winning is to try and make me change what I'm doing."

"I think," said Meadow with determination, "that Jo's ulterior motive is to make everyone better quilters. Why, at our guild meeting, she was instructing each one of us on ways we could improve."

Karen gave her a small smile that didn't quite reach her eyes. "That's very nice." Her voice didn't exactly ring with sincerity.

Beatrice thoughtfully studied Karen. It was interesting that she'd mentioned competitiveness. If anyone appeared competitive, it was Karen. Jo just acted like a know-it-all. "How do you place at shows where Jo judges?"

Karen sighed. "I never win when Jo is judging. She always makes sure I lose. She'll come up with all kinds of reasons why she didn't like them—bad composition, poor execution. I also think she talks to other judges, too, and influences them against me."

"Most likely trying to help you improve," murmured Meadow again. This time Karen ignored her.

Beatrice noticed Opal Woosley walking over to the refreshment table. "Opal isn't wild about Jo, either, is she? I'm surprised to see her here when she knows Jo is going to be here, too. I'd think she'd want to avoid meeting up with her."

"Opal wouldn't miss any opportunity to make a dig at Jo. She lives for these moments. Besides, she has a quilt here in the show—it's not a contender for a ribbon, but it's a nice quilt. I'm sure she's been practicing what she's going to say to Jo today . . . probably for hours." Karen glanced over at the disheveled Opal, who was spilling punch on the top of her blouse and muttering to herself.

The Looney Tunes ring tone on Meadow's phone went off, loudly. Meadow frowned. "That's the ring for Ramsay. Why would he be calling me? He knows I'm at a show."

"If you answer it," said Beatrice through gritted teeth as Looney Tunes merrily played on and on, "then maybe you'll find out."

Meadow raised the phone to her ear. "Ramsay? I'm sort of busy at this show. Can I call you back . . . what? What!" She listened intently for a moment, her mouth rather comically agape. "Oh. Ohhh. Okay. Yes."

"Something wrong, Meadow? It wasn't bad news, was it?" asked Karen.

A loud peal of thunder made them all jump.

"Yes," said Meadow slowly. "Yes, actually, it was bad news. Jo is dead. She drove her car right off the side of the mountain."

Chapter 4

For the next thirty minutes, the quilters clumped together to exclaim over the tragedy and the horrible weather that had surely been responsible.

"Jo always did drive perilously fast," said Opal. She clearly couldn't bring herself to fake any sorrow at Jo's passing, and her elfish face held some barely repressed glee.

Meadow's face was set in grim lines. "We should cancel the show. It's terrible of us to continue on as if nothing has happened. Besides, we lost one of our judges."

Karen quickly spoke up. "Meadow, I think that's a bad idea. We already rented the facility, after all. We've already transported the quilts and spent a long time working to display them. The refreshments and the quilters and the public are already here."

Meadow gave a hesitating nod, but still looked unconvinced.

"Besides, wouldn't Jo have wanted us to go ahead with the show?"

Karen was pushing it.

Suddenly, Opal's eyes opened up wide. She gaped blankly across the room as if she was seeing something that no one else saw. Her mouth dropped open.

Meadow's did, too, as she watched Opal. "She's having a vision!" she hissed at Beatrice.

Opal's mouth snapped shut again. "It wasn't an accident," said Opal in a wavering voice. "Jo Paxton was murdered."

"Murdered!" the women chorused.

Karen shook her head. "Opal, it looks to me like Jo was driving too fast for conditions."

"Why *shouldn't* she have been murdered? It was probably someone's good deed for the day. The month!" Opal Woosley's face was now irrepressibly elated.

Beatrice shook her head impatiently. "Maybe no one liked her, but that doesn't mean that someone murdered her. It's pouring down buckets of rain out there and Jo is driving on narrow, curving mountain roads. It sounds like the perfect setup for an accident."

Opal's eyes were huge. "It was no accident. I saw it—clear as day." She saw Beatrice peering closely at her and explained, "I have the sight, you know. I had a vision of a dark figure going underneath the car."

"You saw a dark figure going underneath Jo's Jeep? When?" asked Beatrice.

Opal shook her head vigorously. "No, no. I *just* saw it. In my head. With the sight." She gave a shudder as if shaking off a particularly sticky spirit.

"Her *gift*, Beatrice," said Meadow in a warning voice. That's right. Meadow hadn't wanted her to upset Opal for fear of paranormal repercussions.

Meadow was already pulling her phone out of her pocketbook. This was going to be interesting. Ramsay clearly had no intention of calling the accident murder or doing much of an investigation of it. He was likely only wanting to go back home, get out of the rain, and relax with some restorative classical literature.

Meadow stuck her finger in her ear to focus on her phone call over the high volume of the excited voices in the room. "Ramsay? It's me. Hey, Opal says that you need to treat the accident like a crime scene. That's right." She paused for a minute and listened hard to the phone. "She does know something about it, yes. She saw the crime happen! Opal saw the Jeep being tampered with!" Another pause. "No, no . . . she saw it in her head. She has the sight, you know." Meadow frowned. "We lost our connection."

Naturally.

"Oh no," gasped Meadow, reaching up to clutch at her throat in dismay. "Jo's husband, Glen, is coming in."

Sure enough, a rain-soaked and rumpled man wearing old khakis and a tired-looking button-down shirt was shaking off the rain and wrestling with a wet umbrella. He turned to walk farther into the room, then stopped with a puzzled expression as he took in the quilters' horrified expressions. "Is something wrong?" he asked.

As he was the only true official in the room, the onerous task of informing Glen of his wife's untimely demise had fallen to Booth Grayson, who handled the job with a brisk efficiency that Glen likely handled better than the weepiness of various motherly quilters. Already upset by the phone call, Meadow was a red-eyed disaster from the morning's drama. It was the final straw to have Glen come by the quilt show to support his wife, only to discover her death. Now, plied with iced tea and brownies, Meadow had subsided into a quieter state.

Booth left the quilt show with relief, glad to have an excuse . . . and a ride. Since Glen wanted to see the accident site, Booth offered to drive him in Glen's car. After the two left, Meadow said sadly to Beatrice, "And now we need to find another member for the Village Quilters again. Back in the same spot! It's such a tragedy!" She loudly blew her nose.

"I'm still not convinced it's totally necessary to find another member," said Beatrice, wanting to avoid the whole hashing-through process that had gone on before Meadow had decided to ask Jo to fill the empty spot. "Besides," she said in a low, pointed voice, "this is hardly the time to figure that out."

Meadow clearly needed distracting. Karen, who'd been pacing up and down the long wall of quilts, joined them again. Beatrice said, "Don't you need to make a decision about the quilt show? You're one of the organizers, right? Do we continue on or try to regroup and set everything up for another day?"

Karen said, "I think we decided it would be a lot of time and expense to set everything up again and rent the space, didn't we? But you and the other organizer need to find a substitute judge."

Meadow started blinking her eyes quickly and giving suspicious-sounding sniffs—the mere threat of tears made Beatrice leap into action. "Meadow!" she cried. "You'll make a fantastic judge. You haven't got a quilt entered, anyway, have you? You know how to be fair and impartial, right?"

Meadow sniffed a little and affected a noble expression.

"You'll be perfect. Just tell the other judges the change in plans, and get to it."

Karen and Beatrice watched as Meadow straightened her shoulders, grabbed a notebook and pen from her huge, quilted pocketbook, and hurried off with an expression of determined duty on her face. "Good job," said Karen, exhaling in relief.

"It was necessary," said Beatrice. "Meadow was on the brink of obsessing over the guild membership, what with our losing members recently and the Cut-Ups getting some really expert quilters. And there's no sense in wallowing in this all . . . better to finish with the quilt show today, then go pay our respects to Jo's family later on. Then worry about the guild roster later." Or *never* worry about the guild roster.

Beatrice tossed and turned in her bed as she replayed the day's events in her head. Fortunately, the rest of the quilt show had gone just fine. Karen won the awards she deserved and Beatrice enjoyed viewing the other quilts that were spotlighted. And Meadow and the other organizer had made a very poignant ending to the show when they gathered everyone in prayer for Jo's husband and in Jo's memory.

Still, there'd been enough drama to keep Beatrice awake into the wee hours. Noo-noo watched Beatrice anxiously from her dog bed, aware of her mistress's uneasiness. Usually at this time of the night, Noo-noo lay flat on her back snoring or smacking her lips in her sleep.

Finally giving up on sleeping, Beatrice got up. Quilting had really helped her sleep the last time she'd had insomnia. She'd grown to enjoy working on simple appliqués—anything elaborate enough to require focus meant the relaxation factor was lost. There was still so much to learn about quilting and so many different ways of experimenting with techniques. She was currently trying needle-turn appliqué. She'd traced some two-section flowers (she was trying to keep it simple) onto freezer paper, labeled the parts, cut them out, then ironed them onto the soft, pastel fabric that Posy had recommended. Then she'd cut out the fabric and pinned it to the background block. Now she was turning and slip-stitching to appliqué it. It seemed to be going well, although she'd like to have a couple of good reference books to look at every once in a while. She'd have to see what Posy had at the Patchwork Cottage, since she hadn't had a chance to purchase any yet.

As she stitched, she mulled over the events of the day. No one had been surprised that the elderly Jeep had gone over the side of the mountain on such a nasty day. Everyone had probably been thinking that the same thing could so easily have happened to any one of them. But it hadn't—it had happened to Jo, who'd made plenty of enemies. And that's what made it suspect.

Was Ramsay going to investigate this accident any further? It must be tempting for him simply to leave it alone . . . let it be a tragic accident. Still . . .

Beatrice laid the appliqué down. Mistakes. She'd made several mistakes over the last few minutes. Quilting was out. And, clearly, sleep wasn't going to happen. Noo-noo continued eyeing her with interest. She squinted at the clock. Three o'clock. The rain had stopped hours before and it had cleared out the atmosphere. Maybe if she stretched her legs and hashed everything over, she'd erase it from her head enough to fall asleep afterward.

"Want to go for a walk, Noo-noo?"

Noo-noo cocked her head at Beatrice as if not certain she was hearing her right. She quickly got over her confusion, though. A walk, day, night, or middle of the night, was *always* a good thing.

Beatrice changed out of her pajamas, grabbed the corgi's leash and collar, and they set out into a beautiful night. The moon was nearly full and there wasn't a cloud in the sky after the storm had blown through with such fury. The night air was the perfect temperature and had that clean, just-rained scent. Noo-noo pulled eagerly at the leash.

As they started off, Beatrice noticed there was a light on at the Downeys' barn. And it wasn't as weak as a night-light. It looked like someone was really up. Beatrice and Noo-noo paused. She couldn't just go up and knock on the Downeys' door at three in the morning. That would scare the living daylights out of them. Wouldn't it? But it certainly was tempting to see who was up and to maybe hash over Jo's death—particularly if it were Ramsay who was awake. Beatrice bit her lip, thinking it through.

Finally, she squared her shoulders and headed for the barn. It wasn't as if Meadow didn't ever call on *her* at the worst possible times. Not, to be perfectly honest, that these visits had ever been in the middle of the night, though. Still . . . Meadow didn't simply pop by—she came by with that great beast of hers that was always yanking food off Beatrice's counters. She glanced ruefully down at Noo-noo. She had her furry friend with her, too. But Noo-noo was a much better behaved guest.

Before rapping with the large door knocker, Beatrice peered tentatively through the large window next to the door. Apparently, neither of the Downeys worried much about pulling the curtains. She saw, at their huge wooden kitchen table, Ramsay—very respectable in pajamas and a navy bathrobe, wearing reading glasses perched on the end of his nose, and reading a thin, hardback book with what appeared to be avid interest.

Beatrice gently used the door knocker and watched as Ramsay glanced up with mild surprise, but no alarm. Their dog, Boris, barely lifted his huge head to stare at the door, then dropped back down and off to sleep. Some watchdog.

Ramsay laid the book down and walked over to let Beatrice in. He took off his reading glasses and motioned Beatrice and Noo-noo inside. "Hi there, Beatrice. Couldn't you sleep, or is something wrong?" His kind eyes looked searchingly at her.

She shook her head, still feeling a little silly for coming by. "It's insomnia. And I'm sorry to drop by here. . . . I saw your light and figured you'd be the perfect person to talk everything over with." She held out her hands. "Although why you'd want to on your off-hours, I'm not sure." It suddenly didn't seem like such a great idea.

Ramsay wasn't a bit concerned. He reached in the fridge and took out the milk container. "Would you like a glass of milk maybe? I was just about to have some myself."

She nodded, sitting at the kitchen table and giving an absent pat to Noo-noo, who was still trying to figure out what they were doing there.

As he was bringing out glasses from the cabinets, Beatrice glanced at the book he'd laid down on the table. *Walden*. You'd never have guessed at Ramsay's sensitive nature by looking at him.

She glanced around the interior of the barn. Besides Meadow's delicious cooking, the barn was the best part of coming over to the Downeys'. In the daytime, skylights lit the huge interior beautifully. Even in the dim light you could see the exposed rafters and posts of the soaring, cathedral-like ceiling. And Meadow had quilts everywhere. As Jo had pointed out, Meadow paid a special homage to the crazy quilts—hanging them haphazardly on the walls and draping them over most pieces of furniture.

"So you were disturbed by Jo's accident?" he asked, setting down the milks and sitting across from Beatrice at the table. He thoughtfully studied her. "Meadow was, too. But y'all were smart to refocus her by having Meadow substitute for Jo as a judge for the show. She loved it. And it tempered all the bad news."

"She's asleep now, I guess?" asked Beatrice.

"She was sleeping like a baby when I got up." He sighed. "Even after all my years of working accidents, it still gets to me."

"Just a softie at heart," said Beatrice, smiling.

"Meadow did have some worries, though, before she dozed off. She kept muttering about Opal."

Beatrice said, "Actually, that's what I wanted to talk to you about, too. Not about Opal," she added, with a dismissive wave as Ramsay's eyebrows shot up with surprise. "But what Opal was talking *about*."

"That Opal had a psychic vision and believes that Jo was murdered?" Ramsay's nose wrinkled in disgust at the word *murder*. "Beatrice, you're a reasonable woman. In fact, you've been a beacon of sanity in this quirky town since you moved here. You're well aware of the kind of weather we had yesterday. I can attest to the fact that Jo wasn't the most careful of drivers. I've stopped her and given her a ticket, believe it or not, while she was on her route." He took a soothing swallow of milk.

"I'm sure that's all true," said Beatrice, with a nod.

"That Jeep wasn't exactly brand-new, either. Jo was quite rough on those brakes," added Ramsay.

"I bet she was," said Beatrice.

Ramsay blinked with dismay as he realized Beatrice wasn't going to let the subject drop. "What makes you think Jo's accident could be murder?" Boris lifted his great head off the floor at the anxious pitch in his master's voice, and smacked his lips a little as he squinted at the shadows in the room for possible sources of the anxiety. Seeing nothing, he immediately lay back down and dropped back to sleep.

"For a very simple reason—no one liked her," said Beatrice. "I've gotten the very distinct impression that there were at least three people who were delighted to see Jo dead."

Ramsay's face brightened. "Well, but that's different," he said cheerfully. "There are *plenty* of people whose death wouldn't make me lose any sleep." He cast a longing look at *Walden*. Right now perhaps even Beatrice would make his short list.

"It's more than that," said Beatrice, spreading out her hands imploringly. "Karen Taylor and Jo were practically screaming at each other at the Patchwork Cottage the other day."

"Artistic differences?" asked Ramsay.

"That appeared to be the basis of it," said Beatrice. "But it could have been anything . . . the *why* didn't matter. It was the emotion itself and the way they seemed to hate each other."

Ramsay stared down at his milk glass and swirled the last bit of the drink around in his glass.

"And Opal Woosley was livid whenever Jo's name came up or whenever she was around her. Again, I'm not real clear on the *why*, but the important thing was her reaction. When I picked up the cake for the guild meeting, she told me she had reasons for disliking Jo. At the quilt show, she was clearly elated at the news of Jo's death."

"Well . . ."

Beatrice quickly added, "And what about the mayor? You saw the incident between Jo and the mayor unfold with your own eyes at the town hall. Remember how Jo insinuated that she had something damaging that she could use against Booth?"

Ramsay gave a rather pathetic sigh. "Yes, that was troubling. Although it could easily have been an empty threat."

"For an empty threat, it made Mayor Grayson absolutely furious."

Ramsay thought intently for a few moments, without speaking. Then he said, "I'll get a mechanic to check out the car for me—just in case. I suppose I can spare that money from the police budget. But please don't let on to anybody that I'm even considering the possibility it was murder. Especially not Meadow."

"Especially not Meadow *what*?"

They turned to see a sleepy, but rapidly waking and curious Meadow behind them. "Are y'all having a party and didn't invite me?" Meadow jammed her hands on her wide hips. She was wearing a large red T-shirt and green fleece pajama pants. The pajama pants were inexplicably covered with question marks. "Or are y'all having a romance?" She gave her loud, whooping laugh that made Noo-noo growl softly. The growling, naturally, got Boris all wound up. His throaty, booming bark made Noo-noo even more alarmed. It became very, very noisy for the middle of the night. And suddenly, Beatrice did feel very tired and sleepy.

She decided to leave all the explaining to Ramsay and head back home.

Chapter 5

Apparently, Ramsay *had* explained because the next couple of days were blessedly Meadow free and quite quiet. In fact, the only times Beatrice had even left the house were to take Noo-noo on walks on different trails off the Blue Ridge Parkway.

She hadn't really even thought about Jo. She walked, she tried reading a psychological thriller for the first time, she worked on her appliqué, she had supper with Piper one night after Piper's in-service training was through, and she even practiced her biscuit-making ability for breakfast one morning, since her attempts at baking usually ended in disaster. It was blissfully mellow in her cottage and felt very much the way Beatrice had always fondly imagined retirement to be. For a little while, Beatrice felt very much at peace.

Which, of course, meant it couldn't last. It would be a short-lived idyll. Sure enough, the quiet ended with a doorbell's ring and a breathless Meadow on her front porch.

Meadow had an excited Boris on a leash, and seemed to have been pulled the entire way to Beatrice's cottage. The beast immediately galloped in and helped himself to Noo-noo's water bowl. Boris' owner shuffled in and helped herself to most of the sofa, sprawling across it while she tried catching her breath.

It didn't take long for Meadow to recover from the sudden, intense exercise of her walk. Beatrice stuck a glass of iced tea in her hands and Meadow guzzled it down, then panted, "Beatrice! It *was* murder!"

Beatrice sank down into an overstuffed gingham armchair. "Was it? What did Ramsay say?"

"I've got to hand it to you, Beatrice. I don't know how you managed to get Ramsay to investigate that accident, but you did! I could have told him and *told* him it was murder until the cows came home and he'd never have checked Jo's car out."

"What did he find out?" asked Beatrice. It wouldn't do to try and rush Meadow. Resistance was futile. She'd have to wait for her to tell the story her way.

"Maybe it's because I brought up Opal and the whole psychic thing," said Meadow in a musing tone. "Ramsay's very funny about the supernatural. He's not a believer." Boris finally finished draining Noo-noo's water bowl and plopped onto the hardwood floor, thumping it loudly with his tail to express his excitement over the visit. Meadow stared blankly at the dog while Beatrice got back up, filled the water bowl again, and sat back down. "What was I talking about before we got started on Opal? Oh, right." She sat up a bit straighter on the sofa and leaned forward. "Jo was murdered. The brakes on Jo's Jeep were tampered with."

Beatrice said, "Ramsay's mechanic could tell they'd been tampered with? The Jeep is old—there wasn't just a natural brake problem?"

Meadow shook her head vigorously. "Nope. He said the mechanic mentioned that the brake lines to the front and rear brakes were cut open enough to make for a slow leak of brake fluid. They weren't completely severed, but were very clearly deliberately cut— probably with wire cutters. Which everyone has! Don't *you* have a pair of wire cutters?"

"No, I sure don't. I didn't have the need for anything like that in my Atlanta apartment. I had a pair at the museum, but I never brought them home."

"Well, we have some. Although I certainly had no desire to murder Jo! I was thrilled that she was going to fill our empty spot in the guild. Now we're back to square one."

Beatrice started counting to ten in her head. If Meadow went off on that train of thought, she wouldn't return to the station for a while.

Luckily, Meadow was able to stay focused on the murder this time. "Anyway, whoever cut the brake lines was pretty careful. The brake fluid didn't leak out right away—if it had, Ramsay says, then Jo would have noticed the brakes were gone before she even left her driveway. Whoever did it wanted there to be a slow leak so that after she'd been driving for a while, the brakes would have finally completely given out . . . and she'd have been on those mountain curves with no brakes."

Beatrice said, "Couldn't she have used the emergency brakes? Seems like that would have stopped the car or at least slowed things down long enough for Jo to regain control of the Jeep."

"Not really, according to Ramsay's mechanic. The emergency brake works with the rear brakes only, so she'd have ended up with only twenty percent or so of her braking power. At the speed that Jo was driving, going downhill on mountain curves in the pouring rain, she might not even have had the time to react enough to pull up on the emergency brake. At any rate, the mechanic said that the emergency brakes hadn't been used."

Beatrice sat quietly for a moment, digesting the information. "So I'm guessing they ordered an autopsy done on Jo?"

"Ramsay called in the state police as soon as the mechanic reported back to him. They ordered the autopsy right away. But Jo's body was fine—the only injuries resulted from the trauma of the crash."

"Doesn't it sound like her killer would have had to be someone with some knowledge about cars?" asked Beatrice. "A mechanic or someone whose hobby involved cars?"

"Not really. Ramsay said that anyone with an Internet connection could easily and clearly find out about sabotaging brake lines. You can find out anything on the Internet these days—there's all sorts of information on any kind of illegal activity you're interested in."

Beatrice said, "Somehow, I can't see these quilters creeping around under Jo's Jeep with a flashlight during a tremendous rainstorm to find the brake line."

"They certainly could! There's nothing tougher than a quilter," said Meadow, fiercely defending the murderous potential of her fellow quilters.

"They're tough, for sure," said Beatrice, thinking of Patchwork Cottage fixture Miss Sissy. She wouldn't want to be on that old woman's bad side. "Since the autopsy is finished, I'm guessing the funeral will be soon?" Traditionally, in the South, bodies were very quickly buried . . . a practice that was likely rooted in the pre-air-conditioning era.

"I'm hearing that the funeral is arranged for tomorrow. I'm going to take Jo's husband—that's Glen—a frozen chicken casserole. You know he's going to end up with all this food, and these poor men sometimes don't know what to do with it all—and they end up tossing tons of it out and then going hungry weeks later and having to learn to cook before their mourning period is over." Meadow shook her head sorrowfully. "So I'm going to bring it frozen with taped instructions stuck on the top for defrosting and cooking the casserole and I'll stick it right in his freezer."

"Maybe I could bring something like pimento cheese sandwiches," said Beatrice slowly. Having lived by herself for so many years in a city like Atlanta, she'd fallen somewhat out of the habit of cooking. It had been very easy to simply pick up ready-to-eat or ready-to-cook meals from her favorite grocer's deli section. Her husband had died when Piper was still in high school, and after Piper had left for college, she'd found it wasn't exactly fun to cook for one. "At least then he'll have some decent food for lunch, too."

"Make sure you don't cut the crusts off," Meadow reminded her sagely. "Men don't like to eat sandwiches without crusts. They think it's sissy."

"I'll be sure to keep that in mind. By the way, Meadow, I was wondering who you thought might go to Jo's funeral?"

Meadow shrugged, still planning her casserole in her mind. "Pretty much the whole town, I'd think. There's really nothing else going on tomorrow, after all. And she *was* the mail carrier for Dappled Hills. There's not a soul in town who doesn't know her."

"Well, sure, but whom from our group? Which quilters might be there?"

Meadow thought for a moment, tapping her fingertips together. "Why do I have the feeling that you're already thinking about murder suspects? Let's see. I'm sure that Karen will *not* be there. She'd know how hypocritical it would make her look to go to the funeral. On the other hand, I think that Opal *will* be there. She would want proof that Jo is really dead."

"And how about someone like Booth Grayson?" asked Beatrice.

"He'll probably go. He's running for reelection, so he'll be shaking hands and kissing babies wherever two or more people are gathered together. Ramsay said that he's going to the funeral . . . a sure sign he thinks suspects will be in attendance. He's now rereading one of his favorite books and he wouldn't go to a funeral unless he absolutely had to," said Meadow, with a wave of her hand. "And, Beatrice, I know someone else who will be attending the funeral."

Beatrice would have asked who, except she knew Meadow's we-have-a-secret smug smile a little too well. She sighed.

Meadow continued, anyway. "Wyatt. Wyatt Thompson will be there!"

"Naturally, he'll be there. He's a minister, after all, and Jo was a member of our church." Beatrice kept her voice even, although her heart gave a little leap when Meadow said Wyatt's name. Silly heart. It had no permission to do that.

Meadow wasn't at all deflated. "It occurs to me that you need to move forward with this relationship, Beatrice."

"It isn't a relationship at all!"

"Which is precisely my point. You haven't even started *flirting* with him! And you spend more time with my husband than you do with him. It's pitiful. Have you even been to church recently?"

"As a matter of fact, I was there last Sunday," said Beatrice, sounding more defensive than she wanted to.

"And when did you go to church before that?" asked Meadow.

Beatrice stared guiltily down at her shoes. She'd meant to go to church the couple of Sundays before that, but her backyard had been so beautiful and quiet. She'd had her own sort of worship services in her hammock, admiring God's handiwork. She cleared her throat. "You know there's nothing going on between me and the minister, Meadow. Besides friendship, that is."

Meadow rolled her eyes. "I surely do know that. But it doesn't have to be that way. He'd be delighted if you made some sort of move. I mean, look at you! You've got this cute bob of platinum blond hair—"

"It's white hair, Meadow," corrected Beatrice glumly.

"Well, if it *is* white, it doesn't seem white. It looks very blond. Like Marilyn Monroe."

Her analogy stunned Beatrice momentarily into silence.

"You always look classically chic," continued Meadow.

Beatrice blinked down at her khaki capris and pink button-down shirt.

"And if you're a day over sixty, then I'm the Queen of England!" said Meadow, slapping her thigh for emphasis.

"Better go claim your throne, then," said Beatrice in an even glummer tone.

Beatrice could see the wheels spinning in Meadow's head. It was something she didn't like to see. To interrupt whatever matchmaking plans Meadow was concocting, Beatrice quickly switched to a subject dear to Meadow's heart. "What are we planning to do with the Village Quilters membership now? Are you planning recruitment again?"

She felt her shoulders relax a bit as Meadow immediately launched into the convoluted pros and cons of jumping right into recruitment versus waiting in observance of Jo's untimely demise. At the end of her monologue, she said, "But this time I do intend to exercise more caution in placing a member with our group. You were so right about Jo. I simply couldn't see it! We shouldn't recruit someone especially murderable this time. I was thinking that we could get to *know* some prospective members, one on one, you know? What I thought I might do is have a couple of Friends of Quilting dinner parties and invite potential new members. Maybe Karen Taylor for the first one?"

Beatrice frowned. "I thought you said that Karen was entrenched in the Cut-Ups guild. Isn't she happy there? Won't it stir up bad feelings between our groups if we try to solicit members from the other quilt guild?"

"It's up to Karen to decide which group best fits her needs," said Meadow with a pious tone. "We're simply giving her the opportunity to make a choice."

It all sounded like a good way to make enemies. But Beatrice wouldn't turn down an opportunity to quiz Karen on Jo's murder. Karen wasn't someone she was going to run into very often, otherwise. "You'll invite me to your dinner party, Meadow?"

Meadow beamed at her. "I certainly will, Beatrice! Thanks for taking such an interest in our Village Quilters membership."

Or something.

Meadow was perfectly correct with her funeral attendance speculation, a fact that rankled Beatrice. Opal Woosley was at the funeral, with bells on. There were no somber garments for her . . . she wore a party dress covered with vibrantly colored flowers and even had a gardenia in her hair. She had a dazzling smile plastered on her face and exhibited not the slightest inclination to put up a false show of grief.

Also as predicted, Karen *wasn't* there. Most of Dappled Hills was in attendance . . . including Mayor Grayson. It was a beautiful day with puffy white clouds chasing each other across a deeply blue sky and a light breeze cooling off anyone who grew too warm in the bright sun. There was no good reason not to be there, and the entire town had known the mail carrier.

The cemetery itself was almost discordant in its cheeriness. The cheery sun illuminated the graves and all the, mainly fake, flowers propped up on the headstones. The funeral-goers appeared fairly cheerful, too. It was the oddest funeral she'd ever attended.

The funeral home seated Jo's husband, Glen, in the first row under the funeral home tent, and there appeared to be a collection of older men and women near him that must have been either Jo's more-distant relatives (since Meadow had informed her that there was no immediate family besides Glen) or Glen's family. None of them were local residents and none looked particularly sad about Jo's unexpected death.

Except for Jo's husband, Glen. His face was ashen and from time to time he bit his lower lip as if to discourage any strong emotion. He certainly had every appearance of a grieving husband dealing with a sudden and unexpected tragedy.

Beatrice watched Booth cynically. He had an air of detachment as he listened to Wyatt talk about Jo. Like Opal, he clearly had no reason to mourn today, but he

was being less honest about that fact. He sat there under the tent, hands folded, the perfect picture of a local
official paying his respects.

Once Wyatt wrapped up the simple graveside service, everyone stood in small groups among the graves,
talking to each other in muted voices. Meadow walked
up to Beatrice and nodded to some headstones a few
yards away. "That's the Downey plot, right there. See
that blank spot near the big marker? That's my final
resting place." She puffed up with pride at what was
apparently a choice spot in the cemetery.

Beatrice wasn't exactly sure how to respond to
Meadow's comment. "It's a lovely location, Meadow.
On the hill there and everything." Her voice trailed
away at the end.

"We were right, weren't we?" asked Meadow, quickly
changing course. "About the funeral and who was here.
Now, who was it that you wanted to talk to? I know
you're wanting to do a little sleuthing."

"I'm sure this isn't really the time to—"

"Who don't you see on a regular basis? Jo's husband,
Glen, for sure. You don't run into Glen often, do you?"
Meadow pursed her lips doubtfully. "Unless your car
has needed a lot of repairs. He's a mechanic. At least, he
was. The garage laid him off a few months ago. Poor
guy. He was doing some repair work on the side, but
now I don't think he's doing even that anymore."

"No, I don't know Glen. Although I do need some
work done on my new sedan, I think. The alarm is always going off. But I can't see that this is really the
right time—"

"But you know, we don't really need to talk to him here. We'll be bringing him the food later. You *do* have your pimento cheese sandwiches ready, don't you?" asked Meadow.

Beatrice nodded. "The consistency was a little off, though. I don't know if I didn't put enough mayonnaise in this time, or if I put too much cheese in—"

"So we can see Glen when we drop off the meals. We'll try to pick a time when no one else is over there so you can investigate while we're being thoughtful. How about Booth Grayson? Your paths might cross more frequently, I suppose. You're both such serious, studious types. You probably see him at the library when you're reading up on some really obscure Depression-era Southern pottery made with a particular type of clay only found on the banks of certain Georgia creeks," said Meadow.

Beatrice shot Meadow a look.

"Okay, so you don't see him that much. Maybe the mayor isn't as studious as he appears. I thought he'd be in the library reading up on the tax code and trying to figure out ingenious new ways to assess taxes on quilt guilds. Let's go talk to him!"

Meadow pulled Beatrice over to Booth, who'd finished shaking the hands of most of the funeral-goers. He folded his arms, discomfited at seeing them. "Ladies," he greeted them cautiously.

"It's a beautiful day, isn't it, Mayor?" Meadow cheerfully asked. "It couldn't *be* any nicer."

"Perhaps if there wasn't a funeral to attend," noted Booth duly.

Meadow blithely ignored his comment. "You've decided against assessing sales taxes and requiring permits for our quilting guilds, haven't you? I always said you were a reasonable man. Didn't I, Ramsay?" Ramsay, who'd been watching the attendees with some interest, briefly wandered up. Hearing the topic of conversation, he gave Booth a pitying stare, shook his head at Meadow, and quickly walked away again.

Meadow watched him go and said, "Interesting thing about Ramsay—he hates funerals. Absolutely despises them! He's such a sensitive soul that he can't stand to be around folks who are in distress. He's here today," she added, peering at Booth, "because Jo was murdered."

Beatrice sighed. Surely Ramsay wasn't ready for this information to be released.

Before she could deflect Meadow at all, she'd continued. "And Beatrice is the one who convinced him Jo's death wasn't an accident! She likes to do some investigating, you know. Beatrice is a frustrated detective."

Beatrice jumped in. "It's not exactly like that, Meadow."

"Beatrice will get to the bottom of this mess, if anyone can. Oh, my sweet Ramsay *could* get to the bottom of it. If he were only motivated! Bless him, though, he's just not. Beatrice, on the other hand, is just so *discerning*. And smart! She's the very smartest person I believe I've ever met. I'm no young woman, either!"

Booth gave Beatrice a serious and analytical appraisal. Then Beatrice noticed his gaze was diverted by a young woman in a short dress. Men.

"Ramsay told me that Beatrice gave him a list of all the people Jo had been arguing with," said Meadow. Then she glanced over at Booth Grayson and blushed, remembering that he was on the list.

Booth said wryly, "Obviously, I was one of the people you mentioned, Beatrice. Although you wouldn't have had to say anything, since Ramsay was at the town meeting, too. Of course you realize that Jo was fabricating things that night—trying to gain some leverage that didn't exist. She was a woman who clearly cared very deeply about quilting."

"As do most of the ladies here," said Beatrice smoothly. "I'm one of them. And I'm certainly hoping you're planning to reconsider your approach to the Dappled Hills guilds."

"So smart!" murmured Meadow, admiringly.

"If you're interested in protesting the proposed measures," said Booth in a steady voice, "I do have a suggestion for approaching it."

If his droning voice could be bottled, it would do wonders for insomnia sufferers. "Wonderful! What's your suggested approach?"

"If you go online—because we're trying to do as much online now as we can—then you can click on a link to download a PDF of a form . . . let's see. I believe it's form 21-DRV. Once you download that form, you print it out, fill it out, mail it in, and then I'll have an official record of your concerns and can appropriately address them."

"I think I might have a better approach," said Beatrice smoothly. "We'll publicly make our opinion known at the next town hall meeting. Directness is key in these issues, don't you think?"

Booth looked as if he had a mild case of indigestion.

Out of the corner of her eye, Beatrice saw that the minister was walking up with Miss Sissy to join them. Ordinarily, she'd have loved having Wyatt as part of their conversation, but she had a feeling this was going to derail any questioning. Booth was gazing longingly toward a group of older women whom he must have missed politicking with earlier.

"How does Ramsay think the murder happened?" asked Booth smoothly. "It seemed to me that it was an open-and-shut case—a treacherous mountain road and a bad storm. An accident." Wyatt and Miss Sissy stood next to him, and Miss Sissy's face, deeply creviced with wrinkles, grew even more wrinkly as she stared at Booth. She'd apparently taken a strong dislike to the man. Beatrice was beginning to feel sorry for him.

Beatrice cleared her throat. "Someone cut the brake lines. Just enough to ensure that at some point during Jo's route, she was going to lose control of her brakes." Wyatt's eyebrows went up in surprise, and Miss Sissy grunted and leaned in closer to them, cupping her hand over her ear to hear better.

"It sounds like something that was done that morning," said Booth. "If the brake lines had been cut the night before, the fluid would probably have leaked out before she even got into the car. In which case you can remove me from your list of suspects. I was at home, getting ready for the quilt show. I took a phone call from a commissioner about next month's art festival.

Then I got ready to go to the show. Your friend Posy was my ride out there, since you'll remember my saying that I wasn't sure exactly where the event was."

He frowned at the wizened Miss Sissy and added, "And—uh—Miss Sissy was in the car, too. It sounds to me as if you should be searching for a car mechanic. Now, if you'll excuse me . . ." He hurried to catch up with a small group of Dappled Hills residents whom he hadn't yet spoken with.

They watched him go. Wyatt said in a low voice, "So it's definitely murder? Everyone was so convinced it was an accident."

Meadow said in that loud, boisterous voice, "And Ramsay was, too, until Beatrice here persuaded him to investigate." Meadow, Beatrice firmly believed, would someday get her murdered. Fortunately, it was a minister she was talking to now.

And, of course, Miss Sissy. Who wouldn't be forgotten. "Lies! All lies!" Her lips pulled back in a leer. She ran her hands through her hair in agitation, forgetting, apparently, that she was wearing a bun. Now even more strands of wiry hair stuck out.

Wyatt Thompson had the patience of a saint. Or of a Presbyterian minister, anyway. "What lies, Miss Sissy? That Jo's death was murder?"

Miss Sissy hissed, "He wasn't home! He wasn't home! Lies!" She lifted her gnarled fists and shook them at Booth's back as he walked into the parking lot with the older ladies.

Beatrice said, "When wasn't he home, Miss Sissy?"

"Before the quilt show. He wasn't there!"

Miss Sissy was sputtering out now and was distracted by the removal of the quilt that Jo's husband, Glen, had laid on Jo's coffin during the graveside service. Apparently, he was planning to take it back home with him in commemoration of the day.

"I think," said Wyatt slowly, "that today has tired Miss Sissy out a bit. I'm going to go ahead and drive her back home so that she can put her feet up for a while."

"Lies," muttered Miss Sissy.

As they walked away, Beatrice said, "But Booth Grayson *was* at the show. He came in with Posy and Miss Sissy. I remember laughing about it at the time, because I knew Miss Sissy must have been sitting up in the front seat and supervising Posy's driving. It would have been a wild ride for Booth in the backseat with a madwoman muttering in the front. He was there, so at some point he must have been home for them to have picked him up."

Meadow gave a good-natured shrug. "Who knows what Miss Sissy was fussing about? She's forever making these dire, cryptic proclamations. We'll have to catch up with Posy later and see if she can give us any insight. Miss Sissy might be talking about something that happened a month ago, for all we know."

She guessed so. But still, it made you wonder. She'd have to remember to tell Ramsay about it.

Chapter 6

Meadow dropped Beatrice back home for a few hours before they set out for Glen's house with Beatrice's sandwiches and Meadow's frozen chicken casserole. Meadow had apparently had a nap over the afternoon and was in a very perky mood. This perkiness would have been unbearable if she hadn't been offering some information, too. "Ramsay said that the state police found no other evidence of murder. So Jo hadn't been attacked or poisoned or strangled, or drowned, or . . ."

"Got it," said Beatrice drily.

"But Ramsay said the reasonable conclusion drawn from the Jeep's being tampered with is that Jo was the one targeted. It wasn't Glen's vehicle and Glen wasn't known to drive it. He always drives his truck. So it wasn't as if someone sneaked under the Jeep that morning and thought that Glen was going to be the one to die."

"I only really saw Glen for a few minutes at the quilt

show and then a minute at the funeral. What's he like?" asked Beatrice.

"Well, for one thing, he's very well educated," said Meadow. "Ramsay used to hang out with him at the auto repair shop and they'd discuss literature."

Beatrice said, "Really? That's a little unusual for a mechanic, isn't it?"

"Both of his parents were teachers, so he was exposed to a lot of culture through them. He went to college, too. But his parents had always encouraged him to go into whatever interested him—and he was interested in cars. The only bad thing is that when he lost his job as a mechanic, he really didn't have the experience to do anything else. He had the *education*, but not the experience. And, at his age, when he's knocking on the door of middle age, experience is really what matters for an office job."

Studying Glen at his house a few minutes later, Beatrice knew that he was the most likely candidate to be Jo's murderer. The police usually considered the victim's spouse to be the primary suspect. But Beatrice found it hard to imagine that he had anything to do with his wife's death. He was tall, but slightly hunched over as if always bending down to hear what you had to say. He had deep smile lines around his mouth and little ones around his eyes and a generally amiable disposition. He quickly took the dishes out of their hands, then gave them a hug. His eyes were sad.

"Thanks so much for bringing the food over, ladies. It's nice to not have to worry about what I'm going to eat for the next week or so," he said, walking in and putting the food over on the counter.

Meadow said briskly, "Now, if you really pay attention, Glen, this food will last a lot longer than one week. I know you had a bunch of ladies out here right after the funeral with covered dishes. *My* casserole is frozen, so you can stick it in the freezer and then defrost it next week. I've taped instructions on the front."

Glen nodded and gave a vague look at Meadow's casserole. There appeared to be food everywhere—sitting on the counter, in containers on top of the fridge, and stacked on his stove.

Meadow rolled up her sleeves. "Glen, you don't appear to be in any mood to tackle this cornucopia of lovingly donated casseroles. Why don't you and Beatrice sit down and chat for a little while? I'm going to go through everything and see what needs freezing and what needs refrigerator storage." She opened their fridge and peered in. "And maybe I need to make room in your fridge for some of this stuff to begin with." She settled down on the floor and started examining the condiment bottles and jars of pasta sauce in Glen's refrigerator. She glanced up to see that Beatrice and Glen weren't moving. "Go! Shoo!" She waved at them.

They obeyed this time and Beatrice and Glen walked into a small den that was very modestly decorated. Glen sank into a slip-covered sofa and Beatrice noticed for the first time the fine lines around his eyes and how tired he seemed. "This must have been an incredibly difficult day for you. I promise we'll be gone soon. I guess you know how Meadow is—she sees a job to be done and she jumps in with all engines firing."

Glen gave her a faltering smile. "She's nice to take care of it for me. I knew I needed to organize the stuff in there, but every time I opened the fridge door I put it off. You're right. It was a rough day."

They sat quietly for a few moments, the only background noise the sound of clinking glass into a trash bag as Meadow appeared to be throwing out all types of jellies and sauces and salad dressings.

"I'm sure," said Beatrice slowly, "that part of what made it so exhausting is the range of emotions you must be experiencing. For one thing, the unexpectedness of it all."

Glen rubbed the side of his face with a big hand. "That's true. From the moment I showed up at the quilt show, expecting to see Jo there, it's been one surprise after another." He paused, then continued. "I'll go ahead and tell you this—you came with Meadow, so you might already know, anyway. The police are saying that Jo's death was no accident. They're saying she was murdered."

Beatrice hoped her expression had the appropriate amount of surprise on it. But Glen wasn't looking at her, anyway.

"I know that there were some people who really didn't like Jo. But she was a very warmhearted and giving person. She didn't suffer fools lightly, but she was always so giving of her time and talents. Making quilts for the children's hospital and the nursing home. Helping to organize fund-raisers. She cared a lot about people."

Beatrice said carefully, "Does that mean that the police have been asking you questions?"

"Oh, sure. You know how it is—the husband is always the prime suspect if there's a murder." Glen smiled wearily at Beatrice. "They wanted to know if I had the opportunity to tamper with Jo's brakes."

"And you did?"

"Well, sure I did! I live here. It would have been as easy as pie to nip out to the driveway and take a wire cutter and cut the lines just enough so that the fluid would start a slow drip." His own words shook Glen up a little, and his face turned ashen at the thought of what had happened to the Jeep.

"Did you see or hear anybody that morning? See anything suspicious?" asked Beatrice.

Glen smiled at her. "Thanks for thinking that someone else must have done it. I hope everyone in Dappled Hills will be as fair as you. This won't be a fun place to live anymore if everyone is talking about me behind my back or is convinced that I'm a murderer. To answer your question . . . no. I didn't hear or see anything that morning. I sure wish I had. Jo was trying to get ready for the mail route and for judging the show, and I was trying to get ready, too, so that I'd be able to arrive at the show later and give her some support. I wasn't spending time staring out the windows."

"I don't think Dappled Hills will be quick to judge," said Beatrice. "You're someone who's been in town for a long while and has contributed a lot to the community."

Glen brightened a little. "Thanks. I hope you're right."

Meadow walked in. "Okay, Glen, I've got you all set. I cleared out anything from your fridge that was past its expiration date. Then I put in the casseroles and stuff that might not freeze as well. Then I pulled out some old food from your freezer and put in the casseroles that could be frozen. You should be good for a while."

"Thanks, Meadow. You're a lifesaver. I'd have ended up throwing away most of those casseroles, I'm sure, if you hadn't organized it all."

She beamed at him and reached out to pat his arm. "Glen, it was a pleasure. I'm sure you don't feel up to doing it yourself, and it makes me feel good to help out." Meadow turned to Beatrice. "You may not know it, but Glen is a real asset to Dappled Hills. He volunteers his time almost every day out of the week. One day he's at the area food bank, another he's helping with the Crisis Ministry, assisting folks who can't pay their utilities. And you're also helping out with the area underprivileged children and adult literacy, right?"

Glen nodded. "I've been out of work for a while now, and I couldn't stand hanging out in the house and not doing anything. I was driving Jo crazy moping around, so she recommended that I talk to Penny Harris."

Meadow explained to Beatrice, "She's Dappled Hills' top volunteer. Sort of a Super Volunteer."

"Penny explained all the different groups that needed help . . . not all of them in Dappled Hills, of course, since it's such a small town. Some of the other, larger mountain communities needed volunteers, too. I was happy to spend all this extra free time doing something useful. Besides, with me being unemployed for so long, I kind of related to all those folks who needed help. A lot of them were like me—they had a good job, and then they lost it and found themselves in a real spot." He stared down at his hands. "I guess I'll be spending more time than ever volunteering now. Just to keep myself busy since Jo's gone."

Meadow folded her hands to her chest. "So touching, Glen!" Then, in typical nosy Meadow fashion, she asked, "Do you have any ideas about who might have put you in this awful mess? Who could possibly have done this to Jo?"

Glen recoiled a little. "I don't know that I could say, Meadow. It's not something that I have any evidence or proof of, even if I had some ideas. If I did, I'd have let Ramsay know. There were people who didn't like Jo, and that's a fact. But I hate to think that one of those people might have done something like this."

"That's totally understandable, Glen," said Beatrice with a squelching glare at Meadow. "Maybe Meadow should've asked who you knew of who wasn't getting along with Jo very well."

Glen shook his head and said slowly, "Opal Woosley, for one. And I don't think Karen Taylor has ever liked Jo—I think she gets her feelings hurt when she doesn't win the quilt shows that Jo judges. Jo was also telling me something about the mayor the other night. She was upset at something he was doing, I think." He said again, in a stronger voice, "But again, I don't think any of those people could have killed Jo. I can't believe it. Y'all were good enough not to automatically assume that I'd murdered Jo, so we should extend the same courtesy to the others."

But *someone* had murdered Jo. And it sure hadn't been someone who liked her.

The next morning, Beatrice had barely finished her cup of coffee and English muffin when the phone rang. It was Meadow. Naturally.

"I know this is short notice, but Karen Taylor is free tonight for supper. Want to come? I'm going to make something yummy."

Beatrice was trying to remember Meadow's purpose for this dinner party. Meadow took her silence as disapproval and quickly added, "There won't be a lot of people coming—I know you're not crazy about big parties or anything. I just want to get a sense of what Karen would be like as a member of the guild. So it's going to be you and me and Karen and maybe Posy, too . . . I have to ask her."

"And Ramsay?" asked Beatrice.

Beatrice could tell from Meadow's voice that she must be making a face on the other end of the line. "No, not Ramsay. He's being impossible, Beatrice," she said in what she considered a whisper. It was more of a stage whisper and Beatrice heard Ramsay saying in the background, "Meadow! I told you that I don't need to be inviting murder suspects over to dinner! It's not appropriate."

"So Ramsay's clearly not going," said Beatrice drily.

"I guess not," said Meadow with irritation. "I think he'll be eating tomato sandwiches in our bedroom."

"And reading Thoreau and enjoying my solitude!" said Ramsay distantly.

"And missing out on a mouthwatering feast!" said Meadow. To which, there was no reply. Meadow *was* an excellent cook and he'd decidedly be missing out. "Which is very stinky of him. And now I won't have any men there, which throws the balance of a dinner party completely off. Pooh!"

Meadow paused for a moment to think this through.

"Oh! I've had a brilliant idea. I'll invite Wyatt over. Having a minister at the dinner party means that we'll all be on our best behavior. And he's so charming at parties, anyway. Don't you think so, Beatrice?"

Beatrice didn't deign to answer. But her heart gave a little leap at Wyatt's name.

"Anyway, that would make it perfect and more low-key and not quite as unbalanced. Let's see . . . that makes four of us. No, five. Perfect," said Meadow.

"Do you want me to bring anything?" asked Beatrice. She didn't really *want* to bring anything, but figured it would be polite to ask.

"Ummmm." Meadow suddenly was tripping over her words and stuttering in a very un-Meadow-like manner. "Well, you see, I'm not sure if we're going to eat right when everyone gets there or maybe just visit first. Then you'd have to go to the trouble of cooking, or maybe even of going to the store. And we'd have to reheat what you brought. Trouble. Lots of it. Yes. So I'll see you at six, then. Yes." And she quickly hung up.

Apparently, Meadow wasn't much of a fan of Beatrice's cooking.

*   *   *

Beatrice was never exactly sure what to wear to dinner parties in Dappled Hills. But this was Meadow. She guessed she'd be fine in her black pants and white tunic with some dangly jewelry. Ramsay opened the door when she rang the bell. He had a dour expression on his face. "Meadow is still getting ready. I guess. She disappeared into our bathroom. And one of her timers is going off." He straightened up and his eyes pleaded with Beatrice. "I don't suppose there's anything you can do about that?"

Beatrice squared her shoulders. "I can try. She probably needs to pull something out of the oven, right?" They walked over to the stove, where a timer was gently dinging. Very unlike Beatrice's timers, which had a shrill buzz to remind her to stop whatever she was doing. Beatrice peered dubiously into the oven. "Let's take it out, to be on the safe side. It looks done to me." She pulled it out of the oven and placed it gingerly on the counter.

And it smelled absolutely delicious. It appeared to be some sort of bacon-wrapped chicken with a scrumptious sauce over rice. Southern cooking at its finest.

There was a tremendous thumping noise from the back of the barn, and then Meadow appeared moments later with one arm out the top of her dress. "Help! Help, y'all! My zipper broke on this stupid dress and now I can't get out of it. Oh, help!"

There was a tapping at the barn door as Meadow's panicking increased.

"Must be one of my murder suspects, arriving for dinner," said Ramsay grimly.

Beatrice said, "Here, Ramsay, why don't you go into the back and help Meadow with her dress—get her into it or out of it? I'll greet the guests and finish up fixing the supper."

At Beatrice's mention of cooking, Meadow's eyes grew even larger than they already were. Ramsay was pulling her into the back as Beatrice hurried to the door as another timer started going off. Hadn't she taken everything out of the oven? What could that timer be for?

Beatrice opened the door and saw an apologetic Posy standing there with an especially wild-looking Miss Sissy. Posy, as usual, was tidy and sweet with a baby blue cardigan that sported a cute beagle broach. Miss Sissy, on the other hand, looked as though she'd forgotten to comb her hair this morning. "Hi, Beatrice!" said the tiny, bespectacled woman brightly. "Lovely day, isn't it? Are you standing in for Meadow?"

"Just temporarily," said Beatrice, hurrying back to the kitchen. She lifted the lids on the pots. Were these things cooked, or not?

Posy sidled up to her. "Do you think Meadow will be upset?" she asked, blue eyes widening anxiously. "Miss Sissy wandered over right when I was leaving and sort of demanded to come along. She even mentioned being hungry." They both glanced over at Miss Sissy, who was at the kitchen table, steadily consuming the bowl of Goldfish crackers that Meadow had set out.

Beatrice shrugged. "You know Meadow. I don't think she'll really mind. Posy, does this chicken look done to you? The timer keeps going off and I can't figure out what it's for. And Meadow has had some sort of wardrobe malfunction and can't come out yet."

Posy inspected the chicken doubtfully. "Do *you* think the chicken is done?" she asked in her gentle voice.

Beatrice frowned at it. It appeared a little pink. "Are these chicken *breasts* or chicken *thighs*? Because chicken thighs sometimes seem like they're not done yet and they're very done."

There was a knock at the door. Beatrice and Posy gave Miss Sissy a helpless look, but she'd moved on from the Goldfish crackers and onto what appeared to be a plate of cheese olivettes. Beatrice sighed. She'd have enjoyed trying Meadow's version of cheese olivettes.

Posy said, "How about if I try to figure out what's going on with supper and you take care of the door? Everyone's really starting to arrive."

Miss Sissy picked up the plate of hors d'oeuvres and held them close to her chest, glaring ferociously at Beatrice as she passed by.

It was Wyatt at the door. Beatrice cursed herself for putting a hand up to her hair to make sure her platinum white strands were in order. She could never feel totally natural around Wyatt. Fortunately, he didn't appear to notice. He gazed deep into her eyes as if they were the only ones there, and gave that smile that crinkled the edges of his eyes. She cleared her throat and tried to speak. Talking was usually an issue for her whenever Wyatt was around. This was very vexing to Beatrice, since she considered herself an excellent communicator. She'd been a museum curator, for heaven's sake! She'd given tons of talks about folk art—even impromptu talks. But none of them, reminded a little voice inside her, to Wyatt.

She took a deep, sustaining breath. "It's somewhat chaotic inside, Wyatt." She stepped aside and let the minister in. He was wearing khaki pants and a crisply ironed black button-down shirt that complemented his silver-streaked hair. He looked splendid.

There was a shriek from the back of the house that made everyone freeze. They could hear Meadow's voice bellowing, "The zipper caught my skin, Ramsay!"

Beatrice smiled at Wyatt. "Meadow's having a problem with her dress. That's why I'm on door duty and Posy is trying to figure out what's going on with our dinner."

Miss Sissy, who'd polished off the plate of cheese olivettes, hurried up to Wyatt with her odd, galloping gait. He gave her a hug and she smugly smirked at Beatrice. "I didn't know I was going to be able to visit with my favorite parishioner tonight," he said to Miss Sissy. She preened.

Another timer went off, but Posy gave Beatrice a reassuring smile. "Not to worry! I think I've discovered the secrets of Meadow's approach to cooking."

Beatrice said wryly to Wyatt, "I tried to take over in the kitchen for Meadow, but it didn't go so well. I made a tactical error in removing the chicken, apparently. I'd gotten out of the habit of cooking in Atlanta, and I guess I haven't totally remembered the rhythm of it yet."

"You made a really delicious casserole for the covered-dish picnic last month," said Wyatt with a warm smile. "I ate every bit of what was on my plate."

Beatrice said wryly, "No, that would be my daughter's casserole you enjoyed, I'm afraid. Piper made two casseroles for the picnic and I carried one of them in. But thanks." They grinned at each other.

There was another knock at the door. "That must be Karen Taylor," said Beatrice, moving to the door. "She should be the last guest."

It was Karen. She was wearing quite a dress, too. Considering that she was in her thirties, she was able to pull it off pretty well. It was a simple black dress with a fairly deep neckline, cinched at her waist with a gold belt. The hemline fell slightly above her knees, showing off her nice legs to best advantage. But who gets dressed up like that for a group of quilting women?

And a single minister. Beatrice watched as Karen lit up as soon as she saw Wyatt. She muttered out a greeting to Beatrice, then glided over to Wyatt's side, giving him a quick hug, which he returned. "Wyatt, you must have been spying on me to be able to deliver such a perfect sermon last Sunday. It was *exactly* what I needed to hear this week."

Beatrice, walking slowly back to Wyatt, picked her brain trying to remember what the minister's sermon had been about. She'd been in attendance, right on the third row, in her usual pew. She remembered enjoying the pithy message and following along in her Bible as he'd read the perfect verse to put his sermon across. But she couldn't for the life of her remember the topic.

"And you're so right," continued Karen, "that sometimes we get so caught up with life that we don't allow ourselves the time for God to talk to us."

Ah. That was it. Yes.

"I found some really interesting verses in Corinthians during my daily Bible study," said Karen, eyes shining, "that really summed up what you were saying."

Daily Bible study? Beatrice was starting to feel even more incompetent than she had when she'd suddenly been placed in charge of the dinner.

Beatrice thanked the Forces That Be for Meadow's sudden, flamboyant reappearance. She didn't think she'd ever been so happy to see the woman.

"I am *never*," said Meadow, hand to heart in vowing posture, "wearing a dress again. As God is my witness. Never! And y'all make sure Ramsay doesn't bury me in one, because I do believe he might do it out of spite, since he had an epic struggle trying to extricate me from that one." She wore a pantsuit, and her gray braid swung at her side.

Meadow hurried over to greet everyone with a small hug, then she said anxiously to Beatrice, "What happened with the food?"

"Actually, Posy ended up taking over while I greeted at the door," said Beatrice, trying to ignore Meadow's quick sigh of relief. "There were all these timers going off and I couldn't figure out what was supposed to come off the stove or out of the oven."

Meadow walked over to the kitchen, saying over her shoulder, "And some of those timers were for things to go *into* the oven. Posy, how clever of you! You knew that one of the timers was for the bread to go in."

Posy said modestly, "It seemed like the right thing to do." Beatrice then saw Posy move closer to Meadow and speak in a low voice. They both looked at Miss Sissy, and Meadow nodded. Miss Sissy's presence was cleared. Hopefully Meadow had enough food.

While her guests were visiting, Meadow put the food into serving dishes for the table. She motioned Beatrice over and hissed at her, "Shouldn't you be asking Karen about her whereabouts the morning that Jo was murdered?" Meadow scooped some creamy mashed potatoes into a floral vegetable dish.

"I would, Meadow, except that Karen is preoccupied. She's fairly starstruck by Wyatt, I think."

Meadow glanced over to Karen, who was now standing very close to Wyatt and laughing at something he was saying. Meadow's eyes opened wide. "Is she *flirting* with him?" Her voice was outraged, the fact that she was intimidated by Karen's talent forgotten. "But I invited him here for *you* to talk to!" She knit her brows and tossed the pot into the sink with unnecessary force. "That's most annoying! Most annoying indeed!"

Although Meadow was an amiable and loyal friend, Beatrice had noticed that it wasn't a good idea to get on her bad side.

Meadow's eyes narrowed. "I think I need to dictate seating tonight. I wasn't *planning* on assigning seats, but desperate times call for desperate measures. I want Posy and me and even Miss Sissy to get to know Karen better. And that's not going to happen if she's hanging on the minister the whole night."

Meadow bellowed, "Posy and Wyatt? Could you help me put the food on the table, please?"

Both leaped into action. It was amusing to see the minister expertly finding the right dish for each item—and the correct serving spoon or meat fork. It just goes to show how many covered-dish suppers and other meals he'd presided over in his career at the church.

With Wyatt across the room, Karen grew fidgety and glanced at her watch. She settled onto Meadow's sofa, nearly covered in quilts, and ran her hand over one that was draped over the back of the sofa. "She loves the crazy quilts, doesn't she?" Karen winked at Beatrice as if to say there might be a good reason for that.

"She's got that waste-not, want-not mentality," said Beatrice, easing herself next to Karen on the sofa. "Meadow's an ex-hippie, you know. She's a big recycler. Makes sense that she'd be the same way with her fabric."

Miss Sissy had sat down directly across from Karen and was staring at her with fierce fixation. "Meadow is a good quilter!" she barked at Karen as if Karen wasn't properly impressed by Meadow's skill.

Karen said gently, "Of course she is, Miss Sissy. I love Meadow's quilts. I just wish that maybe she'd try something different. She has a lot of talent and enthusiasm for quilting and I want her to explore some of her creativity. That's what I'm doing—experimenting. I guess you don't think much of my quilts."

Miss Sissy shrugged a bony shoulder. "They're

good," she said in a subdued voice. She added quickly, "But they aren't pretty!"

Karen laughed at that. "No. Most times they aren't that pretty. It's funny, but sometimes it takes trying something different—maybe something that's not even really attractive—to catch judges' attention and win shows and get recognition." She was more relaxed as she talked about competitions, clearly a favorite topic.

Which meant it was the perfect time to catch her off guard and ask her some questions about the murder. Beatrice smoothly said, "When I was in the Patchwork Cottage the other day, I heard Jo talking to you about the fabrics you were getting for a quilt."

Karen made a face. "Talking to me? You mean arguing with me, don't you?"

"It did sound like an argument. Is that why Jo left the Cut-Ups guild?" asked Beatrice.

"Jo and I weren't getting along at all. As I mentioned, I'm trying to do some experimental things with my quilts—using different types of fabrics, hand-dying, three-D techniques, decorative threads for unusual stitching. Jo was like Miss Sissy," said Karen, nodding at the still-glaring little woman.

"She didn't think they were pretty?" asked Beatrice.

"She didn't. But more than that, really. Jo didn't think I was emotionally invested in my quilts. She acted like I'm this cold, clinical person, trying to gauge what's going to get me a ribbon. Calculating. Plus, I think she was jealous. I was winning more competitions than she was. She'd get back at me when she could in the quilt shows she was judging—I never placed or showed whenever Jo was a judge." Karen's face was flushed and her eyes were bright. She was clearly still very angry over Jo's bias.

"Refrain from anger and turn from wrath!" Miss Sissy shrieked.

Wyatt walked up and regarded Miss Sissy calmly. "Psalm Thirty-seven, isn't it, Miss Sissy? You have a verse for every occasion." He turned questioning eyes on Beatrice and Karen, as if wondering what exactly that occasion was.

Karen adroitly changed the subject, perhaps to show off more of her biblical knowledge to Wyatt. "Psalms has many more lovely verses, though, don't you agree? Songs to God—what a lovely thought." She stood up and walked over to the table with Wyatt, apparently planning to sit next to him at dinner.

Meadow galloped over, holding a large wooden spoon in a threatening manner. "All right! Seating arrangements for tonight." She cleared her throat. "Karen, I'd like you next to me—to pick your brain on some of the new quilting techniques." Meadow proceeded to tell them all, in no uncertain terms, where they should sit. She pointed to the spots with her spoon.

Karen, crestfallen at first, became more cheerful at the prospect of talking about quilting techniques.

"And, Posy and Miss Sissy, you should listen in, too. Although, Posy, I know you must know all about Karen's type of quilting, what with owning the shop and all."

"Not really," said Posy mildly. "I know enough to

order supplies, but not enough to use most experimental techniques myself. I'd love to know more. Maybe Karen can even teach a workshop at the Patchwork Cottage or at one of our quilt shows. I'm sure a lot of quilters would love to know more."

Miss Sissy was still muttering, "Not pretty!" under her breath.

Chapter 7

The food was, of course, delicious. Southern comfort at its finest. The chicken was smothered with pineapples, chutney, and chopped pecans and served over steamed rice. There were fried green tomatoes from Meadow's own backyard garden and a bowl of collard greens mixed with chunks of chopped smoked ham and bacon. Beatrice carefully pushed her food to the side to make room for some Southern spoon bread on the very edge of her plate.

There must have been two thousand calories on Beatrice's plate, and she savored every single one of them.

Meadow had made sure that Beatrice was sitting next to Wyatt, which she actually hadn't wanted. She really didn't need to talk to him the whole time or even most of the time. She'd only been disturbed, more so than she cared to think about, when Karen had so obviously been trying to catch Wyatt's attention. Even now, as Karen was discussing some of her thoughts on the future of quilting, she stared wistfully at Wyatt. It was startling. She was either infatuated or in love, despite the difference in their ages.

Wyatt appeared oblivious of her gaze. He was asking Beatrice about her life in Atlanta and punctuated her descriptions with nods of interest.

Conversations around the table shifted after a few minutes. Karen was thoughtfully scanning the barn. "You have a ton of quilts, Meadow."

Meadow raised her eyebrows. "Well, when you're an old woman like I am, Karen, and you've been quilting for life, you're bound to have a good number of quilts. Of course, you won't be old like me for quite a while, will you?" She gave her booming laugh. Beatrice could imagine Ramsay in the back of the barn with his Thoreau, wincing.

Karen pushed a hand through her artfully tousled hair and said hastily, "You're not old, Meadow. The only reason I brought up the number of quilts is that I thought you might be able to display them to better advantage."

Meadow glanced around the big room as if seeing it all for the first time. There were quilts draped on the backs of every available object, quilted pillows, quilted quilting bags, quilts on the walls. "Don't I have them almost everywhere I *could* have them? I've even got them stacked in my closets."

"I was just thinking that you could hang more of the quilts. You have an extremely high ceiling, you know. I've been experimenting with different types of hangers—it could really make a difference," said Karen. "I'm sure that Beatrice, with her curator background, would have some other ideas, too."

"Not off the top of my head, no," said Beatrice. Decorating a home was different from setting up a traveling exhibit in a museum space.

Meadow whooped. "Since it's a barn, yes, it *does* have a high ceiling. I'll have to get back to you on that."

Beatrice thought that Karen had probably now scored back the number of points she'd lost earlier in the night. Although the poor woman had no idea she was being judged. Karen seemed very nice and she clearly had no idea that Beatrice had any interest in Wyatt at all. . . . Why would she?

Things wrapped up pretty quickly after dinner. Miss Sissy had gotten tired and started acting out, quoting fire and brimstone Bible verses at Karen in tones of increasing volume and vitriol with her eyes narrowed.

"Aren't you *lively* tonight, Miss Sissy!" said Meadow, blinking at her.

Posy quickly made their good-byes and gently steered Miss Sissy to the door.

"Can I help you clean up the dishes, Meadow?" asked Wyatt.

"Can you help . . . no! Certainly not. But thanks for asking, Wyatt." Meadow beamed at him. Wyatt thanked her for supper and found his keys. Karen quickly thanked Meadow, as well, and picked up her pocketbook so that she could walk out with Wyatt.

But Beatrice didn't move toward the door, instead saying wryly, "I had a feeling you wanted to talk about the evening for a few minutes."

"Yes! An analysis of the events. And I have to say," said Meadow, vigorously scrubbing a baking dish, "that Karen behaved horribly with Wyatt. Very, very tacky of her. Doesn't she know about you and Wyatt?"

Beatrice gave a strangled laugh. "Meadow, there *is* no Wyatt and me. We're merely friends who enjoy each other's company." She ignored the little voice inside her that said there was more to it than that. On her end, at least.

"Whatever," said Meadow with a roll of her eyes. "Anyway, she was obviously hanging all over him. And she's nowhere close to his age. A strumpet!"

"I have to wonder about her interest in Wyatt," admitted Beatrice. She added quickly, "He's very intelligent, spiritual, and attractive—but that age difference made me wonder."

"Which is exactly why you shouldn't worry about the two of them, Beatrice. Wyatt clearly looks at Karen as a daughter," said Meadow.

Beatrice wouldn't go quite that far.

"I'm sure this unhealthy interest of Karen's goes back to the loss of her father when she was just a college student. I believe she's been searching for a father figure ever since. Even so, it's all most irritating. Karen finally won me back with her ideas for better quilt displaying. So that really puts me on the fence. I'm undecided about asking her to be a member of the Village Quilters. How about you?"

Beatrice said, "I'm still undecided whether she's a murderer or not."

Meadow made a *pish* sound. "Beatrice, just because

a woman's a flirt doesn't mean she's a killer. But point taken. We'll reserve judgment and keep exploring our options. I'll sleep on it. Besides, we probably shouldn't replace Jo this week, anyway. It might make us appear insensitive."

The next morning, Beatrice got up, dressed, and resolutely headed to the closet for Noo-noo's leash and collar. Meadow's dinner had been delicious, but now it was time to walk all those fabulous-tasting calories off.

The sun was barely rising in the sky. She loved getting up in time to see the vibrant pinks and oranges of the sunrise light up the horizon. It was cooler in the early morning, too, and the whole day seemed full of promise.

Noo-noo automatically tried steering them in the direction of their usual walks—toward the park in the middle of downtown Dappled Hills. But Beatrice mindlessly moved in the opposite direction. Without taking note of what she was doing, she'd somehow ended up back at Jo's house. Although she should be thinking of it as Glen's house now. Maybe she'd been thinking so much about the murder that her feet automatically moved her in that direction.

Beatrice frowned. Glen's truck wasn't parked in the carport the way it usually was. Surely it was too early in the morning for an unemployed man to be out of the house. It wasn't as if the grocery store was even open yet. Even if it was, Glen couldn't possibly need any food—his kitchen was fairly groaning under the weight of all the casseroles that the good people of Dappled Hills had brought in. Where could he be, then?

She sighed. Now she was turning into the stereotypical nosy Dappled Hills resident. Next she'd be peering through windows and making wild guesses about her neighbors' activities.

Noo-noo suddenly grew alert and turned as if hearing a noise approaching them. Beatrice later wondered what instinct had made her quickly pull the corgi behind her into a cluster of bushes.

A slow-moving Mercedes passed right by them and pulled into the driveway. A moment later, Booth Grayson got out, glancing around him surreptitiously. Beatrice held her breath, but his gaze never rested on them.

Booth strode to the house, peering through the picture window next to the door. Apparently satisfied, he moved to the front door and turned the knob. He wore gloves. Gloves on such a warm morning? An interesting fashion choice for the mayor.

Booth apparently found the door unlocked and darted inside the house. Beatrice released her still-pent-up breath and reached down to give a reassuring pat to the corgi, who was probably wondering what they were doing in the bushes. "Let's stay," she whispered to Noo-noo. She wanted to see how long Booth Grayson was in Glen and Jo's house and what he might leave with.

It was maybe seven or eight minutes before Booth walked out. He was sweaty and rumpled, with none of his usual composure. He clutched something in his gloved hand, which he shoved into a large pocket. She squinted but couldn't make out exactly what the object was. A small camera? A camcorder? It looked like some kind of electronic equipment.

Booth glanced around him as he hurried to his car. Seeing no one, he quickly jumped in and drove off.

Beatrice waited until she could no longer hear his car's engine before she slowly left her hiding place. Booth must have known or guessed that Glen wasn't at his house. He was clearly searching for something and trying not to be seen. At the town meeting Jo had acted as if she'd known something incriminating about Booth. Had he just removed evidence of what she'd known?

Later that morning, Beatrice drove into downtown Dappled Hills to the Patchwork Cottage. After finishing the flower appliqué, she wanted to start working on a new quilt. She hoped that Posy could help her find some new fabrics.

The Patchwork Cottage was fairly busy. Posy gave Beatrice a warm smile but couldn't greet her since she was tied up talking to several women who appeared to be asking her a lot of questions. At least business was doing well.

Posy had gotten some lovely new fabric in. Beatrice was thinking about doing a pinwheel quilt, and there was a bundle of fat quarters of vibrant blue, green, and yellow Woosley prints. And a bundle of fat quarters with red and pink stripes, a delicate floral, a twirly dots pattern . . . it was going to be hard to make up her mind. Or should she look at the yardage and do something that was more uniform? She was at the point where she could *design* something more sophisticated than she could actually create.

Since Posy was still tied up, Beatrice decided to wait for her in the shop's sitting area. There she found Miss Sissy, sleeping on Posy's overstuffed sofa and snoring ferociously. Beatrice sat in the chair across from her and picked up a quilting magazine off the end table.

A few minutes later, she got the feeling that she was being watched. Beatrice glanced up to see Miss Sissy scowling at her with brows fiercely knitted. Beatrice felt the need to explain her presence there. "I'm waiting for Posy," she said with a shrug. "I couldn't decide which fat quarter bundle I should get."

"Posy's talking to the new quilters," barked Miss Sissy. She studied Beatrice for a moment. "You should get the garden one." Miss Sissy was muttering so low that Beatrice had to strain to hear.

"I'm sorry?" asked Beatrice.

Miss Sissy glared at her. "The gardening one! With the flowers and pots and gloves and watering cans on it."

Beatrice wondered if she was going to roll her eyes like a teenager. "But, Miss Sissy. I don't garden." And remembering Miss Sissy's jungle of poison ivy that surrounded her house like something out of *Sleeping Beauty*, Beatrice thought neither did she. Beatrice only replaced plants that she killed. She hardly called that gardening.

"Hmph!" Miss Sissy's expression told her she should start. And immediately.

They sat in silence for a moment. It wasn't a particularly companionable one, so Beatrice cleared her throat and said, "It was good to see you at Meadow's last night."

Miss Sissy said, "I never saw you at Meadow's last night!"

Apparently, some things were getting lost in the black hole that was Miss Sissy's mind. But the thing was, you could never tell what she might *know*, either. She could be a worthwhile source of information. It was simply a matter of getting her to talk about something that pertained to the topic at hand. And possibly to sort out the truth from the fabrication or, perhaps, the madness.

Beatrice used a coaxing voice. "You spend a lot of time here in the Patchwork Cottage, don't you, Miss Sissy?"

The old woman appeared pacified. And she was listening. Catching Miss Sissy's attention was half the battle.

"I bet you know a lot about the ladies who come here and the different things going on around town," said Beatrice. "You certainly seem observant."

Miss Sissy smiled smugly, in an omniscient manner.

"When I was in here the other day, I saw some things going on that I didn't totally understand. Karen Taylor was having a real argument with Jo . . . over fabric. It got pretty heated and I couldn't believe that someone's fabric choice could turn into such an argument."

Miss Sissy narrowed her eyes. "Those two love to hate each other. It's wrong to hate. *The wages of sin is death*."

Now the task was to keep Miss Sissy from getting

distracted by her favorite topic—sinning. "It is. Very wrong! So why did they hate each other?"

"Envy! Wretched envy! Wickedness!"

Beatrice gazed thoughtfully at the old woman. She might have something there. Envy was a very strong emotion, and both those women could have been afflicted by it. Jo would likely be sour at any rising star in the quilting world and determined to shut Karen down from racking up successes too quickly. Karen, on the other hand, sounded very ambitious and determined to obtain both quilting awards and recognition. Her pleasure in quilting didn't seem inherent in the activity itself—she also wanted to *win*. She'd have been jealous of all of Jo's ribbons and her status in the quilting community. And she'd have wanted to confront anyone who stood in the way of her having similar successes.

Miss Sissy was mulling over Karen and Jo, too. "A wicked woman," she hissed, almost to herself.

"Who? Jo?"

"No," she said scornfully. "Karen. Flirting. Wicked." Her face was dark with memory.

Oh. She'd forgotten that Miss Sissy also had a thing for the good minister. He was always kind to her . . . going by her house for visits, bringing her the treats she loved. And Karen *had* been hanging on Wyatt during the dinner party. Beatrice had better move this conversation along before it got completely sidetracked.

"Something else about that day in the shop and then later when I picked up the cake," she said, "was that Opal Woosley was making all these digs at Jo. But I didn't know the story behind it."

If she'd thought that Miss Sissy was animated before, she hadn't seen anything yet. "She killed him!" she said, eyes wild, leaning forward on the sofa, bony elbows jutting out. As if unsure that the import of this statement was getting through, she stressed, "On purpose!"

"Who? Who killed him?"

"Jo!" she bellowed.

"Killed who?"

"Skippy!"

It must have been getting very loud in their corner of the store because several customers were now staring at them. Beatrice smiled at them in what she hoped was a reassuring way. One of them took her smile as encouragement to chat. She asked her opinion on two different fabrics and which she liked better. Beatrice pointed to the one she liked and they talked for a minute. By the time Beatrice had turned back to Miss Sissy, the old woman had fallen asleep again and had resumed her emphatic snoring.

Posy finally finished up with her customers and smiled at Beatrice, her blue eyes holding a friendly greeting. She said, "Sorry about that—there were some novice quilters in from Lenoir to pick up supplies." She glanced over at the sofa. "I'd whisper except I know Miss Sissy won't wake up even if we shouted at each other."

Beatrice gazed at the thin figure on the sofa. "Only babies and innocents sleep that soundly," she said, a little sourly to her ears. She hadn't slept particularly well since moving to Dappled Hills. It was so quiet there—she'd gotten used to the sounds of the city when she lived in Atlanta.

"Posy," she said, "I did have a nonquilting question for you. Who is Skippy?"

Posy gave a vague frown. "I'm sorry?"

"Skippy. Miss Sissy and I were talking about Opal and she said something about Jo killing someone named Skippy."

"Oh, I see. Skippy is a dog. Well, he *was* a dog. But he wasn't just a dog to Opal. Her whole life revolved around him. She'd dress him up in different outfits and talk about the cute things he'd done. And she'd carry pictures of him the few times that she didn't have him with her in her purse. Actually, she'd carry pictures of him even when she did have Skippy with her," said Posy.

"So let me see if I've got this right," said Beatrice slowly. "Opal Woosley cared about her dog as if he were her child. And Jo somehow killed him?"

Posy sighed. "It was an accident, of course. Jo said she never saw the little dog when she was delivering Opal's mail. Apparently, Opal had a package that day and so Jo had to pull into her driveway and walk it up to the house since it wouldn't fit in the mailbox. Jo said the dog was barking and snapping at her ankles. Skippy had never taken a liking to Jo for some reason, you know."

"Not an uncommon problem for mail carriers, I'd imagine."

"Exactly," said Posy. "The dogs just see the constant trespassing on their property. Apparently, Skippy was out that morning, and Jo accidentally ran over him. At least, Jo swore it was an accident. But Opal took it quite seriously and acted as if Jo had intentionally murdered Skippy. She claimed that she had a vision that showed Jo had planned it all."

Posy didn't realize that she'd used the word *murder* in connection with Skippy's death. She continued. "Poor Opal took to her bed. We didn't see her for a couple of weeks, at least. We all brought her food— casseroles, breakfasts, sandwiches. She didn't have the will to keep on going. She really loved that little dog. And she held Jo responsible for his death."

The door to the shop dinged again and Posy said quickly, "Let me show you those new fabrics you wanted to ask me about before I get caught up with more customers!"

This time the interruption came from outside. There was suddenly a persistent honking coming from the parking lot behind the shop. "Mercy!" said Posy in alarm. Even Miss Sissy woke from her deep slumbers, jumping violently at the shrieking sound.

Beatrice sighed and stood up, pointing her key ring in the direction of the noise, which immediately stopped. "I've *got* to get that car alarm fixed," she sighed.

The problem with getting fun, new fabrics was that you wanted to start using them right away. She'd ended up with the pretty Woosleys and was itching to start cutting the triangles for the pinwheels. If she got into the pattern of not finishing what she started, though, she'd end up with a bunch of UFOs—unfinished objects—like Meadow. Uncompleted projects weren't a good way for Beatrice to stay motivated. If she had a precedent for not finishing a quilt, it gave her an out whenever she got bored or started losing her way with it. Instead of moving on to the shiny new object the new fabric represented, she spent the rest of the afternoon and evening finishing up the quilt she was working on: colorful appliquéd flowers on an ocean waves blue-green background.

The next morning, she slept a little later than she usually did. She'd wanted to finish the quilt before she turned in, so she'd been up past her usual bedtime. Beatrice was pouring herself a cup of coffee when Noonoo's ears perked up and she started giving a low growl and her fur stood up on end as she stared at the front door.

Beatrice waited to see if anyone was planning on knocking at her door or ringing her bell—but heard nothing. Actually, she did hear something—a strange snuffling, snorting sound. Feeling the hairs lift on the back of her neck, she moved slowly to the door and peered cautiously out the window. She didn't see anything. She was returning to her coffee when she heard the sound again. This time she looked down . . . and saw Boris sitting to the far side of her porch, grinning up at her hopefully. He wagged his tail and it thumped loudly on her porch.

Somehow, much as Boris annoyed her, she couldn't resist him. He was always in such a bubbly mood. He showed up so frequently at her house that she now had a treat jar full of extra-large treats especially designated for Boris. Noo-noo's expression was horrified as Beatrice opened the door, gave him a couple of treats (she'd seen before that Boris would help himself to anything on her counter if she didn't feed him), and refilled Noo-noo's water bowl. She also opened another jar and gave the corgi a couple of smaller-sized treats. Noo-noo would turn into a tummy with feet if she ate as much as she'd like to eat.

Beatrice glanced at the clock. It was still really too early to make phone calls to the Downey household. Ramsay might have been up late, working the case with the state police. Besides, the now-full and satisfied Boris had curled himself up on Noo-noo's pillow (causing yet another expression of horror on the corgi's face) and was sleeping soundly. Noo-noo begrudgingly napped herself, lying on her back and making small snores. It was all enough to make Beatrice snuggle into the soft sofa, cover herself with a quilt, and read quietly until she, too, fell asleep.

A gentle tap on her door woke them all up. Noo-noo gave sharp warning barks and Boris cocked his head curiously at the front door. Beatrice extricated herself from the softness of the quilt and the sofa and half staggered to the door, still a bit fuzzy from the nap. Meadow's knock was unusually tentative. She peered out the window to the side of the door and saw an apologetic Ramsay there, holding a leash and collar.

"I'm sorry to be coming by so early, Beatrice. You haven't seen Boris, have you?"

Beatrice didn't even have time to answer before the

dog had pushed through the door and joyfully greeted his master by throwing his tremendous paws up on the police chief's stooping shoulders and licking him on the face. Ramsay turned his face to the side and lifted the dog off to the ground. "I'm sorry again, then! We didn't mean for you to have an unexpected houseguest this morning. I've got to figure how he's getting out." He sounded baffled.

She might not have been delighted to see Boris this morning, but Ramsay was a slightly different matter. There were a few things she'd like to ask him, and having him show up on her doorstep this way was most convenient. She could always try to siphon information through Meadow, but then, you could never really be sure about the information you were getting.

"Can you come in for a minute? I was about to pour some coffee—would you like a cup?" asked Beatrice.

Ramsay said, "Oh, that would be great. I didn't get a chance to even drink mine before I realized that Boris wasn't there. Surprisingly, Meadow is still asleep. The coffee that I make is never as good as hers, anyway. I don't think I've ever really figured out the ratio of water to grounds."

Soon they were sitting companionably in Beatrice's tiny living room, sipping coffee and talking about the personalities of dogs. Noo-noo acted more cheerful now that Ramsay was there. The leash and collar that the police chief held probably helped the corgi realize that Boris was a temporary addition to the household.

Beatrice was wondering how to introduce a discussion of the murder into this very relaxed conversation when Ramsay blessedly introduced it himself. "You're a well-read and thoughtful woman, Beatrice," he said in a musing voice. "Have you read *On Walden Pond*?"

"Not recently, but I've read it, yes." Beatrice had a feeling that the seclusion of Walden was extremely appealing to a man like Ramsay Downey. Particularly since he lived with Meadow and her nonstop motion and talking.

"Well, it's made me think. Thoreau, of course, had this ideal of being solitary. But in fact, he had many unexpected visitors. Sort of like you've had this morning," added Ramsay ruefully. "Thoreau lived around a lot of characters himself. And he probably was one of the primary unusual characters."

Beatrice was frowning in concentration by now, trying to follow Ramsay's rather scattered train of thought. He noticed her frown and waved a dismissive hand. "I'm not making sense, am I? It's still so early in the morning. I'm just saying that we can never really know a person, can we? Not even if we've lived around her our whole lives in a small town. People seem easy to understand. But they're not."

"Case in point?" asked Beatrice, trying not to sound too hopeful.

Ramsay studied her thoughtfully for a few moments, then said, "Well, Jo, for instance. I thought she was an open book. She was a little prickly, into her quilting craft, and enjoyed her job as postal carrier. It always looked like she and her husband were trying to make ends meet, particularly after Glen lost his job as a mechanic. Why wouldn't it? Jo wouldn't make much from the post office, and with Glen out of work, it looked like they were really having tough times."

"But she wasn't so easy to read after all?" asked Beatrice.

Ramsay shook his head slowly. "Not so easy, no. Turns out she has a whole ton of money. She was her dad's only child and he owned a string of factories. Sold them, made a bunch of money, died, and left everything to her."

"I guess she and Glen were simply conservative with their money," said Beatrice with a shrug. "It happens. Maybe they liked to live under their means instead of pushing it."

"That's another funny thing," said Ramsay. "Glen acted totally surprised about the inheritance. Like he had no idea there was anything in the bank at all. How could you be married to someone for a couple of decades and not know their financial situation?"

Beatrice wasn't sure. "Are you certain that Glen didn't know?"

"If he did know, he put on a good show of not knowing. But I guess he'd do that if he possibly murdered for money." Ramsay shook his head, bemused. "I somehow can't see it, though. Glen has always been devoted to Jo. In fact, he always seemed sort of under her thumb. He's an interesting fellow himself. Glen is very well educated and well read and we like to hang out and talk to each other about literature sometimes. But he chose a career as a mechanic because that was what he liked to do."

Could Glen have finally gotten fed up with Jo's controlling ways? It had to have gotten old sometimes. "As you said, though, do we ever really know someone? Maybe Glen did know about the money and decided he was tired of living so simply. Maybe he'd have liked to travel or to relax and read all day and buy a big library of books."

"Or maybe he got tired of being pushed around by Jo," said Ramsay, echoing Beatrice's thoughts. "Still— you were there when he got the news about his wife, weren't you? How did he appear to you then?"

Beatrice thought back to the quilt show. "He looked completely shocked. And you're saying he was surprised about Jo's money. Maybe he really is a good actor."

Ramsay shrugged and looked baffled. "That's what I'm saying. It's hard to believe you can live in a town your whole life and not really know a person."

"I guess you would know people pretty well, Ramsay. I bet they probably open up a lot to you, too," said Beatrice.

"Maybe," said Ramsay, tilting his head to one side and looking at her inquisitively. "Is there somebody you can't really make out?"

"Well, Opal Woosley for one," said Beatrice. "She looks like this very stereotypical old maid. But she's supposed to be psychic and she's obviously got some very passionate feelings about particular topics."

Ramsay rolled his eyes. "Oh, Opal gives me fits. Maybe she *is* psychic, I don't know. But if she was so psychic, it seems to me that she could have kept her little dog out of harm's way. She was always telling me that she thought Skippy was in danger from various evil forces—coyotes, mean neighborhood cats, a little girl down the street. Although she never mentioned Jo."

"Who apparently was someone to watch out for," said Beatrice.

"Clearly. But as I mentioned before, Jo wasn't the best of drivers. Opal should have realized that. Here you've got someone who drives to your house *every day* and isn't really focused on driving." Ramsay sounded a bit disgusted and Boris lifted his head to see if there was something he should do to help out his master. Seeing nothing, he groaned and rolled over and fell asleep.

"I gather Opal was on something of an anti-Jo vendetta after Skippy died," said Beatrice.

"Oh yes. And that made another big pain for me. Apparently, Jo Paxton kept having all these practical jokes played on her. She was convinced that Opal was behind them."

Beatrice said, "Well, that's likely, isn't it? After all, who else is going to do something like that? Did Jo have any other enemies?"

"That's something the state police and I are getting to the bottom of. But yes, I think there were some folks who weren't all that crazy about Miss Jo. Opal was the most vocal. However, there wasn't anything I could really do about the practical joking. I didn't have any proof against Opal, and I never caught her in the act of playing a trick on Jo."

Knowing Ramsay, he probably hadn't knocked himself out trying to investigate it, either.

He cleared his throat. "You did mention, earlier, that you thought Karen Taylor wasn't a member of the Jo Paxton fan club."

"That's right. I heard them arguing in the Patchwork Cottage myself. It sounded like Jo was jealous of Karen's ability—well, either that or she really didn't like her quilts at all. Karen is sure that Jo was the judge holding her back from winning a bunch of quilt shows. Karen is a pretty competitive person," said Beatrice. "Nice. But she wants to win."

Ramsay looked as if he'd prefer a philosophical discussion instead of an analysis of his various suspects. "What *is* winning?" he asked with a sigh. "That's what I want to know."

"Being happy," said Beatrice. "But for some people, it's a very complicated emotion to attain."

"Not for me," grumbled Ramsay. "Just give me a quiet house and a good book. It doesn't take much."

"Do you think that Booth Grayson cares a lot for winning?" asked Beatrice curiously.

"What, the mayor? For sure—he wants to keep his job. That means winning elections," said Ramsay.

"I thought that the job of mayor wasn't even a full-time paid position here," said Beatrice.

"You're right. It's not. We couldn't afford for it to be," said Ramsay.

"Then why does he care so much about it?" asked Beatrice.

"Oh, I think he's a fella who likes to have control."

"Ah," said Beatrice. "I can see that. For him, it's definitely not the little bit of salary that he gets. He wants to control the town and the people, to some extent. Like the quilters."

Ramsay looked warily at her. "You're not going to go off on a rant, are you? Meadow started fussing about the mayor last night, right out of the blue. I thought she was safely distracted by the Village Quilters membership, but she suddenly latched right on to the fees and taxes and stuff. Out of the blue!" he repeated again, looking frustrated.

"Like you said, the mayor likes to impose some control. I complained about the fees directly to Mayor Grayson, and he told me to print out this form 21-DRV off the town Web site and fill it out. It sounded to me like the form was going to get buried in his own version of the Circumlocution Office."

"If the man has any sense in his head," said Ramsay, "he'll leave quilting out of it. If there's one thing I've learned in my years of being around quilters, it's that those women can get vicious."

Chapter 8

The guild meeting was not off to a good start, and the other members hadn't even arrived. Meadow was, as usual, flitting around pulling hot hors d'oeuvres out of her oven, dumping ice cubes in a bucket, and placing pitchers of tea and lemonade out. That was all good. In fact, that was the best part of having a guild meeting at Meadow's house. The problem was the words coming out of her mouth.

"So that's why I invited Opal here. I figured that having her at a guild meeting would help us to get to know her a little better in a more relaxed setting."

Beatrice said tightly, "But, Meadow, Opal already belongs to a guild. She's part of the Cut-Ups. And Karen is part of the Cut-Ups, too. Don't you think that the other guild is going to get mad at us for trying to steal away their members?"

"We're not really doing that, though. We're having Opal come and talk a little bit about her quilting process.

So it's more like a program. Besides, we're not inviting both Karen and Opal to join the Village Quilters. That would be a little too sneaky of us!" Meadow arranged some miniature bacon quiches on a plate. "In fact, we might not even have to invite one of them. If Opal is impressed by our hospitality and food, maybe she'll come up with the idea herself!"

"Why can't we recruit women who aren't already in a guild?"

Meadow stared at her blankly. "I don't think there really *are* many women who aren't in guilds. At least, I can't think of any. It's not a very big town."

"Wouldn't Posy know of some unaffiliated quilters?"

"I doubt it. There are lots of women who come in her shop who are just starting out, but they're Dappled Hills tourists . . . only passing through town and not staying long enough to even *go* to a guild meeting."

There was a rap at the door. Meadow bobbed her head at it. "Mind getting that? I want to get all the goodies out before Opal arrives."

Beatrice walked across the barn to the door and opened it to find Opal there. Opal actually appeared like someone expecting to give a program. She'd tamed her frizzy hair and if there were any holes in her hose, she'd covered them up by wearing dress slacks instead of her usually omnipresent dotty skirts. She beamed proudly at Beatrice. "Hi, dear. I'm going to be speaking to your guild today."

There was something slightly ridiculous about Opal Woosley. It brought out the protective nature in Beatrice. "Come on in," she said to Opal. "We're excited to hear you talk about . . ." Beatrice looked in Meadow's direction for help.

Meadow was quickly laying down two more plates, fairly groaning with food, on the coffee table in the den area of the barn. "Bias. Bias and straight of grain."

Opal blinked at all the food. "You're not expecting a huge crowd, are you, Meadow? It's only a guild meeting, right?"

Meadow gave a little laugh. "That's right, only a guild meeting. Although our ladies like to eat, don't they, Beatrice?"

Not that much.

Opal gave a relieved sigh. "That's good. I've never spoken in front of a big group before. Just the thought makes me nervous."

Meadow swooped in for a reassuring hug. "Nothing to be concerned about! Let's get you set up with a plate." She pulled the thin woman over to the food and started heaping a plate with food. "How about some mini pimento cheese sandwiches? Deviled eggs? Fried green tomatoes? And I've got these tasty little biscuits with apple butter in them. . . ."

Opal might never leave the Village Quilters guild meeting, thought Beatrice.

Opal's eyes were about as big as the plate she was carrying. She sat down on a sofa. "And y'all eat like this at every guild meeting? Does everyone cook this much when they host the meeting?" Now she was looking a bit apprehensive. "I know you'd gotten a cake for one of the meetings. . . ."

"No, no!" said Meadow heartily. "I'm the one who provides the food for the guild meetings—no one else has to cook if they don't want to. It's my pleasure!"

Another little cloud of worry appeared. "Meadow, is Ramsay here?"

Meadow made a face. "No, he surely isn't. Busy imposing law and order on the town of Dappled Hills, I believe."

And he probably gave Meadow an earful for inviting yet another murder suspect over to their home.

"I'm only asking," said Opal, running a finger along the edge of the floral plate, "because he came to talk to me yesterday. Along with some policemen from the state force." She gave a nervous laugh. "He thought that I might be involved in Jo's death somehow. They were saying that it wasn't an accident—that Jo was murdered."

Meadow made a *pish* sound. "That silly Ramsay. They're simply exploring all the options, Opal. I'm sure he didn't mean a thing by it. I'm positive he didn't think you're mixed up in murder. He's got to talk to everyone, you know? Besides, you probably had a good alibi, didn't you?"

Opal turned a mottled red. "Yes. Yes, I did." She pulled at the neck of her blouse. "Although I won't pretend to be sorry about Jo dying. You know what she did to my Skippy, of course."

"Such a tragedy!" said Meadow soothingly. "We all know how you loved that little dog."

A tear ran down Opal's heavily powdered cheek. "She did it on purpose, just to get back at Skippy for barking at her every day. But that's what dogs are supposed to do, you know—defend their territory. He was taking care of me and trying to make sure that I was safe. In his mind, Jo was trespassing every day on our property and he was successfully chasing her off. And she hatefully murdered him. I'll never get over it. I'll never forgive Jo. And I'm certainly not sorry that she's dead!" She gave a vindictive bob of her head that threatened to undo the restrained frizz of her hair.

Beatrice and Meadow were stunned into silence by her vehemence. Meadow said brightly, "How about some tea, Opal? Would you like a nice glass of iced tea?"

Despite its inauspicious start, the guild meeting had gone fairly well. Savannah had nodded in agreement so many times with Opal's little talk about bias that she looked like a beaky-nosed bobble-head doll. And Savannah's sister, Georgia, appeared to be taking notes. Meadow smiled at Beatrice several times as if pointing out how well Opal fit their group. Opal looked very pleased to be there; everyone else did, too. It seemed to be going better than Karen's audition. Beatrice learned a lot, too. Plus, she got some tips on appliqué for her future quilts. All in all, it was a very helpful meeting and hadn't been derailed either by Boris the dog (whom Meadow had wisely kept in the back bedroom . . . and who let out a very remorseful cry from time to time) or his owner, who always had the ability to send anything off course.

"Opal!" said Meadow, applauding at the end of her tutorial. "That was inspired! I know so much more now about bias, and I sure didn't think I could possibly learn any more on the topic. Complete brilliance!"

Opal blushed and modestly looked down.

"It's exactly the kind of program we needed after such a stressful week," added Meadow.

Opal looked back up, brows knit in confusion. "Stressful?"

"The *murder*, Opal, the *murder*." Meadow sighed. It sure has made for some stress in my household, anyway.

Opal didn't look particularly fazed at the topic of Jo's death, but nodded quickly. "Oh yes, definitely. Most stressful!"

Meadow leaned forward and said in her loudest stage whisper, "Could you share more with us, Opal? You know—about your vision?"

Opal blinked.

Beatrice said, "I think Meadow means the psychic vision you had the morning of the quilt show—where you saw Jo's Jeep being tampered with."

Opal said in a rush, "You know, I was just in shock that morning, hearing the news about Jo. I think . . . well, I think my brain sort of short-circuited or something. I'm absolutely positive that I was mistaken. Positive." Her eyes were worried, though.

Meadow looked disappointed. "That's too bad. You know how I do love to hear about your amazing visions. And I was hoping to tell Ramsay more details about your vision so he can wrap up this case. He's always so grouchy when he has a case—it takes him away from his books and writing." She suddenly brightened. "Maybe one day you'll have a vision about my son and Piper getting married. I sure would love to have Ash finally unite with his true love. Now, *that* would be a vision." She absently refilled everyone's glass with iced tea, whether they'd originally been drinking it or not. Beatrice sighed.

Opal had made her good-byes and Savannah and Georgia had already left for home on their bikes (with quilting materials sticking up out of the baskets on the front). Posy insisted on helping clean up for a few minutes, and Beatrice also pitched in with the dirty plates, mixing bowls, and baking sheets.

Meadow was very cheerful. "I think that went extremely well," she bubbled. "Opal is an excellent candidate for the Village Quilters guild. She got along well with the others. She's clearly passionate about quilting. And she's very knowledgeable! As long as she's not a murderer, I think we're in good shape. The Cut-Ups guild can surely spare a member from a group as big as theirs."

Posy accidentally dropped a plate she was washing back into the sink. "Murder! Meadow! What are you talking about?"

"Oh, didn't you know? No, I guess you wouldn't, since you weren't at the funeral when we were talking about it. Jo was murdered, can you believe it?"

Beatrice took pity on Posy and explained, "Everyone thought she'd had an accident on the curvy mountain roads in awful weather. But it's more than that. Someone deliberately cut into Jo's brake lines. She was murdered."

"How awful!" Posy's gentle face was shocked.

"It's hard to believe, isn't it?" asked Meadow. "And I must say that I've taken it very personally. Jo was going to be a Village Quilter! This person who murdered her really messed everything up and created a lot of extra work and worry."

Beatrice remembered that Posy had driven both Booth and Miss Sissy to the quilt show that morning. She said, "Posy, you remember how Booth and Jo didn't really get along at that town hall meeting. Jo was making inferences about something that Booth and she knew about, and he got very angry. You drove him to the quilt show that morning—was there anything funny about him that day? Something different about his mood or his actions?"

Posy said, "Goodness. Well, I won't pretend to know Mayor Grayson well. He's a very guarded man in a lot of ways, I think. I only offered to pick him up because I was already picking up Miss Sissy and I knew the venue. The weather was so awful that morning that I admit I thought that if I made it easier for him to *get* to the quilt show, he might be more kindly disposed to our group than if he'd gotten lost and frustrated." She gave a rueful laugh.

So she wasn't even sure that his demeanor was any different from usual since she didn't know him well enough. Beatrice was opening her mouth to ask about Miss Sissy's cryptic statements at the funeral when Posy added, "But there was one thing odd that morning. At least, it wasn't odd at the *time*, but it wasn't what I expected. I'd already picked up Miss Sissy and we were at

Booth's house. I'd half thought that he might be looking out the window for my car since I was there right at the time we'd agreed on. But he didn't come."

Beatrice frowned. "It took him a long time to walk out to the car?"

"To be technically correct," said Posy slowly, "he didn't walk out to the car at all. Not at that time, anyway. I left Miss Sissy in the car—although I had my qualms. Sometimes Miss Sissy gets set in her head to go for a drive, and I wasn't sure if she was going to strand me—and I ran up to the front door and rang his doorbell. He didn't come to the door."

So that was what Miss Sissy had been referring to at the funeral when she'd insisted that Booth hadn't been home. She could have at least mentioned that they did end up finding Booth later on.

"Did you go back to the car and call him on your phone?" asked Meadow breathlessly, as if listening to a riveting bedtime story.

Posy shook her head. "I don't have a cell phone. And neither does Miss Sissy. I'm sure we're probably the last people in the United States not to have one. But I did think we ought to call. Maybe he'd overslept or something? So I drove back home to let myself in and make the phone call."

"Did he answer the phone when you called him?" asked Beatrice.

Posy said sadly, "He sure didn't. Of course, I figured that he was in the shower or something and couldn't hear the doorbell or phone. It was a little odd, though— that a man like him wouldn't be ready."

Meadow said in a robust voice, "Of course it's odd! Men don't spend that long on their appearance. Clearly!"

"The phone line wasn't busy? He'd mentioned something at Jo's funeral about making an important call that morning."

Posy said, "I'm afraid not."

"You did end up eventually bringing Booth with you, Posy. When did you finally end up making contact with him?" asked Beatrice.

"After he didn't pick up the phone," said Posy, "Miss Sissy and I drove back over to his house so that I could try the doorbell again. Miss Sissy was getting quite agitated by this time."

Beatrice could only imagine.

"This time when I rang his bell, he answered. He had a towel in his hand and was patting himself dry. He asked me to wait in the car for him."

Meadow snorted. "So he really *was* in the shower all that time? I wonder if he sings in there. Ramsay sometimes gets very carried away and sings show tunes in the shower."

"A good question, Meadow . . . and who knows? The funny thing was, though," said Posy slowly, "his *clothes* were sopping wet. It wasn't as if it was only his hair that was still wet from the shower. It was his clothes. In fact, when he came out to the car a few minutes later with his umbrella, he'd changed into dry clothes."

Where had Booth Grayson been on such a wet morning? Could he possibly have gotten that wet on a mission to cut Jo's brake lines?

*   *   *

"I've called this special meeting today," said Meadow "to ask for feedback from all of you on our search for a new Village Quilters guild member." She intoned her words in a very formal and serious way, which was instantly destroyed when she started laughing at Noonoo's nap posture—lying on her back with four feet in the air.

Savannah, Georgia, Miss Sissy, and Posy were assembled in Beatrice's backyard. The sun was on its way down and Beatrice had given them each a glass of wine, although Miss Sissy was happily consuming more than her fair share of the large bottle.

"You want us to talk about Opal and Karen?" asked Posy, sounding a little concerned.

Meadow waved her hands in the air. "Not to gossip, just to talk about their suitability for the group. How they might mesh with us, what they might have to offer us in terms of skills—that kind of thing."

It was good that they hadn't had this discussion when Beatrice was first joining the group. She'd had no quilting skills to speak of besides a good eye for art and years of curating at a folk art museum.

Savannah said briskly, "I was extremely impressed with Opal's talk at the guild meeting. She was quite self-possessed and very knowledgeable."

"And friendly," added Georgia with a smile. "She acted like she was really happy to be spending time with us."

"Maybe Posy, Beatrice, Miss Sissy, or Meadow can tell us more about Karen," said Savannah, arching her rather severely drawn on eyebrows. "I don't know her very well. And not all of us were invited to your dinner party for an opportunity to know Karen better." This with a sharp glance at Meadow.

Meadow blushed. "Not enough seats at the table. You understand! But I will say that Karen also sounded very knowledgeable about quilting when I spoke with her about it. She even had some ideas about hanging up some of my quilts to display them a little better."

Everyone kindly refrained from mentioning that Meadow's quilts were really not being displayed at all—just sort of piled up everywhere.

"Although she did strike a couple of bad chords with me," said Meadow in what passed for a murmur from her. It was completely audible, of course, and accompanied by a sideways, meaningful wink at Beatrice.

Posy said, "Karen is an excellent quilter. Oh, I'm sorry. You did want me to talk about Karen a little? Yes. She's very talented and has many, many ideas. And she comes up with fresh ideas for techniques and color combinations all on her own."

Savannah shook her head gravely. "She's very talented, it's true. It's not only talent, though—she's ambitious. . . . I've seen that from some of the quilt shows. I don't think she's getting that much pleasure from the quilting itself. I think she likes the buzz of getting ribbons and recognition."

"Ribbons and wickedness," cried Miss Sissy, briefly surfacing from her glass of wine.

"Aren't you *lively*, today, Miss Sissy?" said Meadow, beaming at her.

Georgia said gently, "Well, of course Karen enjoys winning. She's devoted a lot of time to quilting, and naturally she wants people to appreciate her art. It's only natural."

"I'm not so certain it *is* all that natural," said Savannah, in a grumpy tone, smoothing an imaginary wrinkle from her stiffly starched long floral dress. "Karen comes across like she wants to mow down everyone who stands in her way." She lifted a bony finger to make her point. "People like Jo."

Beatrice and Meadow leaned in a bit. "Did Jo try to stand in Karen's way?" asked Beatrice.

"She certainly did," said Savannah with a bob of her head. "All the time, as a matter of fact. I don't really *know* Karen, but I know what I've picked up about her. You know that I love quilt shows. I'm usually not entered in them, but it's fun going to see all the quilts. I couldn't bicycle to all the events because some of them are almost an hour away in the car. Jo knew that I enjoyed them, and sometimes she took me and Miss Sissy along to the ones she was either entered in or judging."

"Which was quite a few," said Georgia. "Sometimes there was a whole spate of shows in the area, and I didn't see my sister for weekends in a row!"

"At almost every show . . ." Savannah paused and thought about her words, wanting to make them completely accurate. "Let me revise that. At all of the shows that I went to, Karen was there. She'd have at least one quilt entered. Sometimes she'd have a quilt in several different categories, and she'd win each one. And Jo talked about her in the car on both the way over to the shows and back." Savannah's sister gave her a sympathetic glance and Savannah said, "It did make me very uncomfortable."

"What kinds of things did Jo say about Karen?" asked Beatrice.

"Mostly, she'd attack Karen's ideas and approach and the way that Karen was cutting-edge with her design and technique. She thought that a lot of Karen's quilts weren't *pretty*."

Posy nodded. "Jo always did like a pretty quilt. She was a bit of an old-fashioned judge, I think."

Meadow said, "Judging should go beyond pretty, though. There are lots of other things to consider."

"I got the feeling . . ." Savannah paused and pursed her lips as if the words weren't easy for her to say. ". . . that Jo didn't like Karen at all. It wasn't just Karen's quilts. She didn't like Karen's attitude or ambitions or personality. Jo acted very jealous of her."

"So there wasn't one particular incident," said Beatrice, trying to get to the point where they could sum up Savannah's impression of Jo. "This was an impression that you got over a period of time, because of things Jo would say about Karen."

"There *was* one particular incident," said Savannah. She puffed up with importance a little at having such an important story to tell. "It was a gorgeous day at the Patchwork Cottage. I was sitting in one of Posy's armchairs and reading a new quilting book that had just come into the store." She smiled at Beatrice and added earnestly, "It had an interesting chapter on paper piecing."

It seemed important to Savannah that she get some validation for the precision of her storytelling. "Sounds fascinating," offered Beatrice.

Savannah gave a brief nod and continued. "Karen left the shop and Jo must have been right outside the door, about to come in. I could hear them very clearly through the open window. Jo said something very cutting to Karen in this really snide voice—something like she was wasting her time getting fabrics and notions where there was no way on earth that Karen was going to walk away with a ribbon from any show that Jo was judging."

"That was probably a given, wasn't it?" asked Beatrice, suppressing a sigh. She'd heard a very similar conversation between Karen and Jo herself.

"Then she proceeded to explain how many shows she was judging. It was a huge list," said Savannah. "It sounded like Jo was bound and determined to judge every quilt show in the southeastern United States!"

"Did Karen say anything to that?" asked Meadow, now very worried about her guild prospect.

"She certainly did. She said that she'd see her dead first."

Chapter 9

Beatrice was leaving her cottage to run errands when she saw Glen Paxton at her mailbox. She squinted at him a bit. Was he sticking something in the box?

Glen glanced up, saw her, and waved. He held a bunch of fluorescent flyers in one hand.

Beatrice walked over to him. "Hi, Glen."

"Hi, Beatrice. I was about to put a flyer in your mailbox, but I'll hand it to you instead."

Beatrice looked at it. "A food drive? I'm sure I can find some canned goods for you."

"Great! If you just put them out at your mailbox, I'll come by with Penny to pick them up. She's the volunteer coordinator, you know."

"Volunteering is something I was planning on checking into," said Beatrice. Although she'd also made a vow to herself to try to take retirement a little easier and make time to relax. "Is there one organization that sort of spearheads it all for Dappled Hills?"

"Penny Harris runs the Dappled Hills Help Center. But she helps with more than just the town—she knows about all the needs for the whole county. And, believe me, there are plenty of needs. You wouldn't think there'd be so many."

"That was smart of Jo to hook you up with the group," said Beatrice.

"She was a good woman," said Glen. "Despite what people say or think about her. And I do know what people say about Jo." His broad face darkened a little. "Sometimes she rubbed people the wrong way. Of course, living in a small town like Dappled Hills, you can't help running into people you don't get along with."

"What people?" asked Beatrice, hoping she didn't sound too curious.

"Opal Woosley for one," said Glen, heaving a sigh and gazing blankly down at his food collection flyers. "She never did get over Jo accidentally running over her dog." He glanced up at Beatrice. "You've already heard about it? Whatever Opal says, ignore it. Jo loved animals and wouldn't even have run over a squirrel on purpose, much less a dog. That woman treated that little dog like a baby. She gave us the dickens of a time after that."

"Opal was making trouble for you and Jo?" This was what Ramsay had mentioned to her, earlier.

Glen nodded. "You wouldn't believe the trouble. It was all really juvenile stuff, too, like you'd think a kid would do instead of an older lady. Pranks and practical jokes. She taped our mailbox shut with duct tape, glued our newspaper together, toilet-papered our trees, put shaving cream all over Jo's windshield . . ." He rolled his eyes. "She made life difficult for us for a while."

Beatrice said slowly, "You don't think that cutting brake lines would be placed in that category? Making your lives difficult?"

Glen looked startled by the suggestion. "That's a whole different story. No, I can't believe this batty old woman would cut brake lines just because of a dog. That would be crazy!"

But *batty* had been the word that Glen had used.

After Glen left to hand out the rest of his flyers, Beatrice finally made her way to downtown Dappled Hills for her errands. She decided to drive since one of her stops was the grocery store. Walking was usually her favorite way to travel in the little town, though. The place was remarkably beautiful, and you didn't get the full effect in the car.

She pulled up in front of Bub's. The ancient store was constructed entirely of stone and had stood for at least a hundred years. The oldest townsfolk explained to Beatrice that the establishment had originally been owned by a man so devilish that the town had dubbed him Beelzebub. Moss grew on the shady side of the building, and old men warmed the benches outside the store for most of the morning, drinking coffee and cutting up.

Beatrice was getting out of her car when Booth Grayson walked out of the store and headed to the car parked next to her. This was her chance to ask Booth what he was doing the morning that she saw him outside Glen's house.

"Booth!" she called, shutting her car door. He stopped and fleetingly glanced her way. It seemed he almost pretended he didn't hear her as he continued getting into his car. Then he wavered and gave her a perfunctory smile. "Mrs. Coleman, isn't it? Can I help you with something?"

"Actually," she said, "I had a question for you about something I saw." He froze and she added quickly, "Since I've moved to Dappled Hills, I've found that most gossip can be easily explained. Many people don't like easy explanations, though, so they come up with elaborate stories—which can be a lot more damaging in the long run."

Booth's eyes narrowed behind his glasses and he glanced swiftly around them to make sure no one was in earshot.

Beatrice took a deep breath and continued. "I was walking Noo-noo, my corgi, yesterday morning, and I saw you at Glen's house. You let yourself in."

Booth said in a tight voice, "The door was unlocked. It was hardly breaking and entering."

"Which is exactly why I didn't use that term," said Beatrice. He was getting quite defensive already, so she'd have to make it quick. "I was curious what you were up to and I stayed to watch until you left. You took something out of the house a few minutes later and I saw you shove it in your pocket. I wondered what you were doing at the Paxtons' house and what you left with. It was easy to draw my own conclusions, after that town hall meeting, but I thought it would be better if I just asked you."

Instead of appearing concerned, Booth Grayson looked almost relieved. He must be realizing that she didn't know anything specific. What if she did? Would that mean she'd be next to go off a mountain cliff?

Booth said brusquely, "What you saw was nothing. I ran by to see Glen for some equipment that Jo had borrowed from me."

"On the morning after her funeral?" Beatice's voice rose disbelievingly.

"I know that sounds a little crass, but there was something I needed it for. Once I arrived, I was glad to see that Glen clearly wasn't there, and even happier to find the door unlocked. I could find what I needed without bothering Jo's grieving husband." His voice now had a nearly pious tone. Booth Grayson, doer of good. Beatrice realized that she didn't like Booth very much.

He opened his car door and slid in. "Now, if you're curious about this murder—if it is indeed a murder, which I find hard to believe—you should consider talking to Opal Woosley. I'll admit that I did go over to Jo Paxton's house the morning of the quilt show to . . . try to retrieve my equipment then. I didn't go inside their house because I saw another car nearby. That was the odd thing—the car was nearby and not pulled up into their driveway on such a nasty morning. I saw it was Opal—sort of skulking around in the bushes in front of the Paxtons' house. She's someone you ought to be talking to, not me."

Beatrice opened her mouth to ask why he'd acted so

suspiciously himself, scanning for witnesses the morning she'd seen him, but he lifted a hand to cut her off. "Now, if that's all, I really do need to leave. I've got to take these groceries home before I go to the town hall. Good seeing you."

She was sure that he hadn't given her the full story on the mysterious equipment. Whatever he'd taken from the Paxton house, Beatrice would bet it hadn't been borrowed. But Booth did have a point. What was Opal doing at Jo's house the morning she was killed? Playing another practical joke on her? Or was she doing something more sinister? Could it be that the strange vision she'd mentioned at the quilt show wasn't a vision at all—but something she'd actually *seen*?

When Beatrice finally made her way into the grocery store, she was surprised to see Wyatt Thompson in Bub's, too. She chastised herself for being surprised. Ministers had to eat, too, didn't they? For heaven's sake, she was like a child staring disbelievingly at her teacher in the store. Although she did wonder about some of the items she saw in his cart. Sardines? Prunes? Was that liver in there, too? And instant coffee?

Wyatt glanced up and saw her. "Hi there, Beatrice." He looked genuinely pleased to see her, giving a warm smile. "I guess you've figured out this is the place to run into everyone you know." He focused again on the grocery shelves until he found a can of peaches and put them in his cart. "I understand that you're investigating poor Jo's death." His voice remained as even as if he were asking her what she thought the weather would be like tomorrow.

Beatrice blinked. "How did you hear that?"

His eyes twinkled at her. "Meadow is apparently very proud of her friend. Or maybe she's wanting to show Ramsay up or push him into doing more detective work and less reading."

"That's going to be a challenge," said Beatrice.

"Maybe that's why you're interested in stepping forward," suggested Wyatt gently. "You see a need there. And with your background—"

"In art history?" asked Beatrice ruefully.

"—I think you must have spent a lot of time investigating the history of different artworks. How much they were worth, their origins, their story. You were a detective, in a way."

"I suppose art museum curators wear lots of different hats," said Beatrice, smiling back at him. "It's true that I like to dig deeper. Maybe I'm trying to make nosiness sound nicer. I don't know. But people's motives and actions are fascinating stuff. Take yourself, for instance."

Wyatt blinked. "Me?"

"That's right. I'm studying your cart and seeing a mystery there. Sardines? Canned peaches? Instant coffee? I'm going to make a deduction," said Beatrice in a portentous voice.

"Go ahead," said the minister, leaning his forearms on the cart handle and staring attentively at Beatrice.

"I deduce that this food can't possibly be for you. It's not at all ministerial. Or even like regular bachelor food. It seems more like . . . Miss Sissy food. Are you running errands for her today?"

Wyatt gave a laugh and some soft applause. "Bravo! Yes, I ran by her house earlier and she mentioned that she was going to the store after our visit. I offered to pick up some things for her."

"Then you've definitely done your good deed for the day," said Beatrice fervently. "Saving Dappled Hills residents from having Miss Sissy terrorizing the roads." Every time she saw Miss Sissy behind the wheel of her boatlike old Lincoln, she took cover. Miss Sissy's idea of driving was to get from point A to point B—it didn't matter if you drove on sidewalks or over people to get there.

"Well, I'm always happy to help out," he said with a smile. He turned toward the cash register and then said, "You haven't happened to see Opal Woosley as you've been out running errands, have you? She asked me to run by her house this morning for a quick chat. And she wasn't there when I rang her doorbell. That's what made me visit Miss Sissy instead."

"I sure haven't," said Beatrice, "but I've just left home myself. She probably forgot, don't you think? Is she the sort of person who's forgetful?" Opal certainly hadn't given her that impression during the guild lecture she'd given, though. She'd been thoughtful, knowledgeable, and organized, despite her somewhat eccentric appearance.

Wyatt frowned, considering. "Not really. And it was only yesterday that she asked me to come by, so it's sort of recent to forget. Never mind. Something probably just came up."

"I was planning on doing a couple more errands before going back home. I'll keep an eye open for Opal and get her to call you if I come across her," said Beatrice.

She'd thought she didn't need anything that needed to be refrigerated, but then Beatrice remembered she was out of eggs and she was very fond of having a little sunny-side-up egg on toast in the mornings. She dropped off the groceries at the cottage, then headed back downtown.

In the days following Jo's death, the mail delivery had been even more erratic as the post office had scrambled to find a replacement for Jo. Beatrice mailed a small package at the post office before heading off to the Patchwork Cottage. Before she started on a new project, she wanted to do a little technique research. If there was one thing that made her nervous, it was the thought of embarking on something new and different without any kind of road map.

Another good reason to visit Posy's shop was the gossip angle. The Patchwork Cottage was renowned as a Dappled Hills information hub.

Posy's shop was full of customers again. Clearly, the Patchwork Cottage was becoming a magnet for shoppers all around the area. Posy gave her a quick smile when she came in, but had quite a line at the register as well as customers waiting to ask her a question.

Beatrice walked over to the bookshelf on the back wall of the shop and found several books that covered basic quilting techniques. She carried them to the sitting area to leaf through them until Posy had the chance to tell her which one she recommended. Posy might even recommend all of them, since she was the buyer, after all—she must have liked them all.

The sitting area was just as full as the store was. There was a heavyset lady with a large stack of quilting magazines beside her who was clearly in no hurry to leave. She glowered up at Beatrice and spread out her things a bit more on the sofa to discourage Beatrice from sitting next to her. Miss Sissy was successfully taking up most of the rest of the sofa while she enjoyed a noisy siesta.

In one of the armchairs facing the sofa was Opal Woosley, also fast asleep. No wonder she hadn't been home when Wyatt came by. She'd probably come to buy fabric right when the shop opened, and had gotten seduced by the overstuffed armchair. Beatrice would remind Opal when she woke up to check back in with Wyatt.

There was a floral china teapot on the coffee table in the middle of the sitting area with several delicate teacups surrounding it. Beatrice opened the first of the quilting books and became absorbed a lot quicker than she thought she'd be. It was a huge help to read a clearly written explanation of different quilting techniques. Another of the books also had tips for daily, basic quilting techniques like cutting fabric.

Although she found the reading interesting, after twenty minutes the suggestive snoring of Miss Sissy was starting to lull even the alert Beatrice to sleep. The Patchwork Cottage door had kept opening and more customers had come in to replace the ones that left.

Poor Posy could use a clerk to help her out. Maybe she'd have to draft her husband, Cork, from the wine shop.

After twenty minutes of leafing through the books, though, Beatrice had a good feel for which one was going to help her out the most. She stood up to just check out and avoid bothering Posy with her questions. Beatrice glanced over at the still-sleeping Opal and Miss Sissy. Opal seemed even more knocked out than the sprawling Miss Sissy. But Miss Sissy was known for her Patchwork Cottage marathon naps. Was Opal?

Hesitantly, Beatrice laid a tentative hand on Opal's arm. "Opal," she whispered softly. "Could you wake up a second?"

There was no response. The heavyset woman glared at her over the top of her magazine for disturbing the delicate ecosystem of the sitting area.

Beatrice was more persistent this time. "Opal," she said, shaking her gently by the shoulder.

Beatrice peered closer at Opal and noticed she barely seemed to be breathing. In fact, her chest wasn't moving at all. Reluctantly, Beatrice placed a shaky hand to the base of Opal's neck to feel for a pulse—a pulse that wasn't there.

Chapter 10

Beatrice hurried to the front of the store. "Posy," she said urgently, "can I talk to you for a moment? It's important."

Posy bit her lip, then said, "Of course, Beatrice. Oh, I'm so sorry," sighing at the line of customers still waiting to check out.

Beatrice glanced around. "Look, Georgia just walked in. She's covered the register for you before, hasn't she?" She waved her over and quickly asked her to step in for Posy and then pulled Posy over to a corner of the store. "Posy, Opal Woosley is dead. Over there in your sitting area. I don't want to make a big show out of it, but I know the police will want everyone out of the way . . . out of the way, but maybe not gone."

Posy put her hands up to her face. "How awful. Oh, poor Opal."

"Why don't I call Ramsay real quick and see what he wants us to do? If he wants us to clear out the store, or wait for him to question everyone, or what." Beatrice was already pulling out her cell phone and calling Ramsay Downey's number while she talked.

It felt as if she'd only just shoved her cell phone back into her pocketbook when Ramsay hurried into the Patchwork Cottage. He said in his authoritative voice, "Could I have your attention, ladies? If everyone could please step outside the shop? And make sure I've got your name, address, and phone number before you leave the premises."

The quilters all gaped at him for a moment before hurrying to leave. They clearly weren't sure if there had been some horrible disaster—a gas leak, cholera, a bomb threat?—but they were certainly eager to be on their way.

Ramsay asked Posy for the keys and she fumbled through her purse for them, handing them to him with trembling hands as she and Beatrice exited the building. Ramsay stayed in the shop for a few minutes, presumably to confirm Beatrice's report, before grimly striding out and locking the door behind him.

The downside to being the police chief in a very small town would have to be these kinds of occasions—which, blessedly, didn't happen in Dappled Hills very often. Ramsay was really hustling before his deputy finally joined him—he was calling the state police, securing the crime scene, and getting information from potential witnesses.

Beatrice was sure Opal was murdered. But she wasn't so sure how it had happened. Had Opal's tea been poisoned? Had she had some sort of knife wound she couldn't see? Could she possibly even have been strangled or smothered? How could anyone have gotten away with it, as busy as that shop was?

Ramsay was asking customers if they'd been near the sitting area and if they'd seen or heard anything unusual while they were there. If they'd been near the sitting area, he asked, had they seen Opal Woosley awake? Beatrice, trying hard to listen in, thought that it sounded as if most of the women hadn't seen her awake. Unless they were confusing Opal with Miss Sissy. Ramsay was trying to accurately describe Opal, however.

The process took a lot less time than Beatrice had thought. Most of the customers had apparently been intent on their shopping and on asking each other or Posy for their opinion. No one had seen anything unusual or suspicious—even the heavyset woman who'd settled into the sofa. She'd thought that Opal was sleeping, like Miss Sissy.

Once Ramsay spoke with Miss Sissy, Posy briefly left to drive Miss Sissy back home before returning to the store. When she returned, it was finally time for Ramsay to talk to Beatrice and Posy. He'd already let the rest of the women and a few assorted husbands go, and the state police forensics team was arriving at the scene. He spoke with a crime scene technician first, apparently filling him in on the basics. "Let's go next door to the café and get a coffee," he said in a weary voice. "At this point I need to stay out of forensics' way while they take pictures and examine the crime scene. Sorry to make you two wait for so long, but I knew where to find you. A lot of the ladies in the shop had driven over to Dappled Hills from Lenoir or even Hickory, so I wanted to talk to them before they left."

They ordered coffees and sat outside at a round table so that Ramsay could keep an eye on the proceedings at the Patchwork Cottage. "Beatrice," said Ramsay, after taking a long sip from his cup, "did you have any other observations about Opal? Besides the fact that she was deceased, which made you a lot more observant than anyone else on the scene?"

Beatrice thought for a moment before shaking her head. "Not really. I came in, read for a while, then decided to leave since Posy was too busy to talk. I almost expected to see Miss Sissy sleeping so hard, but I was surprised that Opal was so deeply asleep. Wyatt Thompson was over at Bub's Grocery earlier and he said she'd asked him to visit her this morning. Then she didn't answer her doorbell when he'd arrived. I thought that was sort of strange. I was trying to wake Opal up to remind her that Wyatt was trying to connect with her."

Posy's eyes teared up. "I feel terrible about all of this. I should have been paying more attention to what was going on in my shop. I can't believe that poor Opal passed away in the Patchwork Cottage while I was busy answering questions and checking people out."

Ramsay became brusque. "Posy, I'm sure this would have happened regardless of how busy you were at the register. I don't think there was anything you could do."

"Was it a medical condition, then?" asked Beatrice.

"A heart attack or a massive stroke? She looked so natural . . . peaceful." Although she still had that strong feeling that there was nothing natural about Opal's death.

"I don't think it was related to a medical condition, no," said Ramsay, sighing as if he would love to say otherwise. "She was probably murdered."

Posy gasped, and Ramsay continued. "The medical examiner will tell us for sure. But I found it a little hard to believe, after what happened to Jo recently, that Opal Woosley simply died during a nap at the Patchwork Cottage. When I lifted her eyelids, her eyes were bloodshot. The skin around her mouth was very pale, which made me think she might have been suffocated while she was dozing. Of course, the pathologist will look for asphyxia—high levels of carbon dioxide in the blood."

Posy said slowly, as if trying to digest this news, "Smothered. In my shop. How could this have happened? There were so many people there!"

"When did Opal arrive at the Patchwork Cottage?" asked Ramsay. "Had she been shopping for a while, or had she arrived shortly before Beatrice?"

"She'd been there for a long time. In fact, Opal arrived at the shop before I'd even opened up. She was driving by and saw that I was struggling to wrangle a couple of boxes into the store. When I dropped one, she parked her car and hurried over to help me."

Beatrice said, "And she decided to stay?" Then she flashed Ramsay an apologetic smile for interrupting his interview.

"She did. She said she wanted time to leisurely

browse through the fabrics while no one else was there. The fabrics helped inspire her, she said. Opal strolled around the shop while I made the tea and unpacked the boxes so I could put out the merchandise. Then I realized that I'd left another box at home. I called Cork, but he'd already left for the wine shop, so I asked Opal if she minded holding down the fort while I dashed home and got the box," said Posy. "She was already settled into the sofa at that point with her eyes closed. I assumed she was asleep."

Ramsay said slowly, "So Opal's car was parked outside the shop, you'd left, and the Patchwork Cottage hadn't even actually opened for the day."

Posy nodded. "That's right. Well, it was right before it opened."

Beatrice breathed, "Someone could have either driven by or walked up and seen an opportunity to confront Opal . . . or kill her. Maybe our murderer could even have run by the store legitimately to do some early shopping and then seen her opportunity to do away with Opal."

"What I can't understand, though," said Ramsay, "is why she didn't fight back. Opal was an older woman and on the frail side, but if she'd been in a fight for her life, I'd think she would have been able to stop being smothered."

Posy said quietly, "But what if Opal *was* asleep?"

Ramsay said, "It certainly would have been a lot easier for the murderer. She might not even have awakened but for a split second."

"Let's hope that was the case," said Posy fervently.

"Did she say *why* she was so tired?" asked Beatrice. "It's early in the day to be so exhausted that you'd fall asleep in a store."

Posy said, "She said something about not having slept at all last night—that she'd had something on her mind. I'm afraid I was so busy trying to get the store ready to open up . . ." She broke off. "But I did pause to ask her. I wasn't sure if she was trying to talk about something with me or if she was simply mentioning that as a fact. I asked her what she'd been thinking about."

"What did she say?" asked Ramsay.

"She didn't say much. Only that she'd been mulling over the murder and something about it was bothering her. She was evasive, so I didn't push her. I told her that Jo's murder had been keeping me awake, too, and I hoped that they caught the murderer soon." Posy shrugged helplessly. "Then she closed her eyes. With determination, I think. Like she wanted to avoid the subject. That's when I started scrambling to get the store ready."

"What happened when you came back to the store after picking up the box?" asked Ramsay.

"I walked over to thank Opal for watching the store. It looked like she was sound asleep, though, so I didn't bother her. Then customers started arriving. The next time I was over in that part of the store, Miss Sissy had joined Opal and they both appeared to be napping. Then the shop really got swamped," ended Posy in a sad voice. "The next thing I knew, Beatrice was telling me that Opal wasn't asleep at all."

Ramsay glanced over at the Patchwork Cottage. "I think it's time for me to head back over there." He took a last sip from his coffee before tossing it in a nearby trash can. "Posy, you may as well go back home. I think the police are going to be here awhile, and you definitely won't be able to reopen the shop today."

Posy said, "Thanks, Ramsay. And the police are welcome to keep the shop closed as long as they need to. It would be disrespectful to open today, anyway. If it's all the same to you, though, I think I'll get some more coffee and just sit here for a bit. I feel bad leaving the shop and I know that my shoppers will be worried when they walk up to the store and see the crime scene tape and police cars. It would be better for me to be able to explain it all to them."

"I should make a phone call to Wyatt," Beatrice told Posy as Ramsay joined the state police. "I told him I'd call if I saw Opal. He'll want to know."

Posy said, "I'm going in to get another cup of coffee so that I'm not sitting at the café's table and not spending any money. Want anything?"

"No, thanks, Posy. After I make this call, I'm going to head back home for a while. I'm sure Noo-noo is ready to be let out, and I didn't really put my groceries away from earlier—only the refrigerated things."

"I'm so sorry you weren't able to buy what you needed today at the Patchwork Cottage," said Posy, her blue eyes sad. "A new quilting book, wasn't it? And I think you wanted my advice on a good one. What a terrible day."

"I did spend a lot of time reading through them,

though, and I found a few that I liked. I'm in no hurry—I'll buy them the next time I'm at the shop. And, Posy, please call me if there's anything you need. This must have been a huge shock for you."

Beatrice's attempt at kindness made Posy tear up again, and she fumbled in her pocketbook for a tissue. At that moment, Posy's husband, Cork, hurried up and engulfed Posy in a hug that made her start crying in earnest.

Wyatt, as minister, was accustomed to hearing somber news . . . or even delivering it. He listened intently as Beatrice outlined the situation to him, asked Beatrice a few questions, then said, "Poor Opal. What awful news."

"Ramsay will probably be calling you soon. I explained to him that I tried to wake Opal up because she'd missed an appointment with you. Do you have any idea what she was planning on talking with you about? Was Opal someone who usually asked for visits or spiritual guidance?" asked Beatrice.

"She wasn't, actually. And I don't think she was looking for spiritual guidance this time, either. Opal mentioned wanting my opinion about something—something that she was concerned about." He sighed. "I wish I'd asked more questions yesterday when she called me, but it sounded like she wanted to discuss her problem in person instead of on the phone. I don't have the slightest idea what she wanted to talk about."

Later, finally putting her groceries away, Beatrice kept thinking about Opal. Why had she wanted to talk to Wyatt? Had she seen something or known something about Jo's murder that was weighing on her mind? If Booth had seen *her*, had *she* seen Booth? And had he been doing what he said he'd been?

That afternoon, Beatrice tried to pick back up with her regularly scheduled day. The only problem was that her regularly scheduled day was a little on the dull side. This was supposed to be her quiet day to lie in her hammock, read, listen to Noo-noo snore, and perhaps mull over the facts of the case.

This was such a quiet plan that there was no mulling or reading or listening when she climbed into her backyard hammock. There was only napping.

She slept a lot harder than she'd have thought possible. When shadows started streaking across the yard, Beatrice finally jerked awake. Her stomach reminded her that she hadn't eaten in many hours, and she reluctantly walked to the kitchen to poke around for something edible for supper.

The chicken was, naturally, frozen. She didn't really feel like beef. What had she gotten at the store, again? Ah. Well, she could always have cereal. She'd successfully picked up all the things on her grocery list—the problem was that the list didn't have any actual components of a meal on it.

She opened the refrigerator door again and was thoughtfully considering the eggs when there was a knock at her door. Beatrice looked out the window beside the door and sighed as she saw Meadow Downey standing there in a large red caftan that matched her red glasses. But—miracle of miracles—she was holding *food*. Meadow could be kooky, long-winded, irritating, and bossy . . . but she was a marvelous cook.

Beatrice opened the door with unusual alacrity. "Meadow! Come in! Why, what's this? You've cooked something for me? How very sweet!"

Meadow bustled in and was already taking over Beatrice's small kitchen, talking all the while. "Can you believe that I only *just* heard about poor Opal! In *this* town? Usually I hear about things here in Dappled Hills before they've even fully happened!"

Beatrice frowned. "You've been into town and didn't hear about Opal?"

"Well, no. No, I had a little gardening to do. Then I realized that there were some vegetables that needed harvesting. Once I picked the vegetables, I decided to go ahead and do some cooking while everything was fresh and I was inspired."

An inspired dish from Meadow. This *would* be good.

"I thought the vegetables would look gorgeous on a kabob. So then I fired up the grill. I threw the squash and zucchini and tomatoes on there . . . well, you know. I also had some shrimp from Bub's. And some wonderful wild rice that I'd picked up from the farmers' market." She beamed at Beatrice. "I think you'll really enjoy it."

Meadow had clearly gotten distracted. "But Ramsay didn't tell you the news?" asked Beatrice, to redirect her.

"He certainly didn't! I'm completely appalled by him. I didn't think a thing of it that he didn't come home for lunch—I figured that he was busy working on Jo's murder. Then, when he finally came home a little while ago, he disappeared into the bedroom to read Thoreau. Can you believe it?"

She could. The peace and refuge of Walden Pond would be very appealing after a day like today.

"Finally, I brought a plate to him, since he was in no hurry to come out of our room. I asked him how his day was and he sort of grunted and rolled his eyes. 'Murder.' That's what he told me! That his day was murder." Meadow's face was flushed as she took out one of Beatrice's plates and started attractively arranging the skewers and rice on it.

"He probably thought you already knew about Opal," said Beatrice mildly, keeping her eyes on the food.

"That's what he said a few minutes ago when he started asking me questions about Opal. I mean, really. I was wondering why on earth he suddenly cared about poor Opal when he couldn't be bothered to be at the house when she was giving her quilting presentation!" said Meadow huffily.

"To be perfectly fair," said Beatrice in a reasonable tone, "he wouldn't have been expected to attend a guild meeting. Or, probably, even particularly welcomed there."

This Meadow thoughtfully considered. "I suppose. Anyway, once I found out what had happened at the Patchwork Cottage today, I told Ramsay my theory about the murders. It makes perfect sense and it links the two murders together!"

Beatrice said, "What's your theory, Meadow?"

"That someone is killing off potential members of the Village Quilters!" Meadow thrust her hands on her hips and looked fierce.

Beatrice tried hard not to roll her eyes. "But, Meadow, why on earth would someone target the Village Quilters? And how would they know that Jo and Opal were potential members?" Although the way Meadow talked, most of Dappled Hills probably knew.

"Because they don't want the Village Quilters to rule the world!" Meadow waved one of her hands in the air excitedly. "They know that if we end up with another master quilter in our group, we'll be getting blue ribbons all over the place!"

Beatrice gazed longingly at the kebobs on the plate. "Meadow, I can't imagine the ladies in the Cut-Ups guild killing Opal in cold blood."

Meadow exhaled loudly. "Ramsay said the same thing. Y'all have a crippling lack of vision. I told him that he better keep his eye on Karen. She'll be the next target—you'll see that I'm right! She's the only one left!"

When Meadow was worked up like this, there was really only one thing to do. Distract her. Especially since she clearly didn't have any actual helpful information. Before Beatrice could figure out how best to deflect her, Meadow was already charging ahead with her line of thought.

"You were practically heroic today, though, Beatrice," said Meadow, beaming admiringly at her. "So calm and collected at the moment of crisis. Not shrieking or creating a panic or upsetting anyone in the shop. But how horrible it must have been for you."

Beatrice shivered. She'd never really forget that moment she realized Opal wasn't simply sleeping. "I wasn't really heroic; I simply didn't want to create a huge fuss and scare everyone to death," she said briskly. "I only wish I'd seen what was going on earlier. Poor Posy. I hope she won't lose any business from this tragedy."

"Well, of course she will! Who wants to go into a shop where you're murdered if you sit down for a moment?"

"Still," said Beatrice, "I hope people will forget. After all, things had already started settling down after Jo's death. People were still talking about it, but they'd picked up with their usual activities. They were moving on."

"I'll say they were," said Meadow. "Do you know what I saw yesterday? Glen with Penny Harris. Do you know Penny?"

"Ah . . . that's the woman who does all the volunteering, right? Organizes food drives for the county and whatnot? I don't really know her, but Glen has mentioned her a couple of times."

Meadow nodded eagerly, leaning back against Beatrice's counter as if she was in no hurry to leave. "Yes. He's been helping Penny out for a while now— distributing flyers, helping at the secondhand clothing warehouse, working at the food bank. But this is different, Beatrice. I saw Glen *hugging* Penny." Her eyes opened wide. "Don't you think it's awfully early for Glen to be embarking on a romantic relationship?"

"Are you sure it wasn't just a friendly hug? Maybe

Penny was just trying to comfort him, considering Glen's wife just died."

Meadow scoffed, "Of course I'm sure it wasn't just friendly. I might be an old married lady, but I know what romance looks like when I'm seeing it." She sighed. "It makes me wonder if they were involved even before Jo died. Shocking!"

It would be shocking—if it were true. And it would certainly provide Glen with a motive for murdering his wife. But was it true? Beatrice had gotten the impression that Glen really cared for Jo . . . as unlikely as that seemed. Now she had another mystery to uncover.

Chapter 11

The next morning, Beatrice rose early, breakfasted, took a quick walk with the eager Noo-noo, then put on gardening gloves to tackle an area of her front yard. She had an ungainly flower bed right in the front of her cottage. Admittedly, she hadn't done anything really *with* the yard since she'd moved into the cottage a few months ago. She'd been lucky—it had almost tended itself. The azaleas bloomed on cue—the gardenias were just finishing their delicious-smelling blooming. The knockout roses were lovely and she hadn't done more than deadhead them. Ordinarily she killed things on sight, but her yard had been thriving . . . besides this one ailing flower bed.

She stood near the little road in front of her house, studying the bed and wondering whether it needed to be fertilized, weeded, added to, or completely gutted and started over. Beatrice was so absorbed that she didn't hear the sound of an approaching car until the last second when the sound became perilously close. Beatrice glanced up, saw an aging Lincoln just feet away, and stumbled farther into the safety of her yard.

Beatrice rolled her eyes as the car speedily passed over the spot where she'd been standing. Then a bony arm inserted through the car window and a withered fist was shaken at her. Beatrice let a shaky breath out. Miss Sissy. Deadly danger to Dappled Hills. Although Miss Sissy drove on sidewalks and into yards, she always thought that everyone *else* was to blame. Would that license of hers ever expire? Ramsay must just want to stay out of it and pray that Miss Sissy didn't run over someone.

Another car approached, this one actually driving on the road. It was Karen, who lowered her window and asked in concern, "Are you all right, Beatrice? That crazy old woman. Did she scare you to death?"

Beatrice gave an unsteady laugh. "Almost. I'd like to sit down, and the ground isn't very appealing." She expected Karen to continue on to work, which was probably where she was heading at eight o'clock in the morning. But Karen pulled right into her brick driveway, put the car in park, and hurried to give her a supporting arm. It all made her feel somewhat elderly, although her jellylike legs definitely needed the help.

"Piper would have done the same thing if she'd seen Miss Sissy nearly run you down. That old woman should be locked up. Or have her keys taken away from her. Or something," fussed Karen.

If there was one thing Karen was, it was efficient . . . apparently in every aspect of her life. Before Beatrice knew it, she was settled into her sofa, a light quilt over her legs, fluffed pillows behind her back, and a glass of tea in her hand. Karen had continued giving an off-the-cuff, clearly outlined argument for driving tests for the very elderly and how cars were deadly weapons. All the while she was whipping up some eggs with bacon and green onion and toasting some bread with cheese under the oven's broiler. It had taken no time at all.

"Have you and Piper been friends for a while?" asked Beatrice.

Karen nodded, handing Beatrice the plateful of eggs and sitting down across from Beatrice with a small one for herself. "We've been friends since Piper moved here a few years ago. Not that close, though—mainly through the quilting bees since we're in two different guilds. Lately, we've spent more time together and I've gotten to know her better. She's a great quilter; she has a lot of natural ability. And she's very sweet."

Karen was definitely growing on her.

"Piper was so excited when you moved here, and I know she's thrilled that you have gotten into quilting. It's such a great hobby to do together. For me, of course, it's gotten to be much *more* than a hobby. I've been working really hard to get to competition level . . . with my techniques and my designs and my execution of the stitching and handwork. And now I'm lucky to be at the point where I'm winning those competitions a lot." Karen looked both humble and proud at the same time. "I'm very grateful," she said.

"You've got quite a gift," said Beatrice mildly, taking a big forkful of eggs.

"Have you seen my quilts?" asked Karen, leaning forward and piercing Beatrice with her dark eyes. "I know you were at the quilt show, but I wasn't sure if you had an opportunity to see them that day. With all the news about Jo and all."

Beatrice nodded. "I did see one of them. It was stunning. But then, you're right. The day fell apart from that point on."

"I'd love for you to come by my house and see more of my quilts. Maybe for drinks and supper? You and Piper could both come. I'd really appreciate your opinion and feedback on my work."

Her work? She did take it very seriously. These quilts certainly weren't just a way to warm up on a chilly Dappled Hills night to her. "Of course, Karen, I'd love to. Although I'm not sure how much my opinion is worth." She reached over to the back of the sofa and unfolded one of her own, hesitantly constructed, rather shaky quilts. "You can see what I mean. You might be better off asking a longtime quilter like Miss Sissy to give you her advice. She might be crazy, but she knows her quilting."

Karen's eyes narrowed as she assessed the quilt. "You're just new to quilting, Beatrice. There's no reason why you should start as an expert quilter. No, your opinion still matters a lot—from the standpoint of an art curator and appraiser. You saw a lot of folk art make its way through your museum in Atlanta . . . and it's your experience in that area that I'm most interested in. How about supper tomorrow night? As long as Piper can make it, too."

Beatrice said, "I'll look forward to it. Maybe you can give me a few tips for moving forward with my quilting."

"You know the biggest thing you can do to improve? Decide what your goal is. Is your quilting a hobby? Are you wanting to create art that you can hand down, and please yourself with? Are you interested in competing in quilt shows? Then, once you decide that, you'll need to list the steps to take to reach your goal. Break them down into little steps that are manageable . . . and set yourself a deadline. You can do it—but you *have* to know what you're working toward," said Karen. Her eyes were bright and she waved her hands to punctuate what she was saying. This was a subject that was clearly important to her.

Beatrice said, "I do want to enter some shows— eventually, anyway. I've been trying to improve my hand-quilting, but haven't been happy with the results. I skip stitches, pucker fabrics, and sometimes I'll pin-prick the squares and the threads pull right out. A disaster!" She put down her almost-empty plate and got up to grab her current project for Karen's perusal.

Karen studied it. "Your stitches are a little long, Beatrice. Smaller stitches might come automatically if you focus on making your stitches even and consistent. I think the more you practice, the better you'll get. Posy has you set up with the perfect tools and fabrics for hand-quilting. The needle is a size ten between size, which will go through the layers easier. The quilting thread is the best to use—it's stronger and will last longer. The fabric you're using isn't too loosely woven or too densely woven. Now you've got a pattern that's got long, straight lines. That does make it easier for you to quilt, but it does show up the crooked stitches. Maybe next time a pattern with short, curved lines might be more forgiving. But your materials and the tools you're using are top-notch."

"So basically, my quilting problems result from the quilter herself," said Beatrice wryly. She took another big couple of bites of her eggs, polishing them off. Why didn't her eggs ever taste this good?

"As I mentioned, you're a novice. And remember, the mistakes help us learn and grow. At this point, I'd say you have a great eye for design. No surprises there, considering your background. You probably need to read up on technique and spend some time practicing the craft. Nothing beats hands-on practice for improving any skill." Karen grinned at her. She was such a confident young woman. It was hard to imagine her being a novice at anything. She probably jumped into everything as a near expert. And Beatrice hardly thought that Karen took kindly to her own mistakes. She was likely a lot less patient with her own learning and growing process.

Beatrice said, "Sadly, I *was* trying to read up on technique, yesterday morning, at the Patchwork Cottage. Of course, under the tragic circumstances, I needed to leave rather abruptly. I'll have to go back later to purchase the books I wanted. And maybe some magazines, too."

"Such a tragedy," said Karen, shaking her head. "Opal Woosley was a truly talented quilter. You know that we were in the Cut-Ups guild together. She was raised around quilters—the women in her family had quilted for generations. For her, it was all *about* practice. She must have made eighty quilts in her lifetime. The only thing that bothered me," she continued, brushing a strand of blond hair out of her eyes, then impatiently brushing it back again when it resettled in her eyes, "is that Opal never tried to take her quilting to the next level. This was very frustrating to me because I knew that the talent was there. I knew that the experience was there. And she never pushed herself." Karen gave a puzzled shrug.

"I suppose, for her, it was more of a hobby," said Beatrice. "There's nothing wrong with that."

Karen looked blankly at her.

Beatrice cleared her throat. "It's so sad, though, isn't it? I've never gotten such a shock as when I realized Opal wasn't simply napping at the Patchwork Cottage."

Karen's face softened and she shook her head. "Poor Opal. I was shocked, too. I couldn't believe the news when I heard it."

"Were you working when you got the news?" asked Beatrice. "You're a Realtor, aren't you?"

"I am. Not only for Dappled Hills, of course, but for a lot of the county. Business hasn't been great lately, but I like having the extra free time to quilt. I wasn't working yesterday morning, though—I was at home with the appliance repairman. It's such an aggravating process, you know. The repair company said they'd send a worker between eight a.m. and six p.m. Well, that's no help at all in narrowing down the time, is it? They never make it convenient. And my oven wasn't working at all. But they did come out the day after I'd called, so that was good. It's ABC Appliance, if you ever need somebody."

Karen wasn't exactly devastated over Opal's death, clearly.

"At least he came early in the day and there was an end to it. So I wasn't in town to hear the gossip. It made me sad when someone told me. Not just sad about Opal, but for Posy. A murder in a quilt shop can't be good for business. We need the Patchwork Cottage to thrive—we all depend on it so much." She carefully scooped up the rest of her eggs on her fork and ate them, then busily took both her plate and Beatrice's to the kitchen, scrubbed them clean, dried them, and put them away.

"So, tomorrow night, then? As long as it's good for Piper. I'll look forward to it," said Karen. And a minute later, she was gone.

Beatrice was back outside, cautiously regarding her flower bed again. If Miss Sissy had gone out, Miss Sissy would return. And if she was having the kind of day where Beatrice's yard qualified as the roadway, then Beatrice needed to listen out for cars while she was working on the bed.

Having such a close call had apparently put some fire in her. Now she was easily able to decide to rip out the flower bed altogether. It was a so-so collection of flowers; nothing was really vibrant, and it didn't match the rest of the yard's colorful Southern coziness. She gingerly plopped down to the ground, put on her gardening gloves, and started pulling up plants.

The sound of a car engine made her jump. Beatrice scrambled to her feet and scooted back a few yards. The approaching car didn't sound like the rattling old Lincoln that Miss Sissy drove, though. Beatrice was relieved to see Posy's car driving up instead. Posy spotted her and pulled into her driveway. She rolled down the passenger window and called out, "Do you have a moment to visit? I'm glad I saw you in the yard. I wanted to call you this morning, but I thought you might be sleeping in, after the day you had yesterday." She shivered.

Beatrice stood up, brushing herself off and taking off her gloves. "Of course we can visit," she said. Apparently, this would be a morning for visiting.

"Oh, don't stop what you're doing," said Posy quickly. "This is one of the best times of the day for gardening. I'll join you. It'd be a shame to be inside on a morning like this one." Posy loved working in her yard almost as much as she loved quilting. Her yard had been designated a backyard wildlife habitat, and she had both bird feeders and birdhouses scattered throughout her beautiful landscaping. Maybe Beatrice could get some advice on this pitiable flower bed.

Posy was wearing very casual clothes. "I've even got gardening clothes on," she laughed, sitting down next to Beatrice on the ground.

Beatrice jumped up. "Let me at least get you a pair

of gloves. Then I'd welcome the help—and the advice. I can't decide what to plant in this spot after I take out these ailing flowers. Maybe you can help me figure it out."

Posy squinted at the bed, considering it, as Beatrice headed to the house for the gloves and some water for them both. When she came back out, Posy suggested, "Have you thought about having several different levels of plants here? Maybe a pretty knockout rosebush to match the others you have in the yard, then some lamb's ears plants and maybe some buddleia? I think the size of the bed is a little too small. You could make it larger and give it more impact and some visual depth with the different plant heights."

Beatrice beamed at her as she set down a tray of water and handed Posy the gloves. "That's a brilliant idea, Posy. I knew you'd know what to do."

"Where's Noo-noo?" asked Posy, glancing around as if expecting to see the little corgi poking through the bushes. "I thought she'd come running to greet me. I could use a corgi cuddle." She and Beatrice glanced up at the cottage and saw the corgi standing up on her back legs to peer out the low picture window on the front of the house. Her mouth was open in a doggie grin and her big ears were alert.

"Poor Noo-noo!" said Beatrice. "I left her inside because I was almost run over by Miss Sissy this morning and I was worried about having her out here with me."

"Ohhh. Poor you, you mean! Are you all right? Did it take several years off your life to have a close call like that? Miss Sissy is quite creative about what qualifies as the road."

"It definitely shook me up. Actually, Karen happened to be driving by at the same time and saw what happened. She led me inside, fed me, and visited for a little while. So the experience wasn't quite as dire as it might have been."

Posy paused for a moment, staring toward the cottage. "Beatrice, would you mind if I go say hello to Noo-noo for a moment? It breaks my heart to see her watching us out the window."

Beatrice nodded and watched Noo-noo perking up as Posy walked up to the house. The corgi quickly disappeared from view as she jumped down to greet her friend.

A few minutes later, Posy was back. "She's such a happy dog. What a sweetheart!" Posy settled back down on the ground and started pulling weeds again. "Oh, and before I forget, I brought along a book from the shop. It's my favorite one on technique. Remind me before I leave to get it out of my car."

Beatrice said, "I'm guessing, judging from the fact that you're here, that the Patchwork Cottage is closed today?"

"It is. For one thing, Ramsay asked me if I could keep it closed in case the police wanted to spend more time in the shop. For another, though, it didn't seem respectful to Opal's memory to open up today. I just drove over to put a sign on the door and to check back in with Ramsay to see if I could be of any help," said Posy.

"Did they have any more information?" asked Beatrice. "Were they able to say anything more about when or how Opal died?"

Posy said, "Sadly, it does appear to be murder. Something about some discoloration indicating an object placed against Opal's face. I'm afraid it was probably one of my cushy pillows that was the culprit. As far as the time of the death goes, they're thinking that Opal was murdered while I was out of the shop . . . and that the timing was opportunistic. Someone saw Opal go in and saw me come out. For them, it was perfect timing."

Beatrice shivered. So Opal had been dead for a little while when Beatrice had sat near her.

Posy said, in a baffled voice, "I can't see why anyone would want to kill Opal. Or Jo, either, really. Although Jo, sometimes, could be a bit combative, Opal wasn't. I don't think I ever saw her being argumentative, except maybe with Jo. But that's because she loved Skippy and missed him terribly. It was no wonder that she acted that way with Jo, since she blamed her for taking her little friend away from her."

"When I was talking with Glen recently," said Beatrice, "he said that Opal was playing some practical jokes on them before Jo's death. Nothing really harmful, but the kinds of things that would really inconvenience the Paxtons or irritate them. Does that sound like something Opal would have done?"

Posy pulled out a weed from the bed. "I could probably see Opal doing that kind of thing. Practical jokes would be a way to get under Jo's skin and feel like she was getting back at Jo for what she'd put her through. Yes, I could see that. She was . . . mischievous. And maybe that could have turned into malevolence under those circumstances."

"But you don't see her escalating it to the point where she'd cut Jo's brake lines?"

"Of course not!" said Posy.

Beatrice thoughtfully pulled up one of the plants. "What if Opal *were* there the morning that Jo died? What if she were there to play another trick on Jo and Glen and she saw someone else at their house? Maybe that person was doing something that Opal didn't completely understand at the time, but then she started wondering about it later. Something was on her mind— that's why she made that appointment to talk to Wyatt. After all, Opal wouldn't have wanted to be seen at the Paxton house—she was up to no good herself."

"But if she were hiding, how would the murderer know that she'd seen him? It only makes sense if the murderer somehow knew and wanted to silence Opal before she could say something," said Posy.

"Maybe Opal wasn't exactly sure what she'd seen. She could even have confronted this person. Opal could have inadvertently alerted the murderer herself." Beatrice sat back on her heels for a minute. Pulling plants was harder work than she'd remembered. "Opal spent a lot of time at the Patchwork Cottage. Did you see her talking to anyone in the last week or so?"

Posy said gently, "She spoke to just about everyone, Beatrice. You know how Opal was. And she loved to talk about quilting and wanted to see what everyone was working on." She gripped a weed and yanked it out of the ground.

"Karen invited Piper and me over for supper tomorrow night. Maybe that's something I can find out more about, then," said Beatrice.

The sound of a roaring engine made Beatrice look up in alarm. "It's Miss Sissy! Clear out!"

Chapter 12

Despite the fact that neither was a very young woman, Beatrice thought she and Posy sprang to their feet and scrambled into the yard with a fair amount of speed. Their efforts were for nothing, though, since Miss Sissy had clearly spotted Posy, who was one of her favorite people on the planet. She puttered into Beatrice's driveway sedately and pulled the boatlike car up gently next to Posy's.

Miss Sissy climbed out of the car and joined them. She glowered at Beatrice. "Shouldn't play in the roads! Almost hit you earlier when I was heading out to town."

Since it was pointless to argue with Miss Sissy, Beatrice bared her teeth in a smile. Anyone who thought she was young enough to play on streets was clearly demented, anyway.

Posy hugged Miss Sissy, then settled back down on the ground to pull up the last remaining plants while Beatrice scouted out a chair for Miss Sissy to sit in, since she seemed prepared to visit. At this rate, soon half the town of Dappled Hills would have stopped by her cottage by lunchtime.

Once Miss Sissy was perched in a striped beach chair that Beatrice was sure Posy and she would have to extricate her from later, Posy said in a musing tone, "You know, Miss Sissy, Beatrice and I were just talking about poor Opal."

"Wickedness!" said Miss Sissy, bright black eyes shining.

"Yeeess," said Beatrice, not sure whether the old woman was talking about Opal's wickedness or the fact that she was murdered. Or maybe she was simply using one of her favorite words for no reason at all. "And that's what I wanted to ask you about, Miss Sissy. You're in the shop so much and you're so observant." Excepting the fact she hadn't noticed a dead woman only feet away from her.

Miss Sissy preened at the compliment. Beatrice continued. "Had you seen Opal talking with anyone? Or, possibly, having an argument or discussion with anyone?"

Miss Sissy nodded vigorously, endangering the loosely gathered knot of wiry gray hair at the top of her head. "With the mailwoman! Arguing!"

Beatrice sighed. Hadn't they all seen Opal arguing with Jo? "Was there anyone else you saw Opal arguing with or maybe just having a private conversation with? Someone in the last couple of days maybe?"

Miss Sissy assumed a thoughtful pose, drawing out her moment in the sun and the suspense. "Yes! With that young mayor."

Who wasn't particularly young. "She and Booth Grayson were arguing?"

Miss Sissy nodded again, pleased. "She was very mad. Very mad!"

Maybe Opal had been confronting him about why he was at Jo's house. Or maybe she'd only been confronting him about the permit the mayor was planning on enforcing.

"And the other one she was talking to. Sneaky, she was," said Miss Sissy, pantomiming someone being furtive.

"Which other one?"

Miss Sissy gave her a disdainful smirk. "The young one. The young quilter with the ugly quilts."

"Karen?" asked Posy.

"Did you hear what they were talking about?" asked Beatrice.

Miss Sissy frowned. "No. Tried to. Couldn't. They kept staring at me."

Posy and Beatrice thought this through. "I suppose they could have been formulating a strategy for the Cut-Ups guild to win the next quilting competition," offered Posy.

"Wickedness!" suggested Miss Sissy.

The flower bed was completely cleared out now. And Miss Sissy was about ready to start foaming at the mouth again. "Posy," said Beatrice, "you're starting to look tired. I'm sure it's got to be stressful having this tragedy at the shop. Why don't you go home and have a quiet lunch?"

Posy nodded wearily. "I think I might just do that . . .

have a quiet day at home. That would be nice." She hugged them both good-bye and got into her car, quickly leaving it again to hand the quilting book to Beatrice.

Miss Sissy was the one who somehow ended up with it. "Miss Sissy," said Beatrice, "that book is far too basic for you. You could *write* a book like this one." Of course, Miss Sissy's version would likely be full of dire and cryptic proclamations.

Even though Posy was gone, Miss Sissy made no move to leave. The next thing Beatrice knew, the old woman had tromped through the cottage to her back-yard with the book and Noo-noo and climbed into the hammock. At least that was easy enough. She'd keep out of the way there and Beatrice could make some progress finishing up her appliqué.

A couple of hours went by before Miss Sissy surfaced from the hammock. She'd apparently fallen asleep and frowned grouchily as if the nap or her dreams hadn't much agreed with her. Noo-noo, however, had clearly enjoyed her own nap and was grinning doggily at both Beatrice and her unexpected guest.

"Can I fix you something to eat?" asked Beatrice politely, although she remembered that it never really paid to be polite to Miss Sissy. She'd almost always take you up on whatever you were offering.

Instead the old woman shook her head impatiently. "Got to get home." She stopped a moment when she caught sight of Beatrice's quilt. "This what you're working on?"

Without waiting for an answer, she crouched down, squinting at the quilt and running her hand over the material. She grunted. "Not bad," she allowed, before squinting again at a particular square. "Except this. Fix this."

Although Beatrice ordinarily took anything Miss Sissy said with a grain of salt, she sure knew her quilting. And she was right—the square was sloppily stitched while Beatrice ruminated on the murders.

Miss Sissy's beady eyes homed in on her keys. She snatched them off the table, grunted again as a goodbye, and scurried out to her Lincoln.

A few minutes later, she was back in the house. "Car is dead," she said. She walked into Beatrice's kitchen and pulled some grape juice out of the fridge.

"It won't *start*?" asked Beatrice. Was she going to be forced to endure visitors all day long? "Here, give me the keys."

She wasn't sure why she'd thought the engine might turn over for her. It didn't, choosing to make odd, clicking noises instead.

Beatrice walked back into the cottage and gazed thoughtfully at Miss Sissy. "I could drive you back home, Miss Sissy, since you were anxious to get back. Then I could call a mechanic and have him either tow your car or fix it in my driveway."

The cronelike old woman was now eating a pimento cheese sandwich with gusto. She waved her hand to show she was busy eating, gulped down more grape juice, and said, "Can't take me home. I'm blocking your car."

"No, you're not." Beatrice looked out the window. "Oh. I guess it was Posy who'd pulled up next to my car. Well, then, I'll go ahead and call the mechanic."

About an hour later, the mechanic came. He got out of his truck, greeted Beatrice, then eyed the Lincoln. "Miss Sissy's car, isn't it?" he asked.

"I'm sure you've worked on it plenty of times in the past," said Beatrice. She noticed Miss Sissy was glaring through the window.

"She's usually pretty particular about her car," said the mechanic. "Is she here? I'm surprised she's not out reading me the riot act about being careful."

On cue, the old woman opened Beatrice's front door. She waved a gnarled fist at them.

"I'll be very careful, Miss Sissy!" he called out to her. She disappeared back into the cottage, presumably to gobble up more of Beatrice's food.

"Sorry you had to wait awhile," said the mechanic. "We've been busy lately at the garage. People are holding on to their cars longer and they're breaking down more. We had a couple of people waiting at the garage for their cars to be done, so I had to take care of them first."

"No worries," said Beatrice. "I totally understand." She watched as the man listened to the car as he tried to start it, then lifted the hood. She cleared her throat. "I think I have a problem with my car, too—that little sedan over there. The alarm keeps blaring at unexpected times."

The mechanic said patiently, "If you wouldn't mind calling the shop and making an appointment, ma'am?

It sounds like it's got a short or something, but I won't be able to tell unless you bring it in."

"Of course. Sorry. It was just suddenly on my mind and I thought I'd bring it up, that's all." Beatrice watched the mechanic poke around under the hood for another couple of minutes, then said, "I guess the shop didn't used to be as busy as it is now? I think I know someone who used to work for y'all."

The mechanic turned around to face her. "You mean Glen? That's right. It wasn't ever really slow at the shop, but we needed to cut costs. We had one too many mechanics there. Glen is a good guy and a good mechanic, but the others were just a little better."

But even a mediocre mechanic would know how to disable a car. Out of all the potential suspects, wouldn't he best know how to cut brake lines? Especially when it meant making sure the lines weren't *completely* severed so that there would be enough brake fluid for Jo to feel comfortable leaving her driveway and going out on her route? Enough so that the brake fluid would finally be depleted on Jo's curving mountainous trek?

Unfortunately, the mechanic had needed to tow the car to the shop. Miss Sissy, also, was completely disinclined to offer any payment for the services rendered. The Lincoln needed to be removed from Beatrice's driveway, so she ended up paying for the tow. But if Miss Sissy wanted to pick up her car from the shop, she was going to have to fork over the money for the repair herself.

Finally, Miss Sissy's car was out of the way. "I'll run

you home, Miss Sissy." Although it was an easy walk, at this point Beatrice just wanted to make sure she was actually gone.

"I have an errand to run!" announced Miss Sissy.

Was this day ever going to end? She said through gritted teeth, "I thought you were returning from errands when you dropped by."

"I was going back out again later to run the other one. It's later," explained the old woman.

"Where is it that you're needing to go?"

"That young mayor," growled Miss Sissy. "Have something to tell him."

Now, this was an errand she'd be happy to take Miss Sissy to. And sit in on. They piled into Beatrice's car. And naturally, the car alarm went off. Miss Sissy made a hissing noise and jumped right back out of the car while Beatrice muttered under her breath and hit various buttons on the key remote. The blaring alarm finally went off when she stuck the key in the ignition and turned it.

"Miss Sissy, you can come back now," called Beatrice to the old woman, who was suspiciously watching her from behind a tree.

"Is it your car?" asked the old woman, peering distrustfully at both Beatrice and the vehicle.

"It is. You might not recognize it because it's new. I wanted four-wheel drive and better gas mileage. But the stupid alarm keeps going off and I don't know why."

Finally, she managed to talk Miss Sissy into the car. The short drive to downtown Dappled Hills took only a few minutes, and Beatrice's mood was somewhat improved by the sight of Miss Sissy shaking her fist at everyone they passed on the way there. It was nice not to be on the receiving end of it for once.

The mayor's office was in the town hall building, which also housed the tiny police department. Beatrice parked and helped Miss Sissy up the stairs to the second-floor office.

Clearly, their visit wasn't expected. Miss Sissy walked right into the small sitting area outside the mayor's office and straight into the room where Booth Grayson sat at his desk. His dark eyebrows shot up in surprise when he saw her there.

"Ah . . . Miss Sissy, isn't it? And Beatrice. Did we have an appointment today?" He frowned at his computer screen.

"We didn't," said Beatrice. "At least, I didn't, and I don't think Miss Sissy did, either. But she has something on her mind, her car is in the shop, and she asked me to drive her over to talk with you."

Miss Sissy had already settled into one of the wooden chairs in the office and was reading the papers on his desk with interest. Suddenly realizing that Beatrice had given her a cue, she frowned ferociously at the mayor and said, "Wickedness!"

Oh no. And Miss Sissy had been doing so well, too. She'd thought she was going to at least give some sort of coherent accusation against the mayor.

The mayor stiffened. "I beg your pardon?"

The old woman leaned forward as if getting closer so that Booth Grayson could hear her better. "Wickedness! With that young girl. I know her mama. Know her grandmama! You're too old to be with her. Leave her alone."

Booth reddened and made a *pish* sound and picked up a file on his desk, then made a point of looking at his watch. "With respect, Miss Sissy, you haven't got the slightest idea what you're talking about. I'm a married man and very fond of my wife. I'm certainly not spending any time with young girls. If you saw me with someone, then you misinterpreted what you saw—it's as simple as that. After all, as mayor I speak in the schools. Perhaps you saw a young person coming up to ask me questions."

Miss Sissy said sternly, "The young person wasn't asking questions. Wasn't talking. You weren't, either. Nothing wrong with my eyes!"

"You couldn't have. . . ."

"I did! Saw you in Lenoir. Jo took me for a quilt show since I don't drive out of town now." Miss Sissy folded her arms against her thin chest and sat back in her chair in satisfaction.

Booth's face was grim as he stared directly in Miss Sissy's rheumy eyes, then turned his gaze to Beatrice, looping her in, too. "You misunderstood what you saw," he said firmly. "And Jo was more than happy to let you. All she cared about was having something to hold over my head, in case she ever needed it. That was the kind of person she was."

"Saw you!" crowed Miss Sissy.

Booth's lips were a thin line now and Beatrice was beginning to think they weren't going to get anything out of him, especially with Miss Sissy in her current mood. "Miss Sissy, do you think you can make it down the stairs to the car? I'll join you in a minute."

"I can do stairs!" said Miss Sissy scornfully. "Going down, 'specially."

The old woman left and Booth tapped at his desk, staring down at the dark wood as if searching there for words to say. Finally, he said, "Beatrice, I don't know you, but you seem like a sensible woman."

"I like to think so."

"Miss Sissy is . . . well, for one thing, she's so elderly that anyone under thirty looks like a child to her," said Booth, making a scoffing sweep of his hand.

Beatrice clicked her tongue. "I wouldn't say that her guesses at age are that far off. Would you?"

"She's completely mistaken that I would ever consider being with anyone who is underage," said Booth. He sat stiffly in his chair and stared out his small office window, a red flush rising over his shirt collar.

"But you would consider being with a woman who was very young. Just not criminally young," guessed Beatrice.

Booth didn't answer for a few moments. Then he said, "The woman in question is over eighteen. I suspect that she's looking for a little excitement in life, and I'm the closest thing she'll get to it until she leaves town for college."

Beatrice arched her eyebrows, studying him. Dark hair, receding hairline. A stomach that was softening a bit with middle age. His glasses were slightly crooked. He just didn't *seem* to fit the role of the passionate lover type. He was more like the type of man who was overly obsessed with 21-DRV forms.

He noticed her appraisal and said ruefully, "Maybe excitement is the wrong word. Actually, no. It's an exciting *situation*, but I'm not an exciting man."

Beatrice said, "Is it an exciting situation? It sounds like a sad one to me. A middle-aged man cheating on his wife of many years with a woman young enough to be his daughter? A young woman with nothing better to do?" She shook her head.

At the word *wife*, Booth Grayson's eyes narrowed a bit. "It doesn't have to be sad, though. It only becomes sad if my wife finds out about it. And there's absolutely no reason for her to learn anything about this. It would only hurt her. The young woman in question will be leaving town in only a couple of months. I've already ended our involvement. It's pointless for Mrs. Grayson to find out."

"If that's the way you want to think about it. I'm glad that my marriage didn't have such a tremendous lie at its core. I haven't met Mrs. Grayson, but I feel very badly for her," said Beatrice.

Booth said briskly, opening his desk drawer. "As I said before, you're a reasonable woman. I'm a man with a secret that I would like to keep from hurting someone close to me. What can I offer to you to forget that this conversation ever happened?"

Chapter 13

Beatrice stared at him. "Excuse me? Are you trying to buy me off, Mayor Grayson?"

"I'm simply offering to make a business arrangement with you that will benefit us both," said Booth.

"An offer that I find completely insulting. And have you forgotten that Miss Sissy is apparently an eyewitness to your shenanigans?"

Booth gave a harsh laugh. "Eyewitness she may be, but no one could call her a reliable one. Why hasn't she spoken of this alleged sighting until now? Why now?"

"Her memory comes in spurts. She's obviously either just remembered or suddenly made the connection that what she saw was important. You're not the only one who would find it important, either, Mayor. . . . I'm sure the police would be interested to hear about this, too. After all, the other eyewitness to this impropriety has been murdered. Covering up a relationship to ensure reelection and to avoid having a spouse find out . . . well, that sure sounds like a solid motive for murder to me," said Beatrice.

Booth's mouth pulled downward, highlighting unhappy grooves in his face.

"What I am interested in is some information. But that's not going to prevent me from talking to the police. The police need all the clues they can get to eliminate the killer," said Beatrice.

"You're going to send them off on a wild-goose chase," said Booth smoothly. "Because I'm not a murderer."

"That may be true," said Beatrice, holding up her hand to stop him from interrupting again, "but it would still be irresponsible of me to withhold information from the investigating officers. What I'd like for you to tell me, though, is exactly what you were bringing out of Jo Paxton's house the day I spotted you there. And where you were the morning of Jo's death?"

Booth heaved an impatient sigh. "I've already told you that I was retrieving some books that Jo had borrowed from me. I tried to get them back the morning Jo died. Then I returned the day after her funeral. That's all there was. I didn't want to worry Glen about them after her death. And the morning of Jo's death, I ended up deciding to come back for them another time because I saw Opal there and I didn't want to get tied up in some sort of visit. She was acting really oddly, anyway."

"I believe there was more to it than that," said Beatrice. "And when I talked to you about it before, you said it was equipment you were there for, not books."

Booth studied Beatrice again, summing her up. Finally, he said, "All right. Yes, Jo Paxton confronted me about what she and Miss Sissy had seen that day in Lenoir. She caught me off guard and I admitted to the relationship and offered to pay her something to ensure her silence. Unfortunately for me, she was more interested in having something she could hold over my head indefinitely. She'd taped our conversation with a voice recording device."

"Which you wanted to recover the morning of Jo's death. But you saw Opal there and decided to go back home," said Beatrice.

He gave a slight nod. "I'd parked my car behind a row of bushes and was already at the house to try to talk sense into Jo that morning. After the way she'd acted at the town hall meeting, I thought she was a loose cannon. She might say anything at the quilt show, simply to put pressure on me . . . or just for her own entertainment."

"She might have continued holding it over you for many years in the future," said Beatrice thoughtfully.

"Exactly."

"So, when you saw Opal, you decided not to talk to Jo about it and you went back home. You were soaking wet, since you'd been outside in the storm."

"From what I've seen," said Booth, "Opal Woosley is a huge gossip. I didn't want to have her asking what I was doing there."

"You mentioned she was acting oddly?" asked Beatrice.

"Odder than usual, you mean?" said Booth drily. "I

thought it was odd that she was outside in a rainstorm. But she had a huge raincoat on. She was peering around, acting as though she didn't want to be seen. And she was carrying a bag with her."

"Did she see you?"

Booth considered this. "At the time, I didn't think so. I'm not sure."

"So you left without the recorder, but returned the day after the funeral, let yourself in, found the device, and took it home with you."

Booth gave a small shrug. "It was easier than the alternative of approaching Glen about it. I didn't know if Jo had even told him about the incident. If he wasn't aware of it, then I sure didn't want him to find out about it."

"And you didn't talk to Opal about seeing her at the Paxtons' house? You didn't try to find out what she'd been doing?" asked Beatrice. "Did it occur to you that she might have been tampering with Jo's car? That she might have had wire cutters in the bag and have slipped under the Jeep and cut into the brake lines?"

"I didn't dwell on the possibility," said Booth with a long-suffering sigh.

Probably because that would involve admitting what he'd been doing there himself.

"What were you doing when Opal was murdered at the Patchwork Cottage?" asked Beatrice.

"Certainly not killing Opal Woosley," said Booth with a cold laugh. "I was at home with my wife, preparing for a day in the office working on next year's budget. She'll back me up on that."

Of course she would. Would she still give him an alibi if she knew the kind of person her husband was, though?

"So, really, the only people who knew anything at all about your indiscretion were Jo, who was murdered, Opal, who was murdered, and an old woman who's demented most of the time."

"And now, it appears, you," said Booth smoothly with an inscrutable stare. "Although, even if you were to say anything, there's no proof at all. It might appear that you had a bone to pick with me about the regulations I'm considering enforcing on the quilting groups. You have no photographs, no recorded conversations, no camcorder footage." He held out empty hands. "And, really, you're only now becoming part of the fabric of our town. You're a newcomer. Would the town be willing to believe you over me? I've been here in a position of authority for years."

"We could always find out," said Beatrice softly. "There's no proof. But in a town like Dappled Hills, the mere suggestion of impropriety will raise eyebrows and generate gossip. Which is exactly the kind of thing you don't want before an election."

Booth said in a tight voice, "As I was saying, what can I do for you? I'd like to prevent that particular experiment from moving forward."

"You can't do a thing for me, Mayor Grayson," said Beatrice, pushing her chair back and standing up. "As a matter of conscience, I'll need to let Chief Downey know about this. Your relationship certainly establishes motive, if nothing else. You tell a fairly convincing story, so I'll let you repeat it to Ramsay and the state police and see if they find it convincing, too. Thanks for your time."

Beatrice felt the mayor's stare boring into back as she walked to the door of the office. She had the strong sensation that she'd made an enemy.

Miss Sissy, who'd been waiting for quite some time in Beatrice's car, had fallen sound asleep. Unfortunately, that nap soon ended when Beatrice's car alarm inexplicably went off again as she tried to quietly insert the key in the ignition. Miss Sissy jumped a mile and gave her a glare that could have fried eggs. A blind in the upstairs window facing the parking lot moved. Maybe she'd bothered Booth Grayson again. Good.

"I'm sorry, Miss Sissy. This is a new car and I either don't know how to work it or else it's got some sort of malfunction." A distraction was clearly in order, since her explanation didn't appease Miss Sissy. "Did you feel like our meeting with the mayor went well? Did you accomplish what you set out to do?"

But Miss Sissy had apparently retreated into Miss Sissy World for the day and either couldn't or wouldn't respond. She grunted noncommittally.

"After you left, I asked him questions about the girl." A blank stare. "The girl you and Jo saw Booth with when you were out of town." Nothing.

Beatrice sighed. "When the garage calls about your car, I'll drive you out there to get it. It sounded like they might need to order a part, though, so it might take a little while." Especially since this Lincoln was at least twenty-five years old. "I'll let Posy know that you're stranded and I'm sure she'll be happy to take you to the Patchwork Cottage tomorrow with her if you don't want to walk there." If the Patchwork Cottage opened tomorrow, that is.

After dropping off the still-unresponsive Miss Sissy, Beatrice ran by the garden center for some flowers for the revamped flower bed. Between Posy's advice and the help from the owner of the shop, she decided she had a nice combination of flowers and heights for the bed. She'd been sure to ask for hardy plants, too—she had a way of killing off perfectly healthy things.

After the garden center, she dropped off a book at the library that she'd had in her car for several days, meaning to return. Then she hesitated before heading back home. A short walk might be relaxing. Her mind was going a hundred miles an hour with all the information she had. And she kept a pair of sturdy hiking shoes and socks in her trunk for exactly these occasions.

She hopped onto the nearby Blue Ridge Parkway and headed for an overlook parking spot. Then she crossed the parkway and started hiking an easy, sloping trail. Too bad she didn't have Noo-noo with her. She'd have to make it up to her furry friend another time.

Booth Grayson could easily be the person behind these murders. He had that cold, calculating manner and apparently, like many politicians, a healthy sense of self-preservation. Would he stoop that low, though? How far would he really go to protect his reputation?

She had to wonder if her strong suspicion of him was colored by the fact that she so heartily disliked the man.

Beatrice was calmer and more focused as she walked up the gently sloping trail. Minutes later, she reached a lookout point where she could see the setting sun cast shadows over the mountain valleys while highlighting the hills. Dappled Hills, for sure. The quiet beauty of the spot made her slow down for a moment and take some relaxing breaths. Sometimes she almost forgot to breathe on busy days.

The sun started dipping lower and the shadows grew longer. Reluctantly, Beatrice headed back down the mountain. Noo-noo would be wondering where her supper was, and she should unload the flowers from her car to plant tomorrow.

The sun seemed to set much quicker than usual and it was nearly dark by the time she reached the bottom of the trail. Her new sedan was waiting for her at the scenic overlook across the street.

As she hurried across the Blue Ridge Parkway, an engine suddenly roared to life behind her. In a split second she realized she had enough time to either dive out of the way or turn around to see what was racing toward her. She dove.

Chapter 14

Beatrice hit the pavement, hands and knees cushioning her blow before she rolled until bumping to a stop into a curb. She heard squealing tires as the car rapidly accelerated and sped off.

By the time she had the strength to lift her head, the vehicle was long gone. Beatrice pushed herself to a sitting position and scrambled out of the road as quickly as possible. The Blue Ridge Parkway was too busy a road for her to stay sprawled there, or else she really *would* be struck by a car. But the next time it would be an accident. . . . She was sure this hadn't been.

Beatrice limped out of the street, fumbling in her pocket for her keys. The alarm immediately started going off and she silenced it quickly as she gasped for breath. She dropped into the driver's seat, closed the door to the car, and pushed the door lock switch.

Someone had tried to kill her. And it wasn't Miss Sissy this time, because her car was in the shop. Someone had either followed her during her errands and to the trail or else spotted her car at the side of the road and realized the opportunity it provided. She peered in the direction the car had come from. There was enough space on the side of the road for a car to pull over and wait—and the curve of the road prevented her from seeing someone waiting there. It would have been easy for the person to wait for her to finish her walk, knowing she'd be crossing the road to return to her car.

Beatrice examined her hands and lifted up her pants to see what her knees looked like. They were both skinned, as were her hands. She hadn't had skinned knees since she was a child, and she'd forgotten how much they stung. But compared to how much worse her injuries *could* have been, she'd gotten off easy. She'd go home and wash the sore skin off, stick some bandages on . . . and probably be very sore when she woke up tomorrow. Better take some ibuprofen, too.

Beatrice started the engine and drove back through town toward home. She paused before pulling into her driveway. She should tell Ramsay about this near miss. Although she enjoyed the intellectual challenge of figuring out who was behind these murders, she had no desire to be murdered herself.

She grimaced as she saw Meadow's car in front of the barn. She'd hoped that Meadow would be out and she could talk to Ramsay without an audience. Meadow tended to hover and cluck.

Sure enough, as soon as Beatrice rather stiffly made her way to the Downeys' door to knock, the door flew open and Meadow gaped at her.

"I saw you getting out of your car. You're hurt? Whatever happened?" Meadow asked, throwing questions like Ping-Pong balls at Beatrice.

Beatrice made a face. "Someone tried to run me down on the Parkway, but I dove out of the way. On the pavement, of course." Meadow's mouth dropped open. Beatrice shifted her weight. "Do you mind if I come in and have a seat, Meadow? I was hoping to be able to talk to Ramsay."

Meadow shut her mouth with a snap and backed quickly out of the way. "Where are my manners? Come in, come in—Ramsay! Ramsay!"

Her calling wakened the Downeys' huge beast, and Boris came galloping across the long living room, barking as he went. Unfortunately, this barking coincided with a headache that was starting to make Beatrice's head throb. She put a hand to her forehead, then winced at the stinging.

"You've got a headache, too?" clucked Meadow. "Here, have a seat." She pulled Beatrice none too gently by the arm and deposited her in a cushy armchair before protectively throwing a quilt on top of her. "Where is that man?" she fretted. "Bad boy, Boris! No jumping!"

In moments, Meadow had disappeared into the back bedroom and returned with a sleepy Ramsay, still wearing reading glasses perched crookedly on his nose and bearing a copy of Thoreau's essay "Walking," which he'd apparently fallen asleep over. He'd finished *Walden* quickly, then.

"She's been *attacked*, Ramsay! By the killer! A near

miss! What is this world coming to when retired curators are mowed down in our streets?" Meadow let go of Ramsay's arm so that she could wring her hands in a very convincing fashion.

Ramsay's gaze sharpened and he suddenly looked awake. "Someone tried to run you down, Beatrice? Are you sure?"

"Well, of course she's sure! How else would she have gotten those skinned hands and knees? You haven't seen her roller-skating around Dappled Hills, have you? She dodged a *car*." Meadow's voice was exasperated.

"Meadow, if you could let Beatrice tell her story, then maybe I would better understand what is going on," said Ramsay in his steady voice. Beatrice honestly wasn't sure how Ramsay refrained from running over *Meadow* in his car.

Meadow opened her mouth as though she might demur, then apparently had some sort of idea pop into her head. "Um. Yes. Well, that's fine, because I've got to make a phone call." And she disappeared into the back of the house.

Ramsay gave Beatrice a measuring look, then opened a cabinet and brought out what appeared to be a bottle of very expensive scotch. He poured a generous amount over ice and handed it to Beatrice. "Here. It's not as if you can't walk home if you're not able to drive. And you've obviously had quite a scare." His eyes were kind as Beatrice took a grateful gulp of the drink. It burned her throat on the way down and made her eyes water.

As Beatrice told her story, Ramsay listened closely. He frowned when Beatrice admitted she hadn't been able to see anything of the car. "Are you sure you don't remember anything at all? Something specific about the engine noise? An impression of whether the car was lighter or darker in color? If it was small or large or a truck or a sedan?"

Beatrice shook her head. "But I was fairly focused on merely surviving," she said in a dry voice.

"Understandably," said Ramsay with a sigh. "Well, I hate to say it, Beatrice, but this might even have been an accident. It's possible," he said, raising his hand when Beatrice protested.

"But the car wasn't just driving along the Parkway. It raced out from the side of the road as soon as I was in the middle of it. I'm sure this was deliberate, Ramsay."

"Maybe it was a teenager or something. You know what their driving is like," said Ramsay reasonably.

"Why on earth wouldn't they have swerved when they saw me?" asked Beatrice in frustration. "They must have seen me."

"Did they?" asked Ramsay. "You have to admit that you're wearing dark clothing. And it must not have been very bright outside at the time. It's dark now."

"I wasn't planning on walking when I set out this morning," said Beatrice a little huffily. "And I still think that if this was accidental, the car would have pulled over to make sure I was all right when they finally saw me."

"Would they?" asked Ramsay. "Hit-and-runs happen every single day in this country. Why? Because people are scared. They're scared of facing the consequences of their actions. I'm not saying this *was* an accident, Beatrice. But it certainly could have been." He gave her a serious look that bordered on stern. "Unless you know something that you're not telling me. Did you possibly find out something that might make a murderer think that you could be dangerous to him?"

"I might have," said Beatrice. "I had an interesting meeting with Booth Grayson today. And I thought you should know what happened during it."

After she told Ramsay about Jo discovering Booth's affair, the voice recorder, and his retrieval of it, Ramsay was more alert. "Did you tell Booth that you were going to tell me about this motive he has?"

"I did. He offered to pay me something to stop me from telling you, as a matter of fact." Beatrice felt her face flush with anger, remembering. "He was determined that the story wouldn't go any further. I wouldn't be at all surprised if he tried to kill me to keep me from exposing his affair and the voice recording of his confession to Jo."

"That's pretty extreme, isn't it?" asked Ramsay in a musing tone. "Just over an affair?"

"But it's not just an affair, remember? Now it's two murders. Now it's a cover-up." Beatrice took another large sip of her drink. The restorative effect of scotch was an amazing thing.

Ramsay rubbed his large forehead as if his head hurt. "So you're saying we should arrest the mayor of Dappled Hills for two murders and an attempted murder? Is that what you're saying, Beatrice? Because I was hoping that instead of arresting a public official to-night, I'd have a peaceful evening at home with Mr. Thoreau."

"No, I'm not saying that at all. We don't have any evidence to that effect. He did give some information that was interesting on its own—that Opal was at the Paxtons' house on the morning of Jo's murder. And Opal was apparently acting oddly lately."

"Like that's anything unusual," said Ramsay with a snort. "Not to speak ill of the dead."

"She obviously had something on her mind that she was trying to tell Wyatt about or consult him over. The murderer clearly realized that she knew something very damaging and made sure to permanently silence her before she could share what she knew."

"It sounds like," said Ramsay in a dry voice, "she might have seen Booth. Considering he's admitting he saw *her*. And again we come back to arresting the mayor, which would not make for a happy day at work for me."

"I'm thinking we should keep an eye on him. That's all."

"Maybe we need to keep an eye on you instead," said Ramsay. "Please try not to be our third murder victim. Is there anyone else who might think that you have some dangerous knowledge that I should keep on my watch list?"

Beatrice thought about Karen and her strange conversation with Opal, about Glen possibly hugging Penny Harris, and the fact that Glen was a mechanic. Slowly, she shook her head. All she really had was a collection of rumors and speculation.

There was a light tap at the door and Boris sprang into action again, leaping to his feet and barking his throaty bark. "I'll get it!" sang out Meadow from the back bedroom, trotting along to the front door, grinning broadly. She obviously had some sort of secret. And clearly it had something to do with whoever was at that door.

It was Wyatt. And he was peering around the corner of the door. "I saw Beatrice's car outside." He frowned, as if sensing something was wrong. "Is something the matter?"

"Oh, Wyatt, it's good you're here. Ministers are always so useful at times like this. Scary times," said Meadow.

Had she called Wyatt just to get him over to see Beatrice? Really, this was going too far. Beatrice frowned crossly at Meadow, who blurted, "I gave Wyatt a call for him to collect the quilts for the church auction on his way home from the church. Wasn't it lucky that they happened to be ready during this time of crisis?"

Ramsay, not really sure what the subtext of the conversation or visit was, but clearly wanting to get back to his nap or his book or both, quickly filled Wyatt in. "And I've given Beatrice a nip of scotch, although she could probably use a dram more. Then maybe you'd be good enough to drive her in her car back home and walk back over to get your own, afterward?"

Police chiefs were good at subtle orders.

Wyatt and Beatrice made their good-byes and Beatrice said quickly as soon as they were outside, "Wyatt, you really don't have to take me home. You sort of got hijacked there, by Meadow and Ramsay. I'm perfectly capable of walking back home."

Wyatt smiled at her as he opened the passenger-side door for her. "Oh, I have no doubt in my mind that you're perfectly capable. But there's simply no reason for it. You've had a rough evening—you've gotten banged up. You need a little TLC. Besides, it's my pleasure."

Beatrice said slowly, "This spate of violence in Dappled Hills must seem unbelievable to you. Having these murders in such a peaceful place."

Wyatt nodded. "They say *still waters run deep.* It's true for people, but it's also true for towns. There are lots of emotions that are brewing under the surface—tension and hurt feelings. They show in different ways . . . and you're right that I find murder a shocking manifestation of it."

He pulled up into Beatrice's driveway and parked her car, carefully applying the parking brake. Beatrice could see Noo-noo's big ears through the living room window. The poor dog must have been wondering where she'd been all day.

She was opening her door and was thanking Wyatt when he stopped her for a moment, staring at her with serious eyes. "I meant what I said about realizing how capable you are. But you need to remember what you're dealing with here. Whoever is behind these crimes is feeling very desperate. I think it's clear to the murderer that you've either learned information that could expose him, or that you're very close to doing so. Please . . . be careful. Very careful."

The concern in Wyatt's voice warmed Beatrice's heart. She nodded. Wyatt gave her hand a squeeze, wished her good night, and set off for the walk back to the Downeys' house for his car, armed with the flashlight they'd lent him.

The next morning, Beatrice was so sore from her tumble on the street that she could barely haul herself out of the bed. Noo-noo watched sympathetically, standing close by the side of the bed.

Fortunately, as she moved around, making herself breakfast, showering, and getting dressed, she noticed that she'd loosened up a little bit. Noo-noo was relieved at her mistress's recovery and eagerly stood next to the hook where her leash hung.

"Sorry, sweetie, I don't think I feel that great yet. But maybe we can sit on the ground for a while and plant those flowers. Miss Sissy doesn't have her car right now, so I think you'll be safe with me in the front yard." Beatrice glanced around the kitchen and out the window for the flats of flowers. "Oh, I never got them out of the car last night," she said sheepishly. It had been the kind of evening where plans went completely awry.

Beatrice brought a small tarp to sit on, retrieved the flowers, and planted as Noo-noo watched. It was sappy to think it, but she felt a sense of renewal out there with the dew and the rising sun and the fresh day starting. It was good to be doing something basic, something mindless out in the dirt. Noo-noo apparently shared her sentiment and dozed peacefully next to her.

The idyll ended when there was a sudden crashing

through the bushes, and Beatrice struggled to her feet. Noo-noo growled and then barked as Beatrice brandished her spade in front of her in a threatening manner and wished she'd brought her shovel outside with her instead.

Another few heart-racing moments of the wordless crashing sounds ... then Boris bolted toward her, tongue hanging out of his mouth, tail wagging ecstatically.

Beatrice shakily exhaled, dropping the spade and wiping her sweaty palms on her jeans. It was ridiculous to be feeling this way. She hated jumping at every little sound.

Boris wasn't exactly a *little* sound, though. "Come on, Boris," she said. "Let's go inside."

She'd learned from experience with Boris that it was best if she was proactive and had food available for him to eat. Otherwise, he'd consume everything in her tiny kitchen that he deemed edible. Which encompassed most of the contents of her kitchen.

Noo-noo was looking particularly put-out by the fact that Beatrice was providing treats to Boris. She pulled out a couple and tossed them her way.

A few minutes later, there was a knock at Beatrice's door and Beatrice opened it to a disheveled Meadow, wearing plaid flannel pajama bottoms and an inside-out burgundy sweatshirt.

"Have you seen Boris?" she asked breathlessly. Leaves and twigs stuck out of her gray braid, attesting to her search through the woods between their two houses.

They heard a joyful, throaty bark from Beatrice's kitchen, and the huge dog barreled toward them.

"Boris! What a bad boy you are!" cried Meadow, showering the dog with kisses.

"Want some coffee, Meadow?" asked Beatrice, already heading back to the kitchen for two cups.

"Please! With cream and sugar." As if Beatrice could forget, considering Meadow's habit of dropping by for nearly daily coffee.

Minutes later, they were sitting on Beatrice's sofa, coffees in hand, and gazing at the two napping dogs. Noo-noo, even in sleep, seemed slightly on alert as if Boris was dangerously close to a complete invasion of her space.

"So, what are you doing for the rest of the day, Beatrice? Lolling around the house?"

Beatrice opened her mouth to sharply answer back and Meadow gave a deep chuckle. "Now, now. Don't get all wound up! I'm only kidding. You never loll, although lolling should be required today. What a scary evening you had yesterday! Are you feeling the effects of skidding across the pavement?"

Yes, especially when Meadow put it that way. "I was pretty sore when I woke up this morning. Although I've loosened up a bit since I've been moving around." And trying to keep your beast from eating up everything in my house.

"Ooh. I bet that was painful. You probably haven't skinned yourself up like that since you were a little kid. So you'll be taking it easy today?"

"Not so much, really. I've started on the flower bed

out there—I'd picked some flowers up at the nursery and started planting them," said Beatrice, leaving the sentence hanging a little, suggestively.

"Oh, when my bad Boris came over?" asked Meadow, clucking at the sleeping dog. "He's a mess, isn't he? I can help you to plant the flowers, if you'd like. I've got a bit of a green thumb."

Judging from the amazing success of her vegetable garden, she had more like a green *hand* than just a thumb.

"It's all right. The planting is pretty calming. And it gives me time to think."

Meadow suddenly fluttered her eyelashes coyly. "Are you thinking about anyone in particular? Anyone special?"

Beatrice frowned, thinking. "Well, probably Glen."

"Glen!" Meadow sounded horrified.

"Sure," said Beatrice. "Why not?" Meadow was the one who'd mentioned that he probably had a possible love interest, which made for an excellent motive for murder. What *was* the matter with the woman? You never could tell what was going through Meadow's mind.

"There's certainly no accounting for taste," said Meadow, rather cryptically. "So that's it for your day? Planting flowers and wondering about Glen?"

"And eating supper with Karen Taylor. She invited Piper and me over tonight."

"Really!" said Meadow. "That's remarkable. I wouldn't have said the two of you would even have gotten along well together."

"I don't think we'll ever be best friends, no. She's pretty strong-willed and very driven. But she's friendly enough. I was interested in seeing more of her quilts. From what I saw at the quilt show, she's extraordinarily gifted," said Beatrice.

Meadow snapped her fingers. "You know, I've been thinking about how to go about formally asking Karen to be part of the Village Quilters. Since Opal and Jo are dead, you know, and we still need someone to be part of our group."

How flattered Karen would feel.

"Maybe if I accidentally sort of popped by tonight. For some reason, whenever I see her, she's all stressed out or in a tremendous hurry. If I drop by tonight, she'll be relaxed from a full tummy, a couple of glasses of wine, and friendly conversation. Maybe she'll accept our invitation right on the spot."

While Meadow got up to pour herself another cup of coffee, still talking about the possibilities Karen would bring to the guild, Beatrice rubbed her forehead. She had a funny feeling that Meadow's intrusion into Karen's dinner party was going to turn this into a very long day.

Chapter 15

That evening, Piper came by to pick her up. "You look nice," she said. "Boy, am I happy to finally get away from the school! The staff development speaker we had today was absolutely awful." Then she frowned. "What happened to your hands?"

Beatrice hesitated. She hated to make her daughter worry over her. Plus, she had a feeling that Piper was going to fuss and tell her that she shouldn't be trying to run her own side investigation of these murders. How *couldn't* she, though, when these crimes had practically happened on top of her? But Meadow, of course, would have told most of the town by now. It might be better to downplay it.

"It's nothing now. I took a tumble out on the Blue Ridge Parkway."

"You did *what*? When?" Piper gaped at her. "You're not one to keel over like that, Mama!"

Beatrice told her story with as little excitement as

she could. "So you see, it all turned out fine. And Ramsay will probably find out who's behind it all very soon and we'll all go back to our quiet lives." Piper was still frowning over the story. "Do you think I'm dressed all right for tonight?" Beatrice asked, in an attempt to change the topic.

"Hmm? Yes, I think so. Didn't I say so a minute ago? I'm still worried over what happened yesterday. I wish you'd called me last night when you got back. I don't think I'm looking out for you like I should be," said Piper.

"Sweetie, I feel the same way about you. I keep thinking I should be inviting you over to supper and filling you up with healthy meals and good conversation. We can't stop feeling guilty, no matter what, can we? And there was absolutely no way I was going to call you last night and worry you right before bedtime. What good would that have accomplished?"

Piper smiled at her. "I guess you're right." She glanced at her watch. "We probably need to go ahead over to Karen's house. It was nice of her to invite us over."

It was nice, for sure, although Karen probably didn't do anything merely to be nice. For her it was more like networking and information-gathering. She'd certainly been very interested in Beatrice's background at the art museum.

Karen's house was a pretty Colonial with a historic marker outside it. Beatrice raised her eyebrows when she saw it. "That's quite a house for a young woman on her own."

Piper said, "It's the house she grew up in. Her mother died when she was a teenager and then her dad passed away a few years later—like he just didn't want to go on without her. Of course, it didn't have a historic marker at the time, but Karen worked hard to get it listed in the register. She's that kind of person, you know."

"Snobbish?" asked Beatrice.

Piper gave a laugh. "Diligent. I don't think she's snobby, but I think she's proud."

"Have you heard anything about her parents or her background at all? I'm curious how she ended up becoming such a supercompetitive quilter. Opal was saying something about nothing Karen did was ever good enough for her parents—something like that."

"Yes. I guess everyone in town knew about it because it was Meadow who actually filled me in on Karen's parents. Apparently, she just about bit a hole through her tongue to keep from butting in when she was around Karen and her folks. Karen's mother was a quilter, too, and was even in the Village Quilters for a while. And she was incredibly critical of Karen apparently—always very negative about Karen's quilts and her ability. I wondered if maybe Karen was determined to win quilt shows just to prove that her mother was wrong about her."

"There would definitely be a sense of satisfaction in getting critical acclaim and awards—especially if you've always been told you weren't any good. Sounds like a healthy way of restoring your ego," said Beatrice.

Karen opened the door before they had a chance to

knock. She was nicely dressed in a black blouse that perfectly contrasted with her shoulder-length blond hair, and wore crisply ironed white slacks and an intricately designed silver necklace. "How are y'all doing today? I'm so excited to have you over for supper," she said warmly, holding the heavy wooden door open wide.

"Mmm," said Piper. "It smells amazing in here."

"Tenderloin with Gorgonzola cheese," said Karen with a smile. "And smashed garlic potatoes and some cheesy biscuits that I've got a real weakness for. The aromas mingle nicely, don't they?"

"They sure do," said Piper. "And what a nice treat for Mama. Especially after the rotten day she had yesterday."

Karen frowned. "Yesterday? What happened yesterday?"

"Only that Mama was almost run down by a car, that's what! She had to dive out of the way and ended up skinning her hands and knees all over the Blue Ridge Parkway."

Ordinarily, Piper's pronouncement would have made Beatrice a bit grouchy. But this time she was more interested in seeing what Karen's reaction was to the news. Where had *she* been last evening?

Karen's eyes widened. "What? But that's insane! Oh, wait. What was Miss Sissy doing yesterday evening? She almost ran me flat over at the church picnic last June. And I was yards off the road." She added to Piper, "Miss Sissy almost ran your mother down yesterday, too. While she was gardening!"

Piper said, "I didn't hear about that, either!"

Beatrice said quickly, "No, Miss Sissy was safely tucked away at home at the time. Carless. Her car died in my driveway, actually, and had to be towed away. So she wasn't the culprit this time."

"Well, that's absolutely terrifying, Beatrice. You must have been scared out of your mind. Did you tell Ramsay about it? Did he think it was an accident?"

"Of course he did! But you know Ramsay. He'd rather stay in denial so he can relax and read Keats and write sonnets." Beatrice was aware some of her irritation was spilling over into her voice. But really, Ramsay could be so stubborn sometimes about not wanting to see crime, even when it was right in front of him.

"You drove yourself away afterward? After such a scare? I'd have been shaking too hard to drive home. I wish I'd seen you last night to give you a ride, but I stayed in to catch up on some work. You know what? There's some ointment that you should try. Bub's carries it. It's like an aloe cream with some other herbs added to it that really helps with scrapes and cuts. I used it when I took a tumble hiking one day. And it smells delicious, too."

"Thanks, Karen. I'll try to find it at the store. It's amazing that the scrapes still sting like they do."

"I've still got some left over. Let's get you set up with some wine, and I'll go dig it out. Wine will take the edge off. White or red?"

While Karen was getting their drinks and the ointment, Beatrice gazed around her living room. Like with Meadow's house, there were quilts everywhere. But unlike Meadow, Karen had carefully taken the time to display her quilts in artistic ways and with an eye for showing them in the best light. She had several quilts draped over an antique ladder that was propped against a back wall. Karen had mounted and framed a few unfinished quilt blocks, which made a stunning visual display over her sofa. Quilts were also hanging from the walls with lighting carefully pointed their way to show them to their best advantage.

Karen came back with their wineglasses on a small tray. "Beatrice, I'm glad you're here. I was hoping you could give your opinion of my display approach for the quilts. As you can see, I've made quite a few and it's a challenge to show them off. But not a challenge for a former art museum curator."

Piper smiled proudly at her mother.

"Actually," said Beatrice. "I think you've done a fantastic job here. You'd mentioned something to Meadow a while back about displaying quilts on the wall, and it made me a little worried. That's such a static way of presenting quilts, and quilts need to be shown off in different ways. Some of them show really well on walls, of course, but too many on walls makes it all sort of stiff. I love the way you've draped some of them. They're really meant to be draped over people . . . to be soft and comforting. And I think you've captured some of that. The quilts' texture."

Karen beamed at her. "That's exactly what I was trying to accomplish. I wanted to show them off in a variety of ways. To me, quilts are art. If I could put them all under glass with spotlights, I'd do it. But recently, someone with a lot of experience and wisdom convinced me to try other approaches." She motioned Piper and Beatrice to follow her upstairs. There they saw a couple of bedrooms that had curtain rods mounted over the beds and draped quilts as textured headboards.

"How did you display the quilts at the folk art museum?" asked Karen. Beatrice started answering, but then was quickly interrupted by Karen, who wanted to show her some of her more unusual quilts. Piper glanced at Beatrice and shrugged. Karen did warm to an audience. It was all right—Piper would have ended up bored to tears if Beatrice had launched into a lecture on the rotation of antique quilts to incorporate a resting time in between displays.

Their supper was delicious and Beatrice was surprised to discover that she was famished. Karen seemed pleased when she asked for seconds. The conversation around the table was lively, and if Karen dominated it, at least she wasn't boring. It was obvious that Karen was very well read on quilting and had very clear goals for herself in the craft. And was competitive. Her eyes gleamed when she explained her plans for winning at national quilt shows. She actually used the word *plans* in regards to winning, instead of *hopes*.

They were finishing their supper when the doorbell gave several merry rings. Karen frowned. "I wasn't expecting anyone." She quickly got up from the table to answer it. Beatrice sighed. Meadow. There went their quiet evening.

Piper whispered, "You act like you know who's at the door."

"It's Meadow. She's planning an ambush. She's going to invite Karen to join the Village Quilters." Beatrice took a rather large sip of her wine. Good thing Piper was driving.

"Right now?" Piper shifted uncomfortably. She was the kind of person who never enjoyed potential conflict. Apparently, she thought that Meadow might be pushy and that Karen might not be interested in the group.

Meadow was loudly apologizing. "Oh my! My! I am so, so sorry, Karen! I had absolutely no idea that you had company here. Hi there, Beatrice and Piper! My most favorite people all in one place. Isn't this *nice*?" Behind her, came a suspicious-looking Miss Sissy. "Uh. Well, I saw Miss Sissy walking down the street and she flagged me down. It was getting dark, you know. . . ." Meadow gave a helpless shrug and watched as the old woman strode across the room and sat down with great determination.

Beatrice thought she saw a flash of irritation in Karen's eyes for the briefest of seconds. She'd have to be superhuman not to feel irritation with Meadow and Miss Sissy, too. But it was impossible to be upset with Meadow for very long—she was almost like a child. Irrepressible and innocent. And annoying. At least, Beatrice was glad to note, Meadow no longer had the twigs and leaves in her braid from earlier in the day.

Karen was smoothly back in perfect hostess mode. "Meadow, can I get you something to drink? A glass of wine, maybe?"

"Yes! That would be wonderful. Oh, bring the whole

bottle, Karen. I think we might have something to celebrate." Meadow winked broadly at Beatrice and Piper
watched them both, curiously.

Obediently, Karen returned with another tray with
the rest of the white wine and also brought along an
unopened bottle of red and a wineglass for Meadow.
"Just in case. I'm never one to shirk celebrating."

Meadow gave a hearty laugh, poured herself a glass
of white wine, and said, now solemn, "Karen, I'd like
to ask you to become part of the historic Village Quilters guild. As a longtime resident of Dappled Hills, you
know that as long as this town has existed, there has
been a Village Quilters guild. For many generations,
women have shared friendship and their talents to create art, and I hope you'll join us in that fine tradition. It
would be an honor to have you as a member."

Piper appeared to be holding her breath. Beatrice
watched as some unrecognizable emotions passed
across Karen's face. Then she quickly grinned and said,
"The honor is mine. I'd love to join the Village Quilters."

Meadow let up a whoop and jumped up to fiercely
hug Karen. "I knew it! I knew you'd do it!" Then she
pulled back and anxiously studied Karen from arm's
length. "The ladies in the Cut-Ups won't hate you, will
they? I know they're going to be sorry to lose you."

"They'll live," said Karen with a short laugh.
"They've got enough members to really not miss me at
all. You know, I've been thinking about leaving the
Cut-Ups for the Village Quilters for a while."

"Have you?" asked Meadow with a wide grin.

"There's a lot of talent in your group. Our group. And forgive me for saying so, but I think some of it is being wasted," said Karen.

"Really?" Instead of sounding insulted, Meadow appeared intrigued. She took a large swallow of her wine.

"I'm afraid so. Let's take Savannah, for instance. Her craftsmanship is absolutely amazing. She puts tremendous effort into everything she quilts. I inspected one of her recent projects and couldn't believe how densely stitched it was. But she doesn't experiment with her talent or choose projects based on their artistic merit. It's almost like her quilts lack creativity."

That was certainly true. But Savannah was a bit eccentric. Her idea of a perfect pattern was something rigidly geometric where she could really shine in the constraints. And she did.

"And, Beatrice," said Karen, turning toward her. "You've got a real eye for art. I think your compositions have been striking and I've overheard some of your conversations at quilting bees—ideas for others' designs. You've got some fascinating ideas and I really want to pick your brain. But you don't have any skill."

Beatrice nodded calmly, ignoring Meadow's shocked gasp and Miss Sissy's dire mutterings. What Karen said was true. And she'd been in the art world long enough to retain at least a modicum of distance from any artwork—even her own.

Meadow, though, was clearly distressed at the direction that the conversation was taking. She drained her glass of wine and gratefully took more when Karen offered it. "Well, *isn't* it wonderful that you're going to be a part of the group? I'm sure you do have many fabulous ideas to share with us, too. Uh . . . hey, weren't you telling me about your quilt poster? Something like that? Displaying quilts on posters? Something?" Poor Meadow was now grasping at straws to prevent her new inductee from possibly stepping on more toes.

Karen, always willing to show off some of her work, quickly made the transition. "I was showing Beatrice and Piper some of the ways I'm presenting my quilts before you came in. But I have other displays I've done, too. I found this antique quilt at a flea market and the poor thing was literally falling apart at the edges. I was shocked they'd even tried to sell it. I guess they know there are people like me who'll have ideas for threadbare quilts. So I used corkboard, wire cutters, and a staple gun to attach a portion to the board and make a display. Now, it's not the thing to do if you have something really valuable and you're trying to preserve it," she said quickly, sensing some objection from the retired curator. "But it's great for something that was unusable to begin with.

"And I've used scraps to make Christmas ornaments for craft fairs. They sell like hotcakes. They're really easy to make with foam balls, Christmas fabric scraps, wire cutters, and ribbon. See, we could do things like this as the Village Quilters and really raise some money in our coffers with a minimum of time or effort."

"If it's not all taxed to death by the good mayor," said Beatrice drily.

"So sweet!" said Meadow a little unsteadily, looking at one of the ornaments. "Such a sweet thing. Ha!" She hiccupped. Piper and Beatrice glanced at each other. "I can drive her back home," said Piper in a whisper.

"Might be a good idea," said Beatrice.

"Did you hear about what happened to Beatrice yesterday?" asked Meadow. She sloshed a bit of white wine from her glass as she stumbled and caught herself on Karen's sleeve.

To her credit, Karen was unperturbed by the spill or the stumble. "Piper told me about it earlier. So horrible."

Meadow nodded solemnly. "Awful. Dappled Hills is falling apart. Jo, Opal, now Beatrice!" She clucked and hiccupped again.

"I'm glad that I had y'all over for supper tonight, then. It's good to have something fun and relaxing happen for a change."

"And the food was so delicious!" said Piper, helpfully chiming in.

"Food is always comforting, isn't it?" said Karen with satisfaction. "I baked myself extravagant breakfasts every day last week—just to keep my spirits up. Well, except the morning when I had the repairman out. I picked up breakfast that day . . . and I made sure it was decadent . . . doughnuts. The other days, I had blueberry baked French toast, garlic cheese grits, a breakfast casserole . . ."

"We could have had leftovers for supper!" said Beatrice. "At my house, that's almost certainly what we'd have eaten."

"This talk of food reminds me . . . what in heaven's name am I going to do about cakes now?" asked

Meadow in exasperation. "Dappled Hills is bakerless without Opal around! So thoughtless of the murderer."

"So we don't have a cake for the next show?" asked Karen, looking concerned. "Everyone counts on them being there. I think some people show up so they can eat cake."

The rapidly frying synapses in Miss Sissy's brain momentarily connected with each other. "June Bug!" she barked.

Meadow frowned vaguely at her. "I beg your pardon, Miss Sissy?"

"June Bug. She bakes cakes. Quilts, too."

Meadow tilted her head to one side, considering this information. "Now, that name is familiar to me. Is that the little woman who cleans for Opal Woosley? Or *cleaned*, I guess I should say now." Meadow sniffed sadly at the thought, and Beatrice quickly jumped into the conversation to head off a full-fledged cry.

"That's June Bug. I saw her when I was there to pick up the cake for the guild meeting. Surely her name can't be June Bug, though."

"It is!" said Miss Sissy fiercely, waving a gnarled fist. "It is."

"I guess it is," said Meadow, raising her eyebrows. "So she can bake cakes, too? She's a good baker?"

"You ate her cakes, didn't you? Ate them all," Miss Sissy growled.

"I . . . no, I don't think so, Miss Sissy. I've never had the pleasure of eating a June Bug cake," said Meadow pleasantly.

"Yes, you did! She baked all the cakes. *She* did." Miss Sissy became more agitated than ever. "She is my friend and she brings me cakes every visit!" She stamped her foot. Miss Sissy must have made a formidable toddler back in the day.

"I guess Opal decided to subcontract her baking," said Beatrice drily. "Maybe business picked up and she couldn't keep up with the demand."

Meadow's brows knit. "It all sounds a bit fraudulent to me. But okay. I suppose it's a type of business model. I'll ask June Bug to make some cakes for the next quilt show . . . the one in Lenoir. Where would I find her? Do you have her phone number?"

Miss Sissy glared at her. "Don't have a phone!"

"Oh, that's right. I forgot you don't make phone calls."

"She comes to my house on Thursdays," offered Miss Sissy, a bit more helpfully.

"To clean?" asked Meadow in a doubtful way. Miss Sissy's house wasn't exactly in pristine condition.

"To visit," proclaimed Miss Sissy smugly. "And to bring cake."

"Well, all right, then. I'll have to drop by your house Thursday," said Meadow.

"June Bug? I'm remembering now. Isn't she the really slow woman?" asked Karen.

Meadow frowned. "Slow? Do you mean disabled? She seemed able-bodied enough to me."

"No, I mean dim-witted. She always ran away whenever I knocked on Opal's door," said Karen.

"I think she's just shy, Karen," said Beatrice briskly.

Karen exuded confidence—her manner was probably very intimidating to such a shy woman.

Miss Sissy scowled and shook her fist at Karen, not taking kindly to her friend being labeled dim-witted.

Karen shrugged, losing interest in the conversation, so Meadow said quickly to her, "You're such a wonderful cook that I *know* you're going to find a wonderful husband. The way to a man's heart . . ." She frowned as she lost her train of thought. "Anyway, I'm surprised that no one has put a ring on your finger yet."

Karen gave her guest a rather tight smile.

"Are there any contenders?" asked Meadow sweetly, taking a gulp from her wineglass. "You and Wyatt were fairly friendly at my dinner party. Isn't he a lovely man?" She turned to Piper and Beatrice. "Isn't he? I just think he's lovely. Handsome, smart, ethical. What's better than that?"

A slight flush crept up Karen's neck. She *did* fancy him.

To her horror, Beatrice heard Meadow dragging her name into it. "Of course, Beatrice and Wyatt have a special connection. Don't you think so, Beatrice? You always look so well together. And you're both always smiling and laughing and pleased to be together. I really do think you're at the brink of a wonderful relationship with each other."

Beatrice gritted her teeth and Karen's flush grew. Miss Sissy made a growling sound.

Piper jumped in. "Did you hear the rumors about Glen and that lady who does all the volunteer work in Dappled Hills. What's her name?"

"Penny?" asked Meadow with a concerned eye at Beatrice. "You've heard things about them having a romance?"

Piper nodded. "Well, I've seen them together for a while now, but it was always a volunteer partnership before. At least, that's what I saw. I know they were serving food next to each other at the pancake breakfast fund-raiser a few months ago. And I've seen them doing other fund-raisers, too. But this time, there are rumors that they're an item."

Meadow was staring at Beatrice again. What on earth was going through her head? She couldn't think that Beatrice liked Glen?

Karen's shoulders relaxed in relief by the change in conversation. "That's interesting. But I think it's way too early for Glen to be starting a relationship with somebody else. He and Jo were married for a long time—he should respect her memory a little more. I haven't noticed anything romantic between the two of them, though. I'm like you, Piper—I've just seen them volunteering together. And I saw Penny by herself the other day, coming out of the county hospital when I was driving to meet a client."

"Penny is probably running the Pink Lady program over there," said Piper. "That's sort of a long drive for such a big commitment, though."

Karen shook her head. "That's what I thought, too. But when I asked her the next time I saw her, she acted real flustered to see me. Then she said that she was there to have tests run. She apparently has some very aggressive form of rare cancer."

"What a pity!" said Meadow. "Oh, I hope that she pulls through it all okay. She does a lot of good things for Dappled Hills."

"It's a good hospital and she's in good hands. I'm sure she'll be fine. But when I asked her if she was going to be admitted to the regional hospital for any kind of treatment, she shook her head and said that the only hospital that really knew the most about her illness was a place up North. They had some kind of experimental treatment. And it was going to cost too much money for her to be able to get it. Such a shame," said Karen.

Beatrice said, "I'm not even sure I'd recognize Penny if I saw her. I haven't crossed paths with her, I guess. And I've been thinking about putting in some volunteer hours for Dappled Hills. I never got the chance to do it while I was working, and now that I'm retired, I'd like to be able to help out in the community a little."

Piper raised her eyebrows. "I thought you'd decided to learn how to relax first before you got involved in any more activities."

Beatrice sighed. "Maybe I'm not cut out for relaxing. But I think I'm better. Now I can spend a few minutes in the hammock and not immediately leap right back out of it because I've thought of something I needed to do. I'm working on it. But if I could even fit volunteering into one weekend a month, or something like that, I'd be pleased."

"I'll introduce you to Penny!" said Meadow eagerly. "I can't believe you two haven't met—she's such an important part of Dappled Hills. And she's sick? I have to do something for her, then, since she's done so much for everybody else!"

Karen shifted uncomfortably. "You know, I have a feeling that she wasn't wanting a lot of people to know about her condition. It sounded like she didn't really want to talk about it."

Karen definitely messed up by telling Meadow, then.

"Pooh on that! All I'm going to do is show her some support and give her some good home cooking and a few hugs. I'm not going to go around gossiping about her or anything. You can come along with me, Beatrice. We leave tomorrow!"

Karen frowned uneasily and Beatrice said to her, under her breath, "Don't worry. Tomorrow morning she probably won't remember any of this. If she has more wine, she probably won't even remember that she was here tonight."

Chapter 16

But the next morning, Meadow *had* remembered, no matter how foggy she'd seemed when Piper had finally taken her home.

The phone rang early and Meadow sounded surprisingly composed and organized. "So, what I was thinking," she said briskly, "is that I could bring Penny a lunch and a supper. And maybe something for the freezer. You wouldn't have to bring anything, since you haven't even been formally introduced. I'm going to start cooking now and I'll call ahead and let Penny know we're coming by."

"Won't she be working? It sounds like she spends most of her time with her volunteer groups."

"I meant that we'd drop by her office. She has a small room off the back of the town hall, same as Booth Grayson and Ramsay. They have a kitchen in the building with a full fridge and freezer. But those men might try to eat some of the food, so I'm going to write dire warnings on some sticky notes. And I'll tell Ramsay it's for Penny, since she's so sick."

Poor Penny. She had no hope of keeping that illness of hers under wraps.

A few hours later, Meadow was tooting her car horn outside Beatrice's cottage. "I don't see how you cooked this so quickly," said Beatrice, noticing the dishes in the backseat. "There's enough food here to feed an entire army."

"Oh, it's nothing. Besides, I doubled the recipe so that I'd have supper for Ramsay and me tonight, too."

If only Meadow would do that every day and bring Beatrice some meals! She'd gotten very tired of her own, uninspired cooking very quickly.

In minutes they were at the town hall. And only a few moments later, they were barging into an office so tiny that Penny could barely fit a desk in it, a desk that was nearly buried in flyers, papers, and a bunch of files. Penny was also tiny—a little woman with a warm smile. But, Beatrice noticed, with worried eyes. She looked like the complete opposite from Jo Paxton. Jo had dark hair and was difficult, where Penny was fair with a sweet disposition.

"We brought you some food!" said Meadow in her booming voice. "I thought I'd show it to you before I stuck it in the kitchen fridge. Chicken salad sandwiches, chicken *cordon bleu*, and a frozen hamburger casserole for later. And they're all covered with sticky notes warning of cataclysmic disaster befalling anyone who eats it besides you."

Penny looked somewhat taken aback, but gave

Meadow a tentative smile. "What's the occasion, Meadow? You're such a great cook that I'm thrilled to get these, but . . . why are you bringing them to me?"

"Because you're sick, of course!" Meadow might have remembered Penny's illness, but had clearly forgotten that Penny was trying to keep it quiet.

Penny's brow furrowed. "But I haven't told anyone that I was sick."

"Sure you did! I heard it through the grapevine," said Meadow.

Penny was obviously still trying to figure out how Meadow had heard the news when Meadow bubbled on. "And where are my manners? Let me introduce you to Beatrice Coleman. She's one of Dappled Hills' newer residents. You probably know her daughter, Piper."

"Of course I do," said Penny warmly. "It's very nice to meet you."

"Nice to meet you, too," said Beatrice. She turned to say something to Meadow and saw she'd already trotted out to put the dishes in the fridge. She smiled at Penny and shrugged. "I wish I had a fraction of her energy."

"Me, too," said Penny. Her eyes were sad.

Beatrice cleared her throat. "I'm sorry to hear that you're not feeling well. That's miserable."

"I'm sure I'll be fine," said Penny in a comforting tone. "It's not really so bad. For the longest time, I didn't even know that I was sick."

"I've heard so much about you," said Beatrice. "You do a lot to help the people in Dappled Hills, and the

rest of the county, too. I'm planning on doing some volunteer work myself soon."

Penny passed Beatrice one of her business cards. "I
hope you'll give me a call when you decide to. I help
coordinate volunteer work so we can get volunteers to
the places where they're most needed. And I try to
match people's talents with the volunteering they do."

Meadow came back in, smiling with satisfaction.
"Well, that's all put away. And I don't think either
Booth or Ramsay will touch them."

"Thanks again, Meadow. That was really thoughtful
of you." Penny hesitated. "I had a question for you, so
it's lucky for me that you dropped by. I hope you won't
mind." She paused again.

"Ask away!"

"It's . . . it's actually about Ramsay's case. Or cases, I
guess. You might know that I've been spending some
time with Glen. He started volunteering after he lost
his job."

Beatrice raised her eyebrows. Were they about to
hear that Glen and Penny were dating?

Penny bit her lip. "But I've been concerned about
him lately. I know that when married women are murdered, the husbands are the prime suspect. I was wondering what you thought Ramsay might be thinking."
She waved a hand quickly. "I'm so sorry to be asking
about this. I know I'm putting you in a spot."

Meadow, though, was perfectly happy to talk about
Ramsay's cases. Probably a lot happier than Ramsay
would have been, in the same position. Whatever she
didn't know, she was delighted to speculate on.

"Well, of *course* he doesn't think that Glen murdered Jo. He's known Glen forever—everybody knows the kind of man he is. No, he's definitely considering other suspect options," said Meadow breezily.

Penny spoke quickly, words tripping up over each other. "Oh, that's so good to hear, Meadow. Thank you. You see, Dappled Hills is such a small town. And he was in the hardware store a couple of weeks ago, buying wire cutters. I heard that wire cutters were probably what was used to cut Jo's brake lines?" she asked.

Beatrice and Meadow nodded.

"So I was sure that the hardware store owner was bound to tell Ramsay. Like I said, it's such a small town, and he would probably remember something like that. It's not like the store is superbusy all the time."

Beatrice said, "Why did he buy the wire cutters?"

"He was looking for ways to make a little money, on the side. He loved volunteering, but he said he was feeling bad about Jo being the breadwinner. He's always been handy and a little crafty, and he noticed that the store signs in downtown looked worn. He decided to offer to make replacement signs for the stores—nice wooden ones that had a sort of retro feel to them. He made a sample one. But he had to have wire cutters to make the signs." She shrugged. "That was all."

"Well, I certainly can't see how that would be considered suspicious," said Meadow with a laugh. "He has them for business reasons! Besides, probably half the people in town have wire cutters. They're helpful to have around."

Penny's face brightened. "That's true. It's just that . . .

you know. What with him having been a mechanic and all, I was worried that Ramsay might add it all up and think that Glen was responsible for killing Jo. And I know he loved her and would never have done anything to harm her."

So there were no confessions of undying love here. Penny could easily be concerned about Glen solely through friendly interest.

"Anyway," said Meadow confidently, "he has alibis for the times of the murders, right?"

Penny's brow wrinkled. "Not for Jo's murder. But that's because he lived in the house with her. The only person who could have given him an alibi was Jo."

"Understandable! But what about for Opal's death?" said Meadow.

Penny said eagerly, "I know exactly what he was doing that day. He went by the Patchwork Cottage first thing in the morning to ask Posy if she was interested in getting a sign for the shop made. She wasn't there, so he came right here to the town hall and he and I spent the rest of the day at the county library for adult literacy." She stopped quickly as she saw Meadow's and Beatrice's faces. "What? That's all right, isn't it? Opal died in the afternoon, didn't she?"

Beatrice said softly, "I'm afraid not. The police are saying that Opal was dead by the time that Posy returned to the Patchwork Cottage that morning."

Penny slumped, face white.

Meadow said, "Don't worry, Penny! Like I said, Ramsay has known Glen for *ages*. For ages!"

Beatrice started pulling at her sleeve. "Penny, really,

you shouldn't worry. It was good to meet you. Meadow, we should be going."

Meadow called behind her, "Remember the food in the fridge, Penny. Food always helps!"

As they left the tiny office, Beatrice uneasily found herself staring right at Booth Grayson, who was heading up the flight of stairs to his own office. He glowered at her and Beatrice lifted her chin to stare him down. There was no way that a man like Booth Grayson was going to intimidate her.

Meadow was apparently completely immune to being intimidated. "Booth! I was going to call you later. I know you were so disappointed not to be able to see a *full* quilt show last time."

Booth hardly appeared crushed or incomplete by this omission.

"I know you had to leave early because of the circumstances and being an official of Dappled Hills," said Meadow. She sounded a little uncertain about this, as well she should. In Beatrice's mind, there was absolutely no need for the mayor of the town, no matter how small that town might be, to go to the scene of an accident. Even if it ended up not being an accident. He'd been searching for an escape route.

"But we ended up having the quilt show after all, since we were all set up and had the space. Of course, it cast a pall over the proceedings. But we soldiered on," said Meadow in a ringing tone.

Booth continued blankly surveying her.

"Since you weren't able to stay to really get a true feel for the event, I'd like you to come to the next one.

And there just so happens to be another quilt show in the area this weekend. We'll also be having a short memorial in honor of Jo and Opal. It's a bit more of a drive, but not too badly—the next county over. I'll call you tonight and give you more exact directions so that you can drive yourself."

"My wife and I won't be in tonight to take your call," said Booth stiffly. He pushed his glasses up the bridge of his nose to more effectively glare at Meadow.

"Perfect!" said Meadow, grinning. "It would be better for me to leave them on your answering machine, anyway. That way you could rewind the tape if you get confused with my directions."

"I believe we might have already had plans for Saturday," said Booth.

"That's fine for us, then," said Beatrice. "Since it certainly wouldn't be considered fair for you to levy taxes and other fees on the group without a full understanding how it operates. You'll have to hold off. To be fair."

Booth's eyes flashed at her. She was right—she'd definitely made an enemy. And now he apparently thought that she was putting pressure on him. And he could be right.

"Look, here comes yet another suspect in this case," said Meadow in her too-loud whisper as Glen Paxton walked toward the town hall from the parking lot. "Ramsay should have your luck. Maybe you should be the policeman and he should be the retired person."

For once, Ramsay would likely agree with Meadow. Glen smiled at them, deepening the smile lines around the corners of his mouth. Beatrice said, "Coming to get another volunteer assignment? I met Penny— she's a delightful person."

Glen said, "She is, isn't she? Yes, I needed to see her this morning and figure out what time we're picking up the food from the food drive on Sunday."

"Thanks for the reminder. I have a few cans that I need to put in the collection bag," said Beatrice.

Meadow leaned in and Beatrice sighed. Here it came. Meadow had clearly not gotten the memo about keeping Penny's illness quiet.

Meadow said, "We heard about Penny. She's in my prayers." She reached over and gave the startled Glen a hug. Meadow clearly still believed Glen and Penny were having a romantic relationship.

"Oh," he said, looking confused. "You know about Penny's illness? She wasn't really telling people about it. I was trying not to mention it, either. You know how it is when you're working closely with someone in a small office. You start overhearing calls from the doctor's office— by accident, you know. . . ."

Meadow said, "Glen, we know all about you and Penny. I think it's so wonderful that you're finding love again." She obviously *didn't*, though, and made a slight wincing face as if the words tasted bad.

Glen's eyes opened wide. "Do people think that Penny and I are having a relationship? A romantic one?" He turned a mottled red color. "Penny and I are just friends and coworkers. I do care a lot about Penny, but only as a good friend. I loved Jo—I'm still trying to work through the fact that she's suddenly gone. Does the whole town think that Penny and I are . . . having an affair?"

Beatrice said, "It doesn't really matter what the rest of Dappled Hills thinks, does it?" But even as she said the words, she knew that it *would* matter. If you live in a small town, you don't want to have to face disapproval . . . day after day.

Meadow blushed, obviously remembering her role in spreading gossip about Glen and Penny.

Glen gave an uncertain sigh. "If you could, please help spread the word that Penny and I are just good friends. And thanks for inviting me to the quilt show and for having the little memorial for Jo. Penny wanted to go to that with me to be a supportive friend. You don't think other people will misinterpret that, do you? Or that it's inappropriate?" he asked in a rush.

"I certainly don't," said Meadow staunchly. "I think it would seem odd to everyone if such a good friend didn't support you."

Glen relaxed a bit. "Hopefully these murders will be solved soon. Right now I feel like I can't exactly do anything—I'm sure I'm a suspect in Jo's murder, since I'm her husband. Penny has been really worried about me, actually."

Meadow nodded. "She was asking me what Ramsay might be thinking. I can't believe you have anything to worry about, Glen, and that's what I told Penny."

"She was also telling us about the morning of Opal's murder—how you were at the Patchwork Cottage to

ask Posy about having a new sign made for the shop."
Beatrice abruptly stopped talking as Glen's face went
white. "Glen?"

He cleared his throat. "Penny was mistaken. I wasn't
at the shop that morning. It was the morning before. I
slept in that day and didn't get out until it was time to
be a reading buddy at the elementary school."

Beatrice frowned. "Really? Penny was certain that
was the day. I was going to ask you if you'd seen anyone or anything. . . ."

But Glen was vehemently shaking his head. "No.
She's wrong about that, but who could blame her, with
everything she's got on her mind? And now, if you'll
excuse me, I've got to go in; I don't want to be late for
my next assignment."

And before they could even say good-bye, Glen was
inside the town hall.

Chapter 17

Meadow and Beatrice got into Meadow's car. "Well, that was certainly interesting," said Meadow. "Especially our chat with Penny. Although I don't understand how you managed to bring up the subject of the investigation. It really worried her."

"*Me?*" said Beatrice. "I had nothing to do with it! Remember, she wanted to ask you what Ramsay thought about Glen's involvement."

"Oh. Well. Anyway, she sure seemed worried about it all," said Meadow.

"And for good reason, I think. Look at it from the police perspective, Meadow. Here we have two people who are rumored to be having an affair. One of them is married to someone who has a lot of money but lives a very simple life. The other has a life-threatening illness and her only hope is to get expensive experimental treatment at a distant hospital. She can't afford it."

"But Glen could help her—only if he gets access to

that money. And his wife obviously isn't going to just *give* him the money . . . especially considering what he wants it for," said Meadow, light dawning in her eyes. "And she's sort of a frugal person, anyway."

"Right. And not only is this man a former auto mechanic, but he also has a pair of wire cutters that he's recently purchased. He chooses to disable her car's brakes on a morning when it would look like a complete accident and probably never even be investigated. It would have been easy for him to slip out into the driveway while Jo was in the shower. He knows her mountainous mail route well. On a stormy morning, the police were certain to write off the tragedy as a horrible accident."

"And they would have," said Meadow, "if you hadn't convinced Ramsay to investigate. Oh, I tried to tell him, but he wouldn't listen to me."

"That might have had something to do with the fact that you were telling him that Opal Woosley had a vision about the car," said Beatrice in a wry voice. "You should've known that wasn't exactly going to fly with Ramsay."

"I guess. So, do you think that Opal saw something to do with Glen?" asked Meadow. "In one of her psychic visions?" Meadow was obviously completely enamored with the supernatural.

"I think she probably actually *saw* something. With her eyes. We already know she was at Jo's house the morning that Jo died—Booth Grayson kindly gave that information, as I told Ramsay," said Beatrice.

"Right. So Opal might have seen Glen messing with

Jo's car? But that would have seemed perfectly normal at the time," said Meadow. "Unless maybe she had a vision about it! Seeing into the future."

"She looked as shocked as the rest of us at the quilt show that Jo had died. Although that might have been the moment when she realized exactly what she *had* seen. If it actually was Glen that she saw. We still don't really know that," said Beatrice. "And he insisted that he and Penny aren't having an affair. But we don't really know that's true. The two of them are awfully close."

"Run through it again for me, Beatrice," said Meadow. "Booth was over at Jo's house to try to get the voice recorder, Opal was over there to play another practical joke on Jo, and maybe Glen was outside tinkering with Jo's car."

Beatrice nodded. "Opal could have been wandering around the Paxtons' yard to make mischief and not even seen Glen immediately, since he was under the car. Then she *did* see him and hurried out of there. Later, she thought about what she'd seen and contacted Glen about it. Maybe she simply wanted to ask him what he was doing, if she might have misinterpreted what she'd seen."

"So he was onto her and saw her car that morning when he was downtown trying to ask the shop owners about replacing their signs," said Meadow.

"When he realized she was alone in the store, asleep, he took advantage of the situation," said Beatrice. "Did you see how eager he was to make sure that we didn't think he was in the Patchwork Cottage the morning Opal died? He was obviously trying to cover that up."

"And he tried to run you down, too?" asked Meadow breathlessly. "He somehow realized you were getting close to the truth? It scares me silly to think that we've been talking to a *killer*."

"This is just one scenario that fits, Meadow. But it might not have happened this way. I'll admit that all the pieces fall into place, though. And it's hard to imagine that Glen would do these things—but when people get desperate and when they're in love, they sometimes act out of character. He could be lying to us about the nature of his relationship with Penny."

Meadow glanced sideways at Beatrice. "I'm glad your crush on Glen is over now. At least, I'm guessing it is, since you've revealed that he's a two-time murderer and a liar. Plus, there's the fact that he tried to kill you, too."

Beatrice struggled to control her temper. "Meadow, let's get this straight. I have never for one second entertained the thought of being romantically involved with Glen Paxton. I promise. I think that you somehow got that impression one day when I said I was going to be thinking about him. I meant about his connection to this case."

"If you're sure," said Meadow with a shrug. "You certainly seem very passionate when you're talking about him."

Beatrice's blood pressure pounded in her ears and she was about to really tell Meadow off when she abruptly changed subjects again.

"You're going to the quilt show, I hope. You can help keep an eye on Glen, since he's a mass murderer. Oh, and thankfully, I did get the food set. I had a cake tasting at Miss Sissy's house and sampled June Bug's baking. Delicious! Every bit as good as Opal's cakes. Well, I guess they weren't Opal's cakes at all, if Miss Sissy is to be believed."

"The tasting must have been interesting," said Beatrice, smiling at the thought of Meadow invading Miss Sissy's house and wrangling cake from the old woman.

"Indeed it was! I thought Miss Sissy was going to be completely inhospitable and not even let me have a crumb of June Bug's cake! She was being quite piggy over it."

Beatrice wished she could have witnessed that scene. Meadow and Miss Sissy wrestling over cake.

"But back to the end of your crush," said Meadow briskly. "That's really wonderful news. Not only because Glen is a depraved killer and pathological liar, but because it means that you're still available to explore a rewarding relationship with a man who's a lot higher on the moral plane—Wyatt."

For a split second, Beatrice entertained the thought of opening the door to the slow-moving car and stepping out.

"It's been obvious to me for some time that Wyatt has feelings for you," said Meadow, a matchmaking sparkle in her eye.

Beatrice took a deep breath to calm herself. "Meadow. I know you mean well. But I promise you that Wyatt and I are just friends. However, if you keep interfering with our friendship, that might soon *not* be the case."

"I wouldn't dream of interfering! All I want to do is to maybe increase the chances that your paths cross, that's all. You're barely at church at all, so I know that you're not going to meet up with him where he spends most of his time," said Meadow.

"I'm at church every Sunday!"

"Well, but you're not there Wednesday nights. Or Sunday nights. Your Sunday morning attendance is a bit spotty, too. And he has little events and Bible studies there on different nights during the week. Or you could always volunteer with the youth—they meet on Thursday nights. . . ."

"Being there on Sunday mornings works well enough for me, Meadow," said Beatrice stiffly. They pulled into Beatrice's driveway. "Thanks for the ride."

As she was getting out of the car, she heard Meadow say, "Fine, then. But you're making this all much more difficult."

"Do you think that you'll be able to take Miss Sissy to the quilt show on Saturday?" asked Posy in a hopeful voice. "If you're planning on going, that is."

Beatrice had been wavering on going since she didn't have a quilt in this show and she didn't think that Piper did, either, with all the training she'd had lately for school. But when Posy called to ask her for a favor, she found it hard to say no. Besides, if Meadow was going to make Booth Grayson go to the show, maybe it would give her an opportunity to talk to him again. "Of course I will," said Beatrice. "It's an out-of-town show, isn't it?"

"It's in Lenoir, so not too far away. I've got to go

early with Meadow to help set up, and Miss Sissy would end up getting bored, I'm afraid. Unfortunately, her car repairs are taking much longer than expected and she really misses driving," said Posy.

"She's the *only* one who misses her driving," said Beatrice.

"She asked if she could borrow Cork's car and drive to Lenoir herself," said Posy with a sigh. "But Cork didn't think that was a good idea."

Posy was likely censoring whatever Cork had actually said in response to that suggestion.

"No, Posy, it's no problem at all. I'm sure Miss Sissy will get her driving fix soon—the part won't take *that* long to come in. Better that she doesn't drive anyone else's car, especially in Lenoir, where there's a lot more traffic."

"I really appreciate it, Beatrice," said Posy.

"Are y'all expecting many people to come to the show?" asked Beatrice.

"Meadow feels pretty confident about the attendance," said Posy. "We're planning to do a special recognition of Jo Paxton and her years of showing and judging quilt shows. We'll also have some time devoted to Opal and bring in some of her quilts as part of the memorial. I think some people who might not have come to the show will be coming to listen to those memorials. Glen is definitely planning on making it."

"And he's bringing Penny with him," said Beatrice, without thinking. She stopped short. "Oh, Posy, keep that under your hat. Glen said that he's taking Penny with him as a friend."

"I heard a rumor," said Posy, looking uncomfortable, "that Penny and Glen were having an affair. And I do understand two people coming together in a time of grief—but it does seem awfully early, doesn't it?"

"Glen told me that there's nothing going on between him and Penny," said Beatrice. "Have you heard or seen something that made you think otherwise?"

"Not really. But there was this one incident. I've hesitated mentioning it because I didn't think it really made a difference to the murder investigation, but . . . well, maybe it does somehow in a way that I can't see. One evening I was coming out of my shop and I heard Jo talking to Penny. Jo must have been on her mail rounds and she had come across Penny on a volunteer errand downtown or something. Jo was asking all these questions about Penny's health—and not in a very nice way."

She could imagine. Jo didn't have the softest of approaches.

"Apparently, Jo had been delivering a lot of medical bills and statements and test results to Penny's house. I could tell that Penny was trying to avoid talking about it, but Jo was really pushing. Then Glen came up. I guess he must have been volunteering with Penny. He was furious when he saw that Penny was upset. And very angry with Jo for bringing up the subject. None of them noticed me, and I was frantically trying to just lock up the shop so I could avoid overhearing their conversation."

"It must take a lot to get Glen really angry," said Beatrice. "He seems like a pretty laid-back guy to me."

"Oh, he *is*! But Jo—well, she was pushing it. You know. She was being sort of nasty and Penny hadn't done anything, the poor woman. Jo simply wanted to get the inside scoop on something that Penny was clearly trying to cover up," said Posy.

"And it was enough to trigger Glen into action to defend her," said Beatrice.

Posy said, "It was. His defense of Penny made Jo furious, though, and she demanded to know if there was something more than friendship between Penny and Glen."

Posy had worded that delicately. Beatrice was willing to bet that Jo hadn't used the same wording.

"What happened then?" asked Beatrice.

"There were people who were starting to look their way. They *were* right in the middle of downtown Dappled Hills, after all. They finally noticed that I was standing there, too. Penny left in a hurry and Glen told Jo that she was imagining things. The way he said it sounded like the truth. He told Jo that he cared about Penny—because she was a good friend and a good person. Then he left, too. Jo was the only one who wasn't in any hurry to leave," said Posy.

"But it sounds like she might still have had mail to deliver," said Beatrice drily.

"That was probably true. I know she could be a difficult woman, but Jo was a wonderful quilter and could be a good friend, when she wanted to be," said Posy. She looked wistful. "I rather miss having her around the shop. And now we're all about to memorialize her at the quilt show. It's all so hard to believe."

"You were saying there would be a good number of people coming to the show?" asked Beatrice, hoping to distract her friend before she started feeling too sad.

"Oh yes. I think some of Jo's quilting friends from other towns will be there, too—she really made the rounds as a judge, so there were lots of people who knew her in the quilting community."

"A pretty good turnout, then. I guess Karen will have a quilt in the show?"

"At least one! In fact, I think she'll have three. I count my blessings every day with Karen as a Patchwork Cottage customer. I think she could keep the entire shop afloat with her purchases alone. You don't have anything to submit, Beatrice?" asked Posy.

She felt a bit of a pang. She really wanted to have something in the show. She wanted to be an active part of the art world again, even approaching it from the artist side. But she didn't want to participate until her quilts were really *good*. She still had so much to learn and read about and observe. "Not yet, Posy. Maybe sometime soon. Or maybe I'll pump Miss Sissy for some tips when I drive her to Lenoir. I'm still learning the craft."

"Remember," said Posy gently, "we're not all there to judge you. We're your friends and we want to celebrate your art and enjoy it, too. There are judges at quilt shows, but they're not the only ones attending. Don't worry about being perfect."

As she wrapped up the phone call, Beatrice thought wryly that she should have those words tattooed on her somewhere.

*   *   *

Miss Sissy was sitting in a faded rocking chair on her front porch on Saturday morning, completely ready to go to the show. The vines that surrounded her house, like the ones covering Sleeping Beauty's castle, were encroaching on the porch, as well. If Beatrice had been any later, they might have started making inroads on Miss Sissy herself.

Miss Sissy eyed Beatrice's car, suspiciously, even as Beatrice hopped out of the car and strode around it to open up Miss Sissy's door. "Don't worry, Miss Sissy. It's been behaving itself lately. No alarms."

Miss Sissy nodded and spryly trotted to the car . . . which, naturally, meant the car alarm went off. There did seem to be an increase in the number of alarm malfunctions that was in direct relation to Miss Sissy's proximity.

Miss Sissy covered her ears and glared at Beatrice while she tried pressing different buttons on her key ring to stop the blaring noise. Finally, it shut itself off.

She gave the old woman an apologetic smile. "I'm so sorry. It always goes off when I least expect it."

Miss Sissy climbed gingerly into the car. She fastened her seat belt, rolled down the passenger window, and proceeded to shake her fist at every animal, person, or thing she saw on the way to Lenoir.

Beatrice cleared her throat. "Miss Sissy, at least we should see some people we know at the show. Glen is going to be there to hear Jo get recognized."

Miss Sissy grunted. "Jo was nice. Visited me a lot."

Or maybe just brought her mail every day. "And the

mayor is apparently going to be there." She looked sideways at her passenger.

Miss Sissy raised her spindly arm and shook her gnarled fist. "Wickedness!"

So this was a good-memory day for her. It could be good to have Miss Sissy in her corner.

"On another subject, I was hoping that maybe you could give me some quilting pointers. Oh, not right now—it's not the kind of thing I can listen to and really absorb while I'm driving. But I was wondering if you could come by my house a few times when I'm quilting and give me some help with my approach and technique. I've got what I think are some great ideas for quilt design, but I'm not really sure how to carry them out. It was really helpful when I was starting out and you sat down and quilted with me," said Beatrice.

Miss Sissy was almost cheerful. "Just say when," she said gruffly.

"Maybe a couple of days next week? I'd really like to participate in one of the quilt shows later on this year, if I could. I'd even cook for you, if you come," offered Beatrice bravely.

Miss Sissy made an awful face. Beatrice had forgotten that Miss Sissy had sampled her cooking before.

"All right, you could cook for *me* and I'll supply all the food."

Miss Sissy smiled.

There were a good number of people at the quilt show. Apparently, there were some lectures earlier in the day that were well attended. Beatrice felt a guilty pang that she hadn't gone to any. Lectures and classes would definitely help her improve.

The show was being held in a community college gymnasium. The parking lot outside the school was nearly full, although most of the cars had college parking passes hanging from their rearview mirrors. Either way, it meant that Beatrice would be getting her exercise as she walked to the school from the far perimeter of the parking area. She dropped off Miss Sissy at the entrance, then had to park so far away that the school was merely a speck.

Although the quilt show and the lectures had been going on all day, the idea was that she and Miss Sissy were arriving in enough time for them to view all the quilts before the judges announced the winners in the different categories and before the memorial for Jo and Opal. The sun was already setting as Beatrice walked briskly up to the building.

Most of the quilters in the two Dappled Hills quilt guilds were there, and many of the guild members had at least one quilt they were showing. Meadow waved at her and grinned as Beatrice came in. She also saw Wyatt there and had a feeling that Meadow had had a hand in bringing him there. Glen was politely listening to Karen tell him about a quilt—either one of her own or another one.

Posy came up beside her. "It's nice that Glen is here," she said. "And he even brought one of Jo's quilts to show—not officially or to be judged or anything. But so she could sort of participate in the day."

"That's nice." Beatrice glanced over and saw that

Penny Harris was there, too, but not standing very close to Glen.

"Did Booth end up making it here?" asked Beatrice.

Posy motioned to a corner of the room where Booth was sitting on a bench, scowling. He looked even grimmer when he saw Beatrice. "A regular ray of sunshine, isn't he?" asked Beatrice darkly.

"He certainly does look gloomy. Hopefully he's not planning on taking it out on the quilters when he gets back to his office," said Posy with a sigh. Then she gave a small frown. "Oh dear. Here comes Georgia and she looks a bit grim herself."

Georgia joined them with worry creasing her brow. She greeted them in her usually upbeat way, but there was strain in her voice.

"Is there something wrong, Georgia?" asked Beatrice. There was no point in going through the formalities when she was so clearly troubled.

Georgia nodded. "I think so. Beatrice, you remember Savannah's problem that she sometimes has. And Posy definitely knows it well."

Georgia was referring to her sister's kleptomania. The town was so small and the items that Savannah swiped were so insignificant that the Dappled Hills storeowners either looked the other way or had a special Savannah account for Georgia to pay back later. Beatrice nodded at Georgia. "Has Savannah's problem cropped up again lately?"

"It sure has. Honestly, I think it has something to do with the murders. Whenever Savannah is feeling stressed, it usually starts up again. And this time, she took a couple of things from the Patchwork Cottage," said Georgia, face flushed.

Posy reached out and hugged Georgia. "You seem so worried. You know you don't have to worry about poor Savannah when you're talking to me. I totally understand and I'm not concerned about the *things* in the shop at all. I'm only worried about you and your sister."

Georgia brightened. "I do know that, but it makes me feel so much better to hear you say it. There's something else this time, though, that I'm especially worried about. The timing of when she swiped these things."

Beatrice leaned forward a little to listen.

"When I found the packet of needles, I knew they weren't the ones we usually get, so I asked Savannah about it. You know how she can be when she's confronted, even gently, about her borrowing. This time she acted even more flustered than usual. I asked her when she'd taken the needles and she told me it had been several days before."

Georgia fished the packet of needles from her pocketbook and handed them over to Posy. "But then," she continued, "when I was thinking about it again last night when I was in bed, I realized that Savannah couldn't have taken them when she said she had. That was the morning she'd had an optometry appointment. She couldn't have been at the shop then.

"I asked her about it this morning. She'd gone to Bub's the morning that Opal was murdered because we were out of coffee. I guess she was feeling tense after we learned that Jo's death wasn't an accident after all.

She dropped by the Patchwork Cottage after she'd put the bag of coffee in her bicycle basket."

Beatrice took a deep breath. "So Savannah was in the Patchwork Cottage the morning Opal was murdered? Did she see anything?"

"That was the very next thing I asked. Savannah hadn't wanted to put herself at the scene of the crime, of course. And she hadn't *thought* she'd seen anything important. She said Posy wasn't there and Opal was on the sofa in the sitting area, but she was alive . . . and looking sleepy. Savannah was trying to be sneaky to swipe the needles, so Opal never saw her," said Georgia sadly. "But Glen came in, calling for Posy. And Opal said that Posy wasn't there. He told her he'd come back later."

So Glen had definitely been there. Had he left when he'd indicated?

"And then Savannah told me that Karen was there," said Georgia slowly.

Posy and Beatrice both stared at her. "That morning? While Savannah was there?"

Georgia nodded.

"But she said she was doing something else that morning," said Beatrice, frowning. "She said that she'd been waiting for a repairman to come out."

Georgia shifted uneasily. "That's why I really hate bringing it up. I didn't want to say anything to Ramsay . . . or Meadow, who is practically the same as telling Ramsay. Because maybe she was like Savannah— she didn't want to place herself at the scene of the crime. And maybe she *did* wait for the repairman right after she was at the shop. Maybe she left the shop after she realized that you weren't there, Posy."

Or maybe she'd left after she'd speedily smothered the sleeping Opal. With whom she'd recently been seen arguing.

"Did Savannah see when Karen left the shop?" asked Beatrice.

Georgia shook her head. "No. But she didn't think there was anything special about that morning, either. She was more worried about getting out of the shop, undetected, with her pack of needles." She knit her brows. "Do you think we should tell Ramsay, then? I hate letting him know that Savannah was at the Patchwork Cottage that morning, too."

"I don't think Ramsay will even think twice about Savannah being there," said Beatrice. "He knows all about her little . . . problem. What possible motive could Savannah have? And she certainly didn't have a motive to murder Jo. I wouldn't worry about it. But I do think we need to let Ramsay know . . . just so he can check it out or keep an eye on Karen. As Posy said, it might all have been totally innocent."

Meadow came surging toward them.

"And I think we'd better not say anything to Meadow about it," said Beatrice quickly. "She's too excited about having Karen as part of the Village Quilters. Who knows what she'll do if she hears about this?"

Georgia made an excuse and scurried away and Posy murmured something about checking on Miss Sissy and left in another direction. Meadow was clearly focused on the quilt show instead of the murders.

"Beatrice, I think we have an emergency."

"We do?"

"We're out of ice. And it's getting very stuffy in here. I think people will be wanting some ice soon," said Meadow.

Beatrice said, "Shouldn't a community college have an ice maker? At *least* one?"

Meadow said, "Well, they do have one, but it's broken. Actually, I'm afraid that I might have broken it. This is exactly the reason why the mayor has no business levying fees and taxes on us! Sometimes we have these mishaps happen and then we need to take a little money from our general fund to pay for them."

"So you're wanting me to find some ice."

Meadow grabbed her arms. "Could you? That would be wonderful. I'd leave myself, but I'm supposed to be doing that memorial for Jo and Opal in a few minutes and I don't want to be dripping perspiration any more than I already am. There's a gas station that's right beside the college. Shouldn't take you long to hop in your car and head over there."

Beatrice said drily, "My car is parked so far away that it's practically *at* the gas station. I'll just walk there. There's no point driving the ten extra yards or so. One bag of ice?"

"Two. No, three! Yes, three will be perfect," said Meadow, apparently ignoring the fact that three bags might be slightly heavy for a retired art museum curator to tote around.

Karen, who was standing behind Meadow, asked,

"Do you know when the judges are supposed to release their results?"

"Yes! In fact, they should be finishing up their ballots now. . . ." Meadow hurried away again and Beatrice fished in her pocketbook for some money, not noticing that her keys dropped out as she rummaged.

She glanced up sharply, having the uncomfortable feeling that she was being watched. She scanned the room and saw that Booth Grayson was still glowering at her from across the room. Glen's eyes also met hers and he smiled at her a little warily, she thought. She didn't notice anyone else looking her way and scolded herself for having nerves. Maybe the near miss on the Blue Ridge Parkway had rattled her more than she'd thought.

As Beatrice walked out the door, Miss Sissy eyed the keys lying so invitingly and unprotected on the floor. Swooping down, she nimbly grabbed them and jingled them delightedly, stuffing them quickly into her dress pocket as Posy caught up with her.

Clouds had rolled in and made it even darker outside than it actually was. It looked like at least a mile to the gas station. Fortunately, she'd worn sensible shoes. As if she didn't *always* wear sensible shoes. She walked quickly through the quiet parking lot toward the station, weaving through the parked cars.

"I really *did* like you," came a cool voice from behind her. She gasped and spun around to see Karen standing there, holding a lug wrench in one hand.

Chapter 18

The other woman was completely calm and focused, which was more frightening than anything.

"You're a smart, accomplished woman," recited Karen in a detached voice. "And you've got a great daughter. She's really going to miss you."

Beatrice decided to ignore that last bit. She glanced around her to see if there was anything she could use as a weapon or if she could see anyone who could help her. All she could see was a sea of cars and not a soul around. Maybe if she could somehow swing her pocketbook at her? And if she could stall and keep Karen talking . . .

"If you like me so much, Karen, why are you threatening me?" asked Beatrice in as reasonable a tone as she could muster. "I thought we were getting along so well together, too."

"There are a couple of problems with you, Beatrice. One is that you like poking into other people's business. I wouldn't have thought that about you, but all I've seen lately is you asking questions and trying to connect clues. Maybe you come by it honestly. Maybe it's just the fact that evaluating and appraising art is similar to detective work, too," said Karen.

"But my investigating shouldn't have bothered you that much. It didn't bother anyone else. It only bothered you because you killed Jo Paxton and Opal Woosley," stated Beatrice.

"It worried me a little. I'll admit it. It also bothered me that you're clearly bent on starting a relationship with Wyatt," said Karen, eyes narrowing.

This made Beatrice stare at Karen, openmouthed. "What on earth do you mean? The only kind of relationship I'm interested in having with the minister is strictly a friendship. Or perhaps a spiritual relationship," said Beatrice a bit primly. Who was she trying to convince? "I certainly don't have any designs on the minster. Are you romantically interested in him?"

"Of course I am," snapped Karen. "You had to know that. Meadow knows it, which is why she was making such a point over it at my dinner party the other night."

"Meadow had way too much to drink, which should have been obvious to you. Besides, her comments simply reflect the way Meadow *is*. She lives for making connections with people, even connections that won't work out. Like your inclusion in the Village Quilters," said Beatrice.

"You were trying to edge me out. Me! And you're an old woman," seethed Karen, fingers clenching on the lug wrench.

"Then Wyatt is an old man," said Beatrice drily. "Because he and I are the same age."

Fury twisted Karen's mouth and Beatrice added quickly, still hoping to diffuse the situation, "You're very competitive, aren't you? I've heard that you set out to prove your mother wrong. She thought you were no good at quilting, so you decided to become the best."

Karen's voice was clipped. "Mother didn't know anything. She was jealous because she could see I had a lot of natural talent."

Beatrice continued. "That's really why you were so upset with Jo. Not only was she standing in the way of your winning quilt shows and building a name for yourself, but she was also simply competition for you. Jo was a very solid quilter." Out of the corner of her eye, she thought she spotted some movement through the cars—but when she looked again, she saw nothing.

"She had talent. But she didn't have the imagination to win the much bigger shows," said Karen. "And her vision was totally limited. Jo thought in terms of the Southeast. I'm thinking about winning national competitions." Karen's voice rang with pride. "I try different things. I spend a lot of time creating new designs."

"Which of course I could help you with," said Beatrice smoothly. "Design is really my forte."

Karen gripped the lug wrench again, as if reminding herself it was there and what it was for.

Beatrice kept talking. "So, being the cutthroat person you are, you decided to take out the competition. But it needed to look like an accident, didn't it? I'm sure if Ramsay and the state police were to take your computer right now, they'd be sure to find searches for how best to cut brake lines."

Karen kept quiet.

"The best way to cut the lines, as I'm sure you discovered, was to use wire cutters for some control. You wouldn't want to completely sever the brake lines or Jo would never have left her driveway. She'd have known her brakes were out before she ever got on the road. What I'm wondering," said Beatrice, "is if you'd originally planned to cut the brake lines the morning of the quilt show. I'm thinking that the weather played a huge role in your decision. That particular morning with the sheeting rain made for the perfect day for you to carry out your plan. With weather like that, it was sure to look like an accident, wasn't it?"

"I heard that you were the person who convinced Ramsay to investigate the accident," said Karen in a tight voice. "You had to get involved, didn't you? I knew from the start that I was going to have to keep an eye on you."

Beatrice was still visually combing the parking lot for someone to help her. Her visibility was limited on one side by a few large cars and trucks. It wasn't worth it to scream unless she *knew* there was someone to hear her. And no one was outside at the gas station.

She took a deep breath. "The only problem was that Opal Woosley had seen you at the Paxtons' house. She hadn't really understood at the time what she was seeing, of course. Opal was more concerned about getting away without someone seeing her, since she was there to play her regular pranks on Jo."

"Which was going to have been perfect for me in case Ramsay did investigate the accident and discovered that the brakes were tampered with," said Karen. "Glen knew that Opal had been playing pranks on them since Jo had run over her Skippy. He'd be sure to tell the police the kinds of things that Opal had done."

"It made a lot of sense; the only problem was that Opal had actually been out there the morning you were there. Once she put two and two together, she asked you about it. You'd had no idea she'd seen you at the Paxtons' house until she approached you. You were seen having a heated discussion with Opal. It was then that you knew you had to get rid of her," said Beatrice. "Your motive for Jo's murder was to get her out of your way. Opal's murder was a matter of necessity."

Karen said, "She obviously wasn't going to be able to keep quiet about it. The woman couldn't keep quiet about anything."

"You were out that morning, early, to get some breakfast since your oven was out. You saw Opal's car, alone, at the Patchwork Cottage. Posy had already left to run back home. You quietly entered the shop and saw the perfect opportunity to get rid of Opal Woosley," said Beatrice. She unobtrusively hefted the weight of her pocketbook a little. She always carried a big bag. Was it heavy enough to stun Karen enough to drop the lug wrench? If she hit her in the face with the purse maybe?

Karen shifted uneasily and Beatrice hurriedly continued. "You really took a chance with your alibi, didn't you? Especially considering that Opal's murder wasn't planned. You did have a repairman over to fix your oven. But the repairman could have come by your house while you were out and then the police would have known you were out. As it was, you messed up your alibi by telling Meadow, Piper, and me that you'd gone out for breakfast the morning you'd been waiting for your repairman. But you'd also told me that the repair company was very responsive . . . that you'd only called them the afternoon before they came out the next day. So you'd gone out the morning of the murder."

"A girl has to eat," said Karen with a shrug. "I'd no idea at the time that I needed an alibi or to worry over being seen out. It was pure serendipity that I saw Opal's car on the way back from the doughnut shop drive-through. You realize this is all circumstantial evidence, Beatrice."

"There's something else that you don't know about," said Beatrice quickly. "A *living* eyewitness that you know nothing about. One who can nail you on your actual whereabouts during Opal's murder."

Karen's patronizing smile turned into a snarl. "Who is it? Who?" She yanked Beatrice's arm, holding her tightly against her. Her pocketbook was trapped between them and there was no way she could maneuver it out from this position. As it was, she could barely breathe.

She gave a short laugh. "You think I'm going to tell you who saw you, Karen? Why would I tell you who it was? So you could kill that person, too? How stupid do you think I am?"

Karen pushed her hard away from her and Beatrice

went flying backward onto the pavement, on top of her pocketbook.

At that moment, though, something triggered Beatrice's blaring car alarm, only feet away from where they stood.

This time Karen was the one who jumped and spun to look behind her. Beatrice took that opportunity to grab at Karen's legs and pull as hard as she could. Karen fell to the ground with a thud, and the lug wrench clanged onto the pavement.

The alarm wailed persistently as Beatrice strained to reach the lug wrench, scrambling on the cement to grab it. Finally, her hand closed around the iron . . . just as Karen grabbed her foot with a viselike grip.

But Beatrice had the lug wrench. And with one swat at Karen's hand, Karen quickly let go of her foot.

It was a long way back through the enormous parking lot to the community college. Who knew what she'd find as help at the gas station? The best idea seemed to be getting into her car, locking the doors, and driving off.

Her keys, clearly, were in her pocketbook, which had fallen off her arm and was closer to Karen. Beatrice dove for it, then staggered up to run to the car. Karen, furious, grabbed for Beatrice's arm at the same moment and left scratch marks from her elbow to her wrist.

Fumbling inside her purse, Beatrice's fingers scrabbled around the bottom edges for her keys. Not feeling them, she rummaged with increasing desperation. Then she heard a bellow from the direction of the car and saw an agitated Miss Sissy sitting in the driver's seat, beckoning her frantically to the car and pointing at Karen. Beatrice ran to the passenger side of the car, jumped in, and hit the lock button just as Karen flew at the car, beating at it with both hands. In her hurry, Beatrice had dropped the lug wrench. She saw Karen pick it up and swing it at the sedan, breaking off the side mirror and putting a dent in the hood of the car. She lifted the wrench above her head, aiming for the windshield.

Suddenly, the car roared to life. Miss Sissy, a fiendish gleam in her eye, revved the motor loudly. Karen froze, wrench still lifted high, as she saw Miss Sissy's face. With only a split second to react, she dodged to the side as Miss Sissy stomped on the accelerator. Beatrice's heart leaped into her throat and lodged there and she desperately clutched the dashboard as they took off at high speed with Miss Sissy giving a raucous battle cry.

"Miss Sissy," said Beatrice, gasping, "we're at the end of the parking lot. You've got to turn around. There's a sidewalk. . . ." She turned and saw Karen's realization that the car was trapped and then saw the woman sprint after them with the wrench.

Miss Sissy, however, was *not* trapped. She cared nothing for parameters like sidewalks or curbs and instead sped up, popped over the curb and sidewalk and into the gas station, alarm still shrieking as they went.

The gas station attendant rushed outside, dialing on his phone as he gaped at the scene. Beatrice prayed he was calling the police. Any police. At this point she wasn't sure if she was more terrified of the murderous Karen or the maniacal Miss Sissy.

But Karen hadn't yet given up on them, and at this point she couldn't. It was either finish off the two women or else go on the lam, since they'd be sure to spill their story to the police. Miss Sissy saw Karen gasping for breath yet still wielding the wrench, so she laughed, pressing the accelerator down again. The car surged out of the gas station and onto the main road. Or, rather, onto the grassy median *next* to the main road. Karen, quite the endurance runner, sprinted behind them, waving the wrench.

Their wild ride was finally over when Beatrice saw the flickering blue lights of a police car approaching them. She caught Karen's swift expression of horror as she noticed them, too.

Ramsay stopped the car with a jolt and jogged up at a much faster pace than usual. With him was Wyatt, looking both worried and confused. "Here, now," said Ramsay in his usual calm, competent way as if he were talking to someone completely rational instead of someone who'd been waving a lug wrench over her head at a car. "What's all this? Karen? What's going on?"

Karen dropped her weapon and started sobbing at the sight of Wyatt and screeched, "It's all her fault!" Karen pointed at Beatrice as she cautiously got out of her car. "All her fault!"

Ramsay said mildly, "I'd say that's extremely unlikely. From what I saw, you were bent on bashing in Beatrice's car. Beatrice doesn't appear to be armed with anything other than a pocketbook, unless you count Miss Sissy as a deadly weapon. I'm thinking there's not much that Beatrice could have done to be at fault—

except to know too much." He turned to look at Beatrice, who'd weakly stumbled out and was sagging against her car for support. "Is that right, Beatrice? You knew a little too much for your own good?"

Beatrice stared at Karen, whose face was still contorted with both anger and fear, then at Wyatt. He reached an arm out automatically to her as she weakly tried to push herself off the car. Karen howled in frustration and fury at losing.

Yet another quilt show descended into chaos as Ramsay put Karen in the back of the police car. Meadow had seen the police car's lights as she'd peeked outside to see what was keeping her precious bags of ice. And, probably, hoping that it was some sort of tender moment between Wyatt and Beatrice that was creating the delay . . . since she'd trumped up a reason for Ramsay and Wyatt to both attend the quilt show finale.

Instead she realized that there was some sort of arrest or Bad Thing happening and quickly assembled what amounted to a mob of quilters to investigate and make sure Beatrice was all right.

"What happened?" gasped Meadow as she finally reached the group at the far end of the parking lot. "What on *earth* happened?" She saw a figure in the backseat of Ramsay's police car and pushed her way closer.

"Meadow!" barked Ramsay, still in the process of both filling out a report and calling in one to the state police.

But she'd already edged close enough to see who

was in the backseat. "Karen!" She spun around and hollered at the other quilters, "It's *Karen*! And look at Beatrice! She looks *horrible*!"

Beatrice had seen better days, that was for sure. Grappling with the pavement a second time wasn't what her body had needed. Now she had some additional scrapes and already felt the bruises forming. All she really wanted now was a soft bed and the relaxing snores of a napping corgi nearby.

While the quilters gaped at both the injured Beatrice and the cuffed Karen, Meadow whipped out her cell phone. "Beatrice, I'm going to interrupt Piper at the teacher training. This is an emergency—Piper! Everything is fine. Just fine. Except your mama got scraped up again. Yes. But *Karen* is the bad guy. She's been captured, so everything will be back to normal soon." She put her phone away and said to Beatrice, "She's on her way here."

Ramsay, who'd hung up from his own phone call, sighed. "Let's hope it *will* be back to normal soon. I can't stand any more *ab*-normal." He gazed blankly into the darkness for a second or two, and Beatrice imagined he was fondly thinking of a thin volume by Thoreau that was perhaps tucked into his police car somewhere.

He must have been able to read her mind because he said sadly to Beatrice, "I have a feeling this is *not* the kind of wildness that Thoreau was talking about in his essay on nature in 'Walking.'"

Beatrice gave a gasping laugh, still trying to calm her ferociously beating heart. "I'm sure Thoreau would say that Karen just didn't spend enough time outside and that made her unhinged."

"What actually was behind all this?" asked Ramsay. "I know she was ultracompetitive, but why? What made her turn out that way?"

"From what I've gathered," said Beatrice, "Karen desperately needed that validation and support and praise from the quilters. Her parents made her feel that she was never quite good enough. Then she lost them early in her life and ended up seeking that praise, that recognition through quilting. Which made sense—it was something she had natural talent with."

Meadow clucked at her husband. "Ramsay, do you need Beatrice anymore? Because she looks like she's about to drop and I think she should be sitting down and having a wee drop of something to drink. I swear, that's a man for you. No notice of any of the peripheral issues!"

Ramsay said, "No, I think that's all for now. Sorry, Beatrice. Do you want me to call you an ambulance to get you checked out? That was quite a tumble you took."

She shook her head. "I'm fine. Sore, but fine. There's nothing a hospital would do besides put some antiseptic and bandages on me.

"Where's Miss Sissy?" she asked. "She sort of saved me. Well, she saved me, then endangered me, actually. Where did she go?"

"Posy has already hustled her away. She said Miss Sissy had had enough excitement for one night." Meadow stared at the community college, gauging the long walk back. "That's too far for you to walk. And your car looks like it needs a rest, too."

It had a very large dent in it. And had probably suffered a mechanical heart attack from being driven by Miss Sissy. "I think it's drivable, but . . . yes. It's going to need some repairs, and I probably need to get the car alarm fixed at the same time as the dent. By the time I've had a rest, maybe Piper can drive me back home. I'm too shaken up to drive right now, anyway."

Georgia had parked nearby and offered to drive Beatrice to the front entrance. Meadow jumped in Georgia's car, too. But then she hopped back out again and went up close to the police car. "Karen," she called out in her booming voice. "By the way? You lost tonight."

Meadow spun around and jumped right into Georgia's car, nose high in the air.

"But, Meadow," said Georgia as she carefully took her cargo to the entrance of the college. "Karen didn't. She won every single category."

"She certainly didn't! Anyone who leaves a quilt show in a police car with a lifetime in prison ahead of her is certainly not a winner. Certainly *not*!"

Meadow shoved her car door open energetically as soon as Georgia pulled up to the curb and then proceeded to shepherd Beatrice out of the car, clucking as she went. "Murdering two people! Trying to kill you! Trying to kill you *twice*!" Meadow's face was splotched with fury.

Georgia hovered in their wake. "It's awful. Savannah was right about what she saw and when she saw it. I guess she'll be all right to testify about it in court. If it comes to that, which hopefully it won't."

Meadow frowned in confusion, and Georgia quickly filled her in. She finished with "I don't mind you knowing, Meadow, since you already know about poor Savannah's problem. I just hope it doesn't have to go too much further."

"Well, it surely shouldn't. After all," said Meadow, "it should be enough that Karen went berserk out in the parking lot and tried to kill Beatrice!" She seemed stuck on this idea. "I think that should be evidence enough as to her character. With any luck, she's confessed to the whole thing by now."

"She basically confessed to me, anyway," said Beatrice. "So I can always testify against her."

Meadow was ready to fixate back on her favorite theme again. "So she was killing off the new members of the Village Quilters!" she said, through gritted teeth.

"Well, I don't think the Village Quilter connection had anything to do with it," said Beatrice, feeling tired. "She had her own reasons for the murders."

"Which were?" asked Meadow huffily. "I'm also mad that we picked a murderer to be part of the Village Quilters." She passed by the gymnasium and on to a nearby classroom. She turned on the lights, motioned Beatrice to a chair, and then sat down opposite from her. "Wait. Hold that thought. Let's get you cleaned up first. I most definitely don't want Piper to see her mama looking like this."

Fifteen minutes later, Meadow was satisfied with her handiwork. Georgia had returned to Savannah, worried that this latest event was going to make her even more stressed out. Meadow had, amazingly, turned over the rest of the quilt show program to another organizer and hadn't mentioned ice once. She'd been, in fact, very helpful. Meadow somehow scrounged up a first aid kit from the school's kitchen and had cleaned and bandaged up every visible scrape. Then she took a damp towel and was prepared to spot-clean the dirt from Beatrice's clothes like a mother cat cleaning a kitten's coat . . . until Beatrice stopped her. "Thanks, Meadow. I think I can handle that part."

"So, let's get back to the subject. What turned Karen into a psycho?"

Beatrice snorted. "I don't think she was a *psycho*, per se. Although the moment she smashed my car with the lug wrench made me wonder. I think her problem was her ego. At least, that's what I'm going to tell Ramsay."

"Oh, okay. So she had a big head," said Meadow.

"But maybe a little insecure, too. She really, really wanted to win. She was supercompetitive and she didn't want to be held back. And that's all that Jo Paxton was doing, in Karen's opinion—holding her back from winning. Jo had a pretty healthy ego herself, and *she* liked to win. She probably thought Karen was some young upstart. Jo made sure Karen didn't do well at the shows she judged," said Beatrice.

"Hmm. I can see that. And Jo was always insulting Karen's quilts, too, don't you think?" asked Meadow, gazing at the classroom ceiling in a thoughtful way.

"I heard Jo put down Karen's choice of fabric in the Patchwork Cottage. I think that made Karen furious and even more determined to have her meet with an 'accident.' But Opal figured out that Karen was behind Jo's death, so Karen had to get rid of Opal. That way, Karen could stay out of jail and keep winning quilt shows."

"She knew that you were hot on her trail, so she realized she had to get rid of *you*, too," said Meadow.

"I don't think that's all of the reason. She might have been upset that I was poking around too much, but it wasn't like I'd told her I knew she was behind the murders. *I* didn't even add it all up until this evening," said Beatrice.

"So what made her come after you?"

"I think," said Beatrice delicately, "that it was Wyatt."

Meadow gasped. "You mean, because she was competing with you over Wyatt? Because she wanted to win Wyatt's heart and she thought she had to eliminate the competition?"

Beatrice gave a small shrug. "Apparently so. She made some kind of reference to that. It's a little embarrassing, because *as you know*, there's absolutely nothing going on between Wyatt and me. Despite your efforts to the contrary."

Meadow, who was facing the door, suddenly put a stricken hand to her chest.

Beatrice turned slowly to see Wyatt standing there with a small smile, a plate of food and a drink, and a tired look in his eye. If he'd heard what she'd said . . . well, he must have heard it. Couldn't *not* have heard it. But he politely pretended not to. "Beatrice, I'm so glad to see that you're all right. You must have been terrified. It terrified *me*." He handed her the plate of snacks that he'd put together for her and put the cup down on a nearby desk.

Beatrice cleared her throat and said, "I was. You and Ramsay arrived at the perfect time." Because, clearly, Meadow had somehow trumped up a reason for them to be there.

"Meadow's gotten you bandaged up all right? Is there anything else I can get for you?" he asked. She shook her head.

Meadow blinked. "Are you leaving, then? But you're stranded. Ramsay took off with the police car."

"The quilt show has wrapped up for the evening," he said. "Meadow, would you mind giving me a ride back when you head out?"

"Of course I don't mind, Wyatt. That's no problem at all. I have a little clearing up to do . . . but I think I'll come back early tomorrow to do most of it. I'm ready to call it a day," said Meadow.

"I'll throw some cups and plates away while I'm waiting. Glad to see you're all right, Beatrice," said Wyatt with another smile before he ducked back out.

Meadow put her hands on her hips and said severely, "Well, you really stuck your foot in your mouth this time. The very idea of saying that your and Wyatt's relationship is a no-go! But I can fix it all. I've already got some ideas. Now tell me what you were saying about Karen and Wyatt."

"She was absolutely dead set on him. And she thought I was standing in her way, since you'd said at

Karen's dinner party that Wyatt and I were an item. Plus, she was already worried about my poking around in the murders. She decided she needed to get rid of me," said Beatrice.

"Simply ridiculous," said Meadow. She thought for a moment. "I guess we avoided a Tremendous Disaster, didn't we?"

"Did we?" The whole night was fairly disastrous. Aside from the fact that a murderer had been taken off the streets of Dappled Hills, of course.

"We did," said Meadow, looking more cheerful. "After all, Karen was about to be a member of the Village Quilters. With her competitive nature, she'd have slowly eliminated us, one by one!"

Beatrice decided to break the news to Meadow gently, since it hadn't apparently occurred to her. "I don't think Karen really saw the rest of the Village Quilters as competition. She thought we were talented quilters, simply not competition level. Remember how she was giving everyone instructions?"

"But she wanted us to do well," said Meadow.

"No, she wanted the group to beat other guilds. Because she likes to win. But she wouldn't have been happy with our quilters beating her individually. And maybe that was the whole reason she was having problems with the Cut-Ups guild and was ready to leave them."

"But you did beat Karen tonight, Beatrice," said Meadow, beaming. "Karen didn't know, of course, and that's just as well, what with her trying to kill you and everything."

Beatrice frowned. "How could I have won anything? I didn't even have a quilt entered."

"You beat Karen because she was disqualified for being a murderer," said Meadow, waving her hands around excitedly. "And you might have forgotten, but remember back when you were first starting to fiddle with quilt designs? I told you I wanted to try something different from my usual stuff and I asked you to create a design for me."

She did remember. She'd thought Meadow was simply being kind.

"So I did it! I took your design and got all the fabric and I made the quilt. I could enter in the show, since I wasn't a judge. And it won a prize! For best design!" Meadow looked proud enough to pop. "I'm going to run and get it." She trotted off and returned with a stunning quilt that made Beatrice catch her breath with pride. Beatrice had a new take on the old sawtooth pattern design . . . setting the pattern in riotous motion. There were periwinkle blue accents of color with shades of black and tan dominating the color scheme. The design was strong and powerful and there wasn't the usual, static feel to the quilt. It was the kind of quilt that made itself known.

Meadow handed over the ribbon to Beatrice. "Here. You deserve it. It was your design that won. All I did was follow through. Besides, after all you've gone through tonight, a ribbon might make you feel a little better."

Amazingly enough, it did.

*   *   *

The long evening had wrapped up quickly at that point. Piper had come, exclaimed over her injuries and story, chastised herself for not being there, fussed over the rigorous and lengthy conference that had kept her from the quilt show, and quickly taken Beatrice home and tucked her in.

She'd thought there was absolutely no way that she'd be able to fall asleep after all the fear and excitement of the quilt show, but she apparently dropped into a deep sleep as soon as she crawled into bed.

After a quiet morning, she put on some gardening clothes to tend the new flower bed in the front yard. She was watering the flowers when a car pulled up in her driveway. She looked up to see Wyatt and Miss Sissy waving at her. Her breath caught in her throat a bit and she carefully set down the watering can before she dropped it.

Miss Sissy climbed out of Wyatt's car. "Came to teach you to quilt!" she bellowed. She nodded a greeting, then nimbly trotted in, presumably to clean out all the food in Beatrice's kitchen. Was Miss Sissy or Boris the worse unexpected visitor? It was hard to say.

"Is this all right?" asked Wyatt. "I was checking in on Miss Sissy and she said that she needed to have me help her run errands and then come here and quilt with you. She made it sound like an official date, but it occurs to me that you might possibly be surprised by our visit." His eyes crinkled and Beatrice exhaled in relief. He wasn't upset. Or, if he had been, it had passed by now. Ministers must have exemplary temperaments.

"Oh no, this is fine. I did ask her to help me with my

technique. I have all these big ideas, but I don't have the skill to implement them." She gestured to the cottage. "Would you like to come in and have some coffee with us? I'm sure Miss Sissy wants a snack to start out with, and you can leave when we start getting into the quilting. I can walk Miss Sissy back home, since she and I are both without cars right now."

"I'd love some coffee," said Wyatt. "And that's the nice thing about Dappled Hills: you can walk almost anywhere. Let me know when you want to make a big trip to the grocery store, though—I'll drive you to Bub's." His eyes crinkled in a smile again.

They were almost to the cottage door when a sudden frenzied crashing came from the direction of the bushes. It was Boris, of course, leash trailing behind him and big tongue lolling out of his mouth. He spotted Wyatt and jumped ecstatically at him, putting two huge paws over either shoulder.

Meadow huffed and puffed through the bushes behind him. "Bad Boris! No cookie! No treat!" Twigs and leaves stuck from her long gray braid, making it look like a withering vine. "Coffee, Beatrice?" she asked with a hopeful look in her eye.

"I was just inviting Wyatt in for some, so of course, Meadow—come on in," said Beatrice.

Meadow's eyes widened and a smile played on her lips. "Oh, well, I wouldn't want to interrupt. . . ." Then she spotted Miss Sissy and Noo-noo in the picture window at the front of the cottage. Noo-noo was grinning at Meadow, and Miss Sissy was scowling at her. "Looks like you're having a party, though, so I'll take you up on that coffee."

"June Bug's little home is as neat as a *pin*, I tell you! Spotless. And *guess* what was covering every possible square inch of that cute house? Quilts! Yes, quilts. Magnificent quilts all made from everyday fabrics or castoffs or hand-me-downs or whatever. Remarkable! She made art out of scraps. And the most amazing thing is that she didn't recognize or acknowledge her talent whatsoever. June Bug was horrified at the thought of showing her quilts, so I just invited her to join our guild and then the shows will come later. I invited her right on the spot. She doesn't think she's good enough! Imagine."

Meadow's face glowed with excitement. Beatrice had never seen her so pleased.

Wyatt smiled at her. "Meadow, this is wonderful news! I know how you've worried about finding a new guild member."

Even Miss Sissy grinned at Meadow, with her gap-toothed smile.

"Wait," said Meadow, fanning herself with her hand to revive herself from even more excitement. "It gets even better. When I was coming back from June Bug's house, I ran into Booth at Bub's Grocery. He told me that he was completely dropping the idea of assessing fees and taxes and permits on the quilting guilds!"

"That's wonderful news!" exclaimed Beatrice. "It was a silly plan to begin with, but he's such a stubborn man that I was sure he was going to try and stick with it. Did he say what made him change his mind?"

"He said that he wanted nothing to do with the *killer quilters*." Meadow beamed with delight. "Isn't that wonderful? He said that we were too violent a group to try and wrangle with."

Meadow took a restorative gulp of her coffee, to help her regain her composure after her excitement over her wildly successful morning. "I firmly believe," she said with a happy sigh, "that this is the start of a lovely new chapter for the Village Quilters. And," she added, beaming at Beatrice, Wyatt, and Miss Sissy, "a lovely day. There's nothing better than time spent with friends."

And for once, with the promise of a quilt to be stitched, bonds of friendship to be strengthened, and conversation and coffee to be enjoyed, Beatrice had to agree with her.

Quilting Tips

Leftover blocks can be used for table runners, grocery totes, pillowcases, or doll clothes. Batting scraps can be used to stuff pillows.

Empty tissue boxes make good wastebaskets for your work area.

If you're drawing diagonal lines on blocks to form triangles, it's easier to work from the inside out on the corners.

Use adhesive lint rollers to collect loose threads.

Skirt or pant hangers can be used to store unfinished projects or to group completed blocks. Or you can group projects together by putting the pattern and fabric in a large zipper bag and hang it on the hanger.

Magnets are a great way to hold needles while you're quilting.

Recipes

Southern Spoon Bread

2 cups boiling water
1 cup white meal
1 tablespoon butter
1 teaspoon salt
2 teaspoons baking powder
2 eggs
2 cups milk

Pour boiling water over meal, stirring constantly, and boil five minutes. Remove from heat, add butter, salt, and milk. Mix well. Beat eggs lightly, add to mixture. Sift dry ingredients into mixture and mix well. Pour mixture into greased baking dish and bake for 30 minutes in 350-degree oven.

Cucumber Dip

3 tablespoons shredded cucumber
8 ounces cream cheese
2 tablespoons mayonnaise
½ teaspoon Worcestershire
¼ teaspoon celery salt
dash paprika
salt to taste

Blend all and serve with crackers or chips.

Apple Torte

2 eggs
1 cup sugar
½ cup chopped nuts
3½ tablespoons flour
1½ teaspoons baking powder
⅛ teaspoon salt
1 teaspoon vanilla
1 cup chopped apples

Beat eggs well, add other ingredients, and mix. Bake in shallow greased pan 30 minutes at 350 degrees. Serve with whipped cream.

Olive Hors D'oeuvres

1 cup salted peanuts, crushed
small jar pimento-stuffed olives, drained well on paper
    towels

Mix 8-ounce block of cream cheese with teaspoon of
water to soften. Take small amount of cream cheese and
roll around olive in palms, until coated. Roll olive in
crushed peanuts until coated. Store covered in refrigerator.

King Midas Chicken

1 cut-up chicken
1 teaspoon salt
1 8- ounce can crushed pineapple
¼ cup mustard
½ cup chutney
½ cup chopped nuts

Sprinkle chicken with salt. Place skin side up, single
layer, in shallow dish. Mix remaining ingredients and
spoon over chicken. Bake uncovered 350 degrees for 1
hour and 15 minutes.

Read on for a sneak peek at the next
Southern Quilting Mystery
Coming in late 2013 from Obsidian.

Beatrice Coleman looked in horror at her neighbor Meadow Downey. "You mean we're not even invited? We're crashing the party?"

They were in Meadow's aging van, and Meadow was speedily driving them to an elderly quilter's home just slightly outside their town of Dappled Hills, North Carolina. Meadow chortled. "It's not a *party*, Beatrice. It's more like a special quilt guild meeting. And what we're doing is dropping in without calling first."

"What we're really doing," said Beatrice gloomily, "is trying to persuade a sick, elderly woman that we're the best candidates to chair a quilting scholarship committee." She looked out the van window again as the scenery flew by. "Meadow, I think it's going to snow. The sky is that odd mottled gray. I'm getting a really bad feeling about all of this. We should turn around now and go back home."

Meadow glanced away from the road to give Beatrice a reassuring grin. The result was anything but re-assuring, though. Meadow had that fervent look that she had whenever she was all geared up for quilting. Her eyes behind her red glasses were full of it. She'd tried to tame her long gray hair into its customary braid, but must have been distracted while braiding because it escaped in wisps. The overall effect was rather maniacal, Beatrice decided.

"We can't go back, Beatrice. This is the perfect op-portunity for the Village Quilters. If old Mrs. Starnes wants to create a quilting foundation and award schol-arships to ensure the longevity of the quilting craft, I can't think of a better guild than ours to distribute them. I already have a recipient in mind!"

"But, Meadow—the weather. Can't we send Mrs. Starnes or whoever she is an e-mail to express our qual-ifications?" asked Beatrice.

Meadow vehemently shook her head. "No, because Mrs. Starnes doesn't have electronics in her house. She's an eccentric old woman, Beatrice."

Beatrice bit her tongue to keep from pointing out that there was an eccentric old woman sitting right next to her.

"Besides, I'm sure she would have invited us if she'd remembered. She simply forgot about contacting a rep-resentative from the Village Quilters guild. We're help-ing her out," said Meadow in a righteous voice. She paused. "And I'm sure it was also an oversight that she forgot to contact the Cut-Ups guild, but it wasn't my business to contact them."

"We're foisting ourselves on her under the guise of

being helpful," muttered Beatrice to herself. Aloud she groaned. "Look. It's sleeting."

"Pooh. Who cares about a little sleet?"

Clearly not Meadow. Actually, it looked like a combination of sleet and freezing rain. Beatrice had the feeling they were embarking on an adventure. And this adventure was starting with the precarious driveway now facing them.

Dappled Hills was a small, picturesque mountain town full of steep hills. Beatrice was accustomed to rather treacherous driveways. But the driveway Meadow was currently scaling put all other driveways to shame.

"Where are the switchbacks?" asked Beatrice. "We're going straight up. Shouldn't there be switchbacks to keep us at a gradual, safe ascent?"

"This house and driveway are so old that there probably weren't a lot of people using switchbacks when it was being built," said Meadow airily. "We'll be fine."

The narrow, graveled, potholed road stretched through dense trees straight up the side of a mountain. At the crest sat a dilapidated old Victorian house complete with a turret, dormer windows, a wraparound porch, and a steep roof. Its gingerbread trim looked like it had a bad case of rot.

As they finally crested the top of the driveway, they saw a few other cars parked in front of the house. "See," said Meadow. "It's not as if we're interrupting a huge party or anything. Looks like there are probably five or six other people here. Besides, I come bearing food and quilts! Who's going to turn that down?"

Beatrice had a feeling that old Muriel Starnes likely

had gobs of quilts in her aging Victorian mansion. But she'd agree with Meadow on the food. Meadow was a fantastic cook, and Beatrice had been enjoying the aroma of whatever wonderful food she'd cooked all the way from home. She couldn't wait to dig into it. "What did you bring?"

"Poppy seed ham and Swiss biscuits and hot bacon and artichoke dip. Doesn't it smell yummy? Could you help me with these quilts?" Meadow said as she got out of the driver's seat and slid open the side door.

Meadow had flung the quilts into the back of her messy van before they left, and Beatrice eyed them in dismay. "Meadow, these quilts are getting wrinkled and dirty! You didn't put them on hangers or in a garment bag or something?"

Meadow waved her hand dismissively. "Oh, no. Quilts are made to be *used*, Beatrice. Who cares if they have a little dirt on them? That's life! Quilts aren't merely an art form, although I know that's usually how you view them."

Beatrice was a retired art curator who'd moved from Atlanta to the tiny town of Dappled Hills to spend more time with her grown daughter. Meadow was right—she saw quilts through the eyes of a curator. She noticed the artistic merit (or lack of it) of them first, then thought of ways to best display and preserve the quilts.

But before Beatrice could voice more concerns, Meadow trotted brazenly up the warped wooden steps onto the wraparound porch, balancing the bowls of food as she went. The front door had apparently originally been painted black, but now most of its paint had peeled off. She lifted the heavy brass door knocker and rapped authoritatively at the front door.

Beatrice obligingly followed her, a stack of quilts in her arms. A breeze blew up, and she shivered from the chill, hugging the quilts tighter with one arm and pulling her full-length black wool coat around her with the other.

A dour-looking, balding, older man wearing a suit and a frown opened the door. He raised his eyebrows at Meadow's wildly colorful appearance. Meadow was solidly constructed and tall, but had never shied away from wearing large prints and bright colors. He looked somewhat more comforted when he studied Beatrice in her no-nonsense coat, khaki pants, and tamed hair. "Are we expecting you?" he asked doubtfully.

"Mrs. Starnes *should* be expecting us," said Meadow breezily. Meaning, of course, that Mrs. Starnes should have invited them, but hadn't. Beatrice's head started pounding.

"I brought hot dip and chips and ham biscuits," said Meadow with a big smile, as if that guaranteed her entry.

The man opened his mouth to inquire further, but snapped it shut again and frowned as he squinted down the gravel driveway.

Another car was crunching through the gravel as it made its way up the driveway. The man crossed his arms and started looking as if he was going to offer a major roadblock to anybody trying to enter the house.

"It's Posy!" said Meadow delightedly. She explained to the grim man, "It's Posy Beck, owner of the Patchwork Cottage shop in Dappled Hills. She's in our quilting guild."

Beatrice groaned softly. "Look who's with her."

"It's Miss Sissy!" crowed Meadow, who didn't appear to understand that adding a crazy old woman to the mix wasn't going to make it any easier to gain entry to this gathering. The sleet mixed with freezing rain fell harder.

Pulling Meadow aside, Beatrice whispered to her urgently, "Meadow, we need to leave. We're clearly not encouraged to come inside, and the weather is getting worse. How will we get out of here if the ice starts accumulating? We're on the top of a mountain."

There was a cough behind them, and an old woman hunched over a walker gazed steadily at them. The man gave a concerned exclamation and reached to assist her, but she waved him off with irritation. "I'm fine," she grated. "Let these women in, Colton. It's pouring down rain—or something—out here."

Colton still acted reluctant. "Do you know them, Muriel?"

"I know they're quilters because they're holding quilts," she said drily. "It appears as though that other car holds more quilters. They're all welcome here."

Colton tightened his lips as though trying to keep from arguing; then he stepped aside to let Meadow and Beatrice in.

"I have hot dip and ham!" said Meadow brightly to Muriel Starnes.

Muriel gave a small smile and hobbled in with them. "We're all sitting in the library," she said.

Meadow was unfortunately, and as usual, in a very chatty mood. She'd said any number of inane statements before reaching the library, and when she arrived in the library, she didn't seem affected whatsoever by the general atmosphere in the room.

But Beatrice was. The library was a large room, and a cold one. In fact, the entire house was cold. Beatrice shivered and decided to leave her coat on. A stone fireplace held several shards of wood that were quickly burning out. The sight of books ordinarily had a cheering effect for Beatrice, but these books had a depressing never-read look about them. She sniffed delicately. There was definitely a scent of decay and mold in the room.

The gathering of quilters was fairly subdued. Actually, they were completely mute. They nodded a greeting in response to Meadow's over-the-top hello, then took to either looking around the room or staring at their quilts or their hands as Beatrice and Meadow set down the food and the quilts. The women were all of various ages. No one else had brought anything to eat or drink, and Muriel Starnes didn't appear inclined to offer anything. Everyone appeared to be waiting for some sort of speech or official welcome of some kind.

Colton came in with Posy and Miss Sissy. His expression was one of disdain. Posy, fluffy as usual in a pastel cardigan and beagle broach, beamed at everyone and looked completely innocuous, so Beatrice had to assume that it was Miss Sissy who was responsible for Colton's dismay. She was looking even wilder than Meadow—most of her hair had pulled out of her bun, and she wore a long floral dress that had seen better days.

"Wickedness!" proclaimed Miss Sissy, hissing the word as she glared suspiciously around the room.

Posy and Beatrice exchanged glances. Apparently, this wasn't one of Miss Sissy's good days.

Muriel Starnes walked over to a large armchair and carefully sat down, keeping her walker in front of her. "Thanks to everyone for coming," she said in a voice that was weak but still had remnants of authority in it. "It's certainly a tribute to the quilting craft that I have such a good turnout. Perhaps even," she said thoughtfully as she looked at Meadow, Beatrice, and Miss Sissy, "more of a turnout than I anticipated."

Beatrice felt herself blush. Meadow looked completely unconcerned.

"I'm going to let my lawyer, Colton Bradshaw, explain the general setup of the foundation I'm creating and give more information about it," said Muriel, sitting back in her armchair and looking weary.

"Lawyer!" said Meadow, chortling. "I thought he was your butler!"

Colton gave her an icy look and stood up, holding several papers that he appeared to be planning on reading. Beatrice sighed. Judging from that script of his, they might be trapped here for hours.

"Thanks to Muriel Starnes' generosity, the assembled are gathered here today to offer insight and input on finding and vetting qualified and worthy recipients for the quilting scholarships," he intoned.

Beatrice sighed. His delivery wasn't very good, either. Tuning him out, she began watching the other women in the room. It was an odd group. Most of the women were studying Colton seriously. Meadow, on the other hand, was like a wriggling puppy. She could barely stand to wait for Colton to finish before enthusiastically giving her thoughts on the scholarships.

Two of the older quilters had unreadable expressions on their faces. One of the women looked fairly sour, and the other was blankly watching Colton read his prepared statement. Shouldn't everyone be as enthusiastic and excited as Meadow? Weren't they supposed to be selling themselves as good candidates to administer the scholarships?

Muriel didn't appear to be listening to a word Colton was saying, but then, she'd already surely be familiar with his little speech. Her hooded eyes watched the other women closely. Sometimes the quilters caught her staring and looked away.

Miss Sissy was ravenously gobbling down all the crackers, having apparently decided that she didn't care for some component of the bacon-and-artichoke dip. Then she hungrily eyed the ham biscuits.

Colton finally concluded his speech. Or maybe he was only pausing to catch his breath. But Meadow jumped in while she had the chance. "I'll speak for all of us, I'm sure, when I say that I'm absolutely thrilled that you're helping ensure the longevity of the quilting craft through your foundation. And I want to explain how the Village Quilters guild is perfect for administering this scholarship. You see, our guild's amazing history—"

Muriel Starnes interrupted as seamlessly as if Meadow hadn't been speaking at all. "Thank you, Colton. And now I have a confession to make. I haven't been completely honest with you about the reason you're all here."

There was suddenly a great, scary, snapping *pow* outside the window, and the lights went out.

ALSO AVAILABLE
from

Elizabeth Craig

Quilt or Innocence
A Southern Quilting Mystery

Retired folk art curator Beatrice Coleman is the newest member of the Village Quilters Guild in Dapple Hills, North Carolina. Although this isn't how she pictured her retirement, Beatrice is enjoying the lush fabrics, beautiful designs, and friendly faces. Until it all goes to pieces when her fellow quilters become the prime suspects in a crime...

Available wherever books are sold or at
penguin.com

facebook.com/TheCrimeSceneBooks

Sally Goldenbaum

ANGORA ALIBI

A Seaside Knitters Mystery

Coming May 2013

Yarn shop owner Izzy Chambers Perry and her new husband are expecting a baby. Now she's having the best summer of her life—until an abandoned baby car seat and hand-knit blanket spark a terrible premonition.

Unfortunately, Izzy's fear comes true when a young man who did odd jobs at her doctor's clinic is killed during a scuba dive. When Izzy discovers the man was actually murdered and is connected to the abandoned car seat the crime becomes too close for comfort. It'll take the Seaside Knitters' careful attention to patterns—and their fierce commitment to bringing Izzy and Sam's baby into a peaceful town—to knit this mystery together…

OM0097

Amanda Lee

The Embroidery Mysteries

The Quick and the Thread

When Marcy Singer opens an embroidery specialty shop in quaint Tallulah Falls, Oregon, everyone in town seems willing to raise a glass—or a needle—to support the newly-opened Seven Year Stitch.

Then Marcy finds the shop's previous tenant dead in the storeroom, a message scratched with a tapestry needle on the wall beside him. Now Marcy's shop has become a crime scene, and she's the prime suspect. She'll have to find the killer before someone puts a final stitch in her.

<u>Also available in the series</u>

Stitch Me Deadly
Thread Reckoning
The Long Stitch Goodnight
Thread on Arrival

Melissa Bourbon

Deadly Patterns

A Magical Dressmaking Mystery

Bliss, Texas, is gearing up for its annual Winter Wonderland spectacular and Harlow is planning the main event: a holiday fashion show being held at an old Victorian mansion. But when someone is found dead on the mansion's grounds, it's up to Harlow to catch the killer—before she becomes a suspect herself.

"Harlow Jane Cassidy is a tailor-made amateur sleuth."
—Wendy Lyn Watson

<u>Also available in the series</u>
A Fitting End
Pleating for Mercy

Available wherever books are sold or at
penguin.com

facebook.com/TheCrimeSceneBooks